THE BEST LAID PLANS

In one room of Hockleigh manor, innocent and trembling Miss Priscilla Pennington was being told by her mother that she must accept the proposal of the fearfully worldly Lord Richard Devlin.

In another room, the gentle Mr. Caspar Maltby was wondering how he had summoned up the nerve to ask the frightfully beautiful Francesca Waringham to be his unblushing bride.

Meanwhile, Lord Richard was opening the bedroom door of the shamelessly seductive Roxanna Gordon—and, in a forest cottage, Francesca was struggling in the arms of the handsome ruffian hired to dishonor her.

Clearly the course of calculated love had led into a maze of unmentionable mischief. . . .

THE
SENSIBLE COURTSHIP

More Regency Romances from SIGNET

THE
SENSIBLE
COURTSHIP

by
Megan Daniel

Ⓢ
A SIGNET BOOK
NEW AMERICAN LIBRARY
TIMES MIRROR

Copyright © 1982 by Megan Daniel

 SIGNET TRADEMARK REG. U.S. PAT. OFF. AND FOREIGN COUNTRIES
REGISTERED TRADEMARK—MARCA REGISTRADA
HECHO EN CHICAGO, U.S.A.

SIGNET, SIGNET CLASSICS, MENTOR, PLUME, MERIDIAN AND NAL
BOOKS are published by The New American Library, Inc.,
1633 Broadway, New York, New York 10019

First Printing, August, 1982

1   2   3   4   5   6   7   8   9

PRINTED IN THE UNITED STATES OF AMERICA

1

The steaming water of the bath swirled around the young man. He luxuriated in its warmth. He breathed in deep contentment, the water rippling over the hardened muscles of his broad chest and forming rivulets that ran down toward his flat stomach. He felt good.

The comfortable room surrounded him like a cloak, bringing images of his childhood and adolescence. A thick feather mattress and goosedown pillows adorned the high four-posted bed. The fire before him threw cheerfully dancing shadows over the furniture, sturdy but graceful in carved oak. Near to hand sat a decanter of fine old brandy; a welcome pot of tea steeped nearby.

The gentleman was relaxing from a long journey in the best room in the best inn that the city of York could offer. His face, a deeply bronzed and distinctly handsome face, erupted into a broad smile. His deep, throaty laugh rang out. It was good to be back in England.

How many times in the past few years had there been no soothing bath at the end of the day, no hot water at all, in fact? And no good rich brandy, no feather bed, no tea. He had learned to love coffee, to need it even, the kind that was so black and strong you could almost chew it. But there was nothing quite like a good English cup of tea to let a man know that everything was right with the world.

Odd to think he was actually home, that the rolling

hillsides outside his window were populated with Englishmen. Not Indian savages, not French Creole gamblers, not drawling Americans. Just good plain Englishmen. It was odder still to think now that he had been away. Was it really only five days since he had stepped off the gangplank of Captain Witham's neat little schooner, shipping timber out of Boston harbor, to find himself on the quays of Hull?

He had accomplished quite a lot in those five short days, had begun the process of turning himself back into an Englishman worthy of the position he had long been destined to hold. In the yard below stood a shiny new sporting curricle, its seats sheathed in the softest of caramel-colored leather and its wheels picked out in red. It had carrried him from Hull to York, and tomorrow it would take him on to Hockleigh. A few days relaxing with George, his old school chum, was just what he needed to complete his transformation from backwoodsman into gentleman. Then it was on to London.

Neatly laid out across the bed was a newly tailored suit of clothes: cream-colored pantaloons, well-cut dark blue coat of the best Bath cloth, snowy linen. Highly polished and well-fitted boots stood at attention nearby. He had scarce dared to hope he would find anything half so good in York. He hadn't wanted to appear a bumpkin before his friend. When the new clothes had been delivered this morning, he had willingly set aside the poorly fitted broadcloth he had picked up in Boston. More clothes would arrive in the morning.

He sank farther down into the water, watching the play of the firelight on the ceiling. A huge chocolate-colored servant handed him a glass of brandy and a lighted cheroot. He drank deeply from the one and inhaled deeply from the other, closed his eyes, and let his mind drift.

The pungence of cigar smoke and the warmth of good brandy would forever remind him of his Uncle John. The big earthy, life-loving man with a scowl that could freeze icicles and an even bigger smile, had been the closest thing to a father the young gentleman had ever known. He had adored the old man, and it was from that great laughing bear that he had inherited his robust love of life.

But rebellion stirs in the hearts of most of us when the fire of youth burns hottest. Uncle John had been a homebody. His horses, his snug house, and his well-tended acres had been his life. He always expected that they would fill the life of his nephew as well. So naturally the young man wanted no such thing. His soul was filled with adventure. Nothing would do for him but to see the world, to experience it in the flesh, to do it all.

He smiled at the remembrance of his young eagerness. There was precious little he hadn't done in the past five years. No staid Grand Tour for him, "doing" the capitals of Europe. He had headed for India, Africa, even a brief stop in China—and *that* had entailed a hair-raising moment or two—before ending up in the vastness of the North American continent. He had lived with Red Indians, hunted buffalo, broken wild horses, and eaten more than one thing he had never known existed before—and promptly put from his mind afterward.

He took another pull on his brandy, letting the amber liquid roll over his tongue and feeling the warmth flow all the way to his stomach. He wondered idly who he would have become had he been the dutiful nephew and followed his uncle's wishes. When he had come down from Oxford five years ago, Uncle John had simply assumed that he would come home to Kent and burrow in, run the estate, settle down, with perhaps an occasional toddle up to London. He would marry and give the old man several great-nieces and nephews to dangle on his knee. He had always been fond of children, had Uncle John.

A shadow of guilt passed the young man's face. Now Uncle John was dead, and he'd never had a glimpse of

those wished-for great-nieces and nephews. He should
have had that, at least.

But the young man had never before had the least
desire to settle down, never the least doubt of his goals,
to go, to see, to do.

Then he remembered. There had been that one flicker
of doubt, over five years ago now. There had been a
girl. Funny, he had scarce known her at all. They had
met only a few times. It was at some house party or
other that he saw her last. He had already booked his
passage to India, ready to sail in a few days' time.

But one smile from her had been enough to give him
pause, to actually make him consider throwing over all
his plans, his longtime dreams of adventure. Or at least
putting them off for a time. He had come damned close
to selling back that passage to India.

He could still remember that smile. The memory of
her face had faded, but the smile remained, vivid and
warm. She had been so full of life. And there had been a
kiss, a kiss such as he had never known before and never
found again for all the amorous adventures—and they
were not few—the ensuing years had offered up.

It had been rather more than a kiss, actually, and the
memory of it still had the power to stir him. They had
been in some sort of summerhouse. Or, no, it had been a
gazebo, by a lake. Where was it? Somewhere in Sussex,
he thought. Or was it Kent? The banquettes in the
gazebo had been covered in red damask, with a pineapple pattern, and the sun had glinted off the sheet of
water and turned it the color of her eyes. Amber. Yes,
she had had amber eyes.

The kiss, which had started out so innocently, had
quickly taken on an intensity, an urgency, which took
them both by surprise and left them breathless.

The young man looked down at his soapy hands
floating over the soothing water. With mild surprise he
realized they still recalled the shape, the warmth, the soft
round firmness of her young breasts through the thin

muslin of her summer dress. She had offered no resistance as his hands slid down from her shoulders to seek them. She had only kissed him all the more eagerly. She had tasted of strawberries, he remembered. Yes, they had been picking strawberries. They had talked, very animatedly, matching ideas and wits; they had wandered off toward the gazebo; they had embraced.

And then what had happened? His handsome face frowned in concentration. Oh, yes. Footsteps, and a whistled tune, off-key, and the local curate had wandered by. And she had run off.

But what if they had not been interrupted? Odd, he mused. He hadn't thought of that adolescent scene in years. Being back in England again must have brought her back to mind. He wondered whatever had become of her as he soaped his arms.

She had been very like him, that girl. Too much so, in fact. She was impulsive and fiery, the brightest and most independent-minded woman he had ever known. And with far too liberal an education for her own good, as he recalled. But intriguing.

She had stated quite clearly that she wanted the same things for her life that he wanted for his: adventure, romance, experience. Ridiculous, of course. How could a young girl go traipsing around the world on her own?

She had also vowed that she would never give over control of her life to a man, as other women did. Well, she had been but seventeen, after all. By now she was probably settled down with a whole brood of children and a fat, contented husband, with no more such foolish, youthful dreams.

Had he met her when he was a little older himself, a little more experienced, with some of the wanderlust burned out of his soul . . . Well, just as well he hadn't. She had been something special, that girl, but she certainly would not have made a comfortable wife. Passion was all very well. In fact, he planned to experience a great deal more of it before he was through. But in a wife, he was quite ready to settle for comfort. He had learned, through some rather uncomfortable years, that there was a lot to be said for it when all's said and done.

He finished his brandy and snuffed out his cheroot.

A nondescript little tune escaped the young woman's lips as she soaked in the warm scented bath, a counterpoint to the tinkle of the water as it dribbled from her fingertips. The soap, the finest available, smelled of violets from Devonshire and made a rich, creamy lather as she eased it over her white skin, drawing large lazy circles across her shoulders and breasts.

A busy little maid, a pert smile belying her air of industry, stirred up the coals, added more steaming water to the tub, poured in more of the scented oil, and began to scrub her mistress's back.

From the depths of the tub, the young woman let her large amber eyes survey the room. She was familiar with it, for she had visited at Hockleigh once before. Her closest friend was now mistress here. Also, the room was familiar in another sense. In its quality and elegance, it was a mirror of every room she had ever slept in. From where she lay in her bath, she could not see out the windows, now glowing with the last warm pinks and yellows of late afternoon. But she knew what sight would greet her eyes there. Lush, well-manicured lawns, perfectly tended gardens blooming with dahlias and marigolds and other late flowers, an ornamental sheet of water glinting golden in the setting sun.

Hockleigh was one of the finest estates in Yorkshire. The young woman had spent her life on the finest estates of nearly every county in England.

The gong of the dressing bell echoed in the hall outside her door, and the young lady gathered her warmed, relaxed muscles together. It was time she dressed.

A poetic fly on the wall, watching such a maiden rise from her bath, might have been forgiven for likening her to Venus rising from the foam. She was divinely tall and magnificently formed, her full figure well rounded but with no trace of that pudginess which could all too soon turn to fat. Perhaps Diana might have been a more apt choice for the winged bard on the wall, however, for there was an athletic grace about her long limbs and the surety of her movements.

She stepped from the tub and indulged in a long, languid stretch, her arms held high over her head. A pearl hairpin worked itself loose with the movement, and long silken hair cascaded down over her damp shoulders and across her body like a screen of spun gold.

There was an autumn chill in the air beyond the long windows, but the cheerful coal fire and a brisk toweling from the pert maid soon dried her glowing skin. She wrapped herself in a silk wrapper the color of dried roses and sat down before the mirror.

Carnations were set out in shallow bowls on either side of the mirror. That was thoughtful of Sarah, her hostess at Hockleigh, she mused, for Sarah knew them to be her favorite flowers. There were few things Sarah did not know about her, she realized, as she leaned to breathe in the spicy scent of the blooms.

It had been so good to see her friend again this morning on her arrival at Hockleigh. Since Sarah's marriage to the young Duke of Hockleigh a year ago, the two friends had seen little of each other. There had been one brief visit here at Hockleigh, a few encounters in London. It would be lovely to make a prolonged visit. Of course, Sarah would be kept busy with a house full of guests, and her friend would be caught up in the hunting, but surely there would be some leisure for long chats over the teacups.

It was strange that their friendship should be so close, for the two young women were different in nearly every way. Physically Sarah was opposed to her friend, being small and round and soft. Sarah had grown up surrounded by brothers and sisters, cousins and aunts, while her friend, an only child, had been surrounded by governesses and tutors and her father's radical friends. Sarah was often silly, seldom picked up a book, and was the most biddable, compliant, and conformable of wives. The tall golden-haired beauty staring out from the mirror was never silly, was very well read, and she knew that she was far, often too far, from biddable. And she was not a wife.

Her father had brought her up and educated her according to the principles of Mary Wollstonecraft and Mr. Godwin, and she had taken those principles very much to heart. She had, at a very early age, made a solemn vow to become no man's slave.

Now, at the ripe age of three-and-twenty, she had still not changed her mind. She had never met a man who had given her the least cause to do so.

A silver-handled brush was pulled gently but briskly through her long golden hair. The maid worked quickly, deft fingers braiding and piling and twisting, then plucking a mother-of-pearl hairpin from her mouth to secure the knot to her mistress's head. The young woman began to rub a few drops of oil into the bath-warmed skin of her hands, strong, capable hands, but graceful too, with long tapered fingers and delicately rounded nails.

Yes, she still believed in the theories of Mrs. Wollstonecraft. Why should not a woman be educated like a man, have a profession like a man, be offered the same rights and opportunities as a man? And then there was the question of "free love," that most radical of ideas for which the powerful thinker and writer had been most ostracized.

The young woman couldn't help but smile at herself as she dusted the thinnest film of rice powder over her nose. She had once espoused the theory with great vigor herself. She imagined she still believed it in principle. But the only time in her life she had come close to acting on her beliefs, she had run away like a frightened rabbit.

Looking back, she knew it was a good thing that she had run. For the young gentleman in question was the only man she had ever met who might have had the power to tame her independence, to cause her willingly to give up the freedom that was the most important thing in her life.

She had never fully understood what had happened that day five years ago, despite her advanced education. She remembered a white trellis, the wall of some sort of garden house. There were cushions. Red damask cushions, in a pineapple pattern. The walls had been covered with honeysuckle vines; she could still recall their scent. And he smelled vaguely of clove, a spicy, very male scent.

She didn't remember just how the kiss had begun. But she remembered very well that she had no desire for it to end. It was virtually the only time in her life that she could remember feeling truly out of control of a situation. At the moment, she had not minded a bit, though the idea terrified her a short while later. At the time, it had been far too delicious to mind.

How different her life might have been had she not run away from him that day. And what was it that had pulled them apart? Oh, yes, the curate, taking a shortcut across the gardens and whistling a hymn. The girl smiled; she had always hated that hymn, long after she had forgotten why.

She let her mind dwell on that scene in the gazebo; it was the first time in many years that she had done so. She was not, like so many of her contemporaries, completely ignorant of the facts of life and love. Her radical education had seen to that. She knew perfectly well what the logical outcome of that interlude in the honeysuckle-scented gazebo would have been.

What she could not know was how it would have felt, for the simple reason that she had never, since that long-ago summer day, been the least bit tempted to find out. Oh, there had certainly been gentlemen who wished to tempt her. More than she cared to recall. But she had felt nothing for any of them beyond a mild friendship. None of their kisses had stirred her more than mildly. That did not seem enough, somehow.

She was smiling now, a rather wry smile, at her own folly. She had gotten into innumerable scrapes in her day in her search for "adventures." She refused to be confined by antiquated notions of what a young lady should be and should do. She had been setting tongues wagging ever since her come-out.

But it had all seemed empty somehow, and of late she had begun to sink into a dreadful respectability. Despite her odd education, she realized that the deep-seated propriety of her age was as much a part of her as the more radical ideas of her tutors.

And so when the handsome young man had kissed her and held her and made her feel a fire like nothing she had ever known before or since, she had run away, frightened at the intensity of her own feelings, frightened of what he would think of her, and, most of all, frightened of the very real threat to her independence he represented.

And he had let her run away. She had never quite forgiven him for that.

Slowly, almost reluctantly, the gentleman raised himself from the tub and stood to his full six feet. As the water fell away from his glowing wet skin, pink with warmth beneath the deep bronze of his tan, little fingers of steam drifted up and twisted themselves around his head, where wisps of sun-bleached hair curled damply about his face.

The servant, who was nearly as large and powerful-looking as his master, stepped forward with a rough Turkish towel in his hands and began to vigorously rub the gentleman's naked back until it tingled. He submitted with complete enjoyment while the last droplets of moisture were toweled from his body.

The linen shirt was cool and smooth as it slid over his bath-warmed skin; he stretched luxuriously as the servant floated it down over his head. He pulled on the corded pantaloons, which covered but could not conceal his powerful thighs, and settled himself before the mirror. He sipped at the strong dark tea, unable to suppress a smile of remembrance at the flood of memories the taste carried with it.

A vigorous brushing brought some order to his tumbled locks; then he settled to the important business of tying his cravat.

He thought idly that it was a good thing he had spent some time in Virginia and Boston before his return. Those pockets of genteel civilization had given him a chance to relearn a few of the graces and manners that had worn thin during his time in the vast American wilderness. It would not have done to return to his home and his inheritance acting like some sort of savage.

His fingers worked deftly at the mass of starched white muslin, and he was soon satisfied with the result, one attempt being sufficient. The resulting creation was smooth and elegant but understated, impeding neither the movement of his head nor his dignity. The coat, likewise, as it settled smoothly over his fine shoulders, was well cut but easily fitted; it took him but a moment to shrug himself into it.

He stood before the long cheval glass and surveyed the gentleman gazing back at him. He couldn't suppress a lopsided grin at the cool elegance of the fellow. Who would now guess that he had spent much of the past few years in rough buckskins and furs and had, as often as not, slept under the stars and with his boots on?

He carefully pinned a single watch fob to his waist and slid a heavy gold signet ring onto his finger. Lastly, he picked up a high curled beaver hat, brushed to a perfect sheen, and settled it on his head. Adjusting the tilt to a more rakish angle, he let his deep laugh ring out once more. With a mock salute and a grand bow to the polished gentleman in the mirror, he spoke in a voice warmed by good humor and total comfort. "I bid you a good evening, my lord," were his words. He was still chuckling as he decended the stairs.

Richard, Lord Devlin, left the best inn in York to discover what delights the evening might offer up.

The young woman gave her head a shake to bring herself back to the present. The maid scowled as a hairpin worked itself loose, and quickly righted it. Such silly musings and rememberings. She really must hurry or she would be late for dinner. She rose, removed the wrapper, and allowed the maid to slide a silk shift over her head. A tamboured muslin petticoat was tied at her waist. The silk of her demi-gown, a deep dusky rose, rustled as it slid into place; her satin slippers whooshed softly on the Persian carpet. She picked up an exquisite pair of long French kid gloves, a delicately carved ivory fan, a gossamer shawl of silver tissue, and turned again toward the mirror. A perfectly put-together, cool English beauty stared back at her.

She had indeed come a long way from the silly girl who ran, terrified, from a kiss and an embrace in a shimmering summer garden. The young woman staring back at her now would not have lost control, would not have been frightened or humiliated. She would not spend hours wondering: "What if we had not been interrupted?" or "Why did he not come and find me?" A tiny frown creased her smooth forehead.

She looked about the lovely room, then back at her own image. She had never known anything but luxury, beauty, perfect order. She felt certain now that she never would. It was what she had been born to.

It wasn't that she was precisely dissatisfied with her life. She was far too intelligent not to know that her birth had given her privileges enjoyed by only the very few. She had no desire whatever to give up that advantage. She had enjoyed a prank or two in her life. She had experienced much laughter. She was not ungrateful for the ease of her life, for her wealth, her beauty, and her position. She was thankful for a fine education and for a heart not hardened to the pain of others less fortunate than herself.

Neither was she precisely bored. She had a host of friends and was capable of enjoying her own company as well.

But there were times—and they had grown more and more frequent of late—when she would surprise herself in the middle of a crowded and glittering ballroom or sipping India tea from a delicate porcelain cup in someone's elegant drawing room, with the radical thought: "Is this it? Is this my life, from now until forever?"

The dinner bell sounded in the hall below. She was late. She tested out a pleasant smile on the young woman in the mirror. It was returned. Tonight she would simply enjoy being with Sarah again. Tonight she would not worry about the rest of her life.

With a practiced kick at her demi-train, Lady Francesca Waringham turned away from herself and descended the stairs to dinner.

2

Autumn sunshine sparkled off pier glasses and porcelain, gilt-trimmed ceilings and satinwood furniture polished to a high gloss as two young women made their way through room after room and corridor after hallway in the vast, one might say palatial, house that was Hockleigh. A small retinue of servants trailed after them. The young Duchess of Hockleigh was nervous. She was making a last-minute inspection on her home for what was to be her first big house party since becoming duchess. Her guests would begin arriving in less than a pair of hours and everything must be perfect. Thank goodness her best friend was here beside her.

"Oh, Cesca," she cried. "Do you think that I should have added some wood pigeons for dinner tonight? We have the pheasants, and some quail, but George thinks . . ."

"Sarah," said Lady Francesca in a voice of soothing calm. "Indeed, you must stop worrying so. There will be quite enough dishes for dinner. The pheasants will be perfect. Everything will be perfect, and everyone will be enchanted."

"Oh, I do hope you are right. You know what a fearsome reputation Hockleigh has for hospitality. I do so want George to be proud of me." She reached down to plump a cushion as they passed through a charming small sitting room all flowered chintz and ivy-trellised wallpaper. A young maid dusting the mantel dropped a curtsy.

14

The Duchess surveyed the room with a frown. "More roses. It needs more roses, don't you think, Cesca?"

With a placating smile, Francesca turned to the rotund housekeeper behind them. "Will you send to the hothouses for more roses, Mrs. Parish? Yellow, I think."

"Oh," Sarah exclaimed, "and the fire must be lit soon in old Lady Braethon's room. She will want to go up and rest as soon as she arrives, I feel certain, and George says she likes her room like a coal oven all the time."

This time Francesca only looked at the housekeeper, who answered with an efficient nod. "You shall make an excellent hostess, Sarah. I should never have thought of that."

"Oh, Cesca, of course you would have."

"Well, if I had, I would have been likely to decide in my high-handed way that Lady Braethon would be far better off with some fresh air, and I'd have thrown all the windows open."

Sarah chuckled. "You are being nonsensical, for you know very well you have the kindest heart in the world."

Francesca smiled at her friend. Sarah could never see anything but the best in everyone. "No, darling. That honor has already been bestowed." She put an arm gently around the smaller woman's shoulders. "Shall we see to the music room?"

They entered this wondrous baroque chamber and let their eyes wander over its green scagliola columns and red tapestries, its pianoforte and delicately veneered harpsichord. Pink-cheeked cherubs playing gilded lutes greeted them overhead. "The harp!" cried Sarah in dismay. "We never had the harp restrung!"

"It was done this morning." soothed Francesca. "You reminded Mrs. Parish of it yourself only last night."

"Oh, thank goodness. For Mrs. Pennington is certain to want Priscilla to play for us."

"Yes, though why she would subject the poor girl, and us, to such torture is beyond me."

"Oh, Cesca. She doesn't play so *very* badly."

"She does," corrected Francesca. The two of them looked at each other and shared a grin.

"Well, yes, I'm afraid she does," admitted Sarah. "And I shall have to speak to the gardeners about Caspar. He is certain to want to know everything about every strange plant in the garden."

"Caspar?"

"Yes, George's cousin, Caspar Maltby. You know Caspar, don't you?"

"Mr. Maltby. Oh, yes, a botancial sort of fellow, forever prosing on about his roses."

"Yes. I was ever so surprised when he accepted. He never goes anywhere."

She rearranged a huge bowl of chrysanthemums and adjusted the position of a fire screen by about half an inch. She looked at the large gilt mirror over the mantel, frowned, and turned to Francesca, a comment on her lips.

"Yes, yes," said Francesca matter-of-factly, smiling at a footman with a polishing rag in his hand. "The mirror."

The servants had fallen away one by one as various tasks were assigned them. The only companion now remaining to the two girls was Mrs. Parish. "Will you be needing me anymore just now, Your Grace?" she asked. "I should just like to check on things in the kitchen."

"Oh, *please* do, Mrs. Parish," said Sarah. "And please pay Auguste at least one extravagant compliment. He simply must be in good spirits tonight and create us a masterful dinner."

The housekeeper allowed her thin line of mouth to curve ever so slightly upward at the corners. "I shall do my best, Your Grace," she said, and dipping a small curtsy, she hurried from the room with businesslike gait.

"Thank goodness for Mrs. Parish," sighed Sarah. "She

knows simply everything about Hockleigh. But I am so relieved you are here, Cesca. I am so nervous."

"Silly thing. Why ever should you be? Do you remember how nervous we were at our come-outs? Why, you were as white as your muslin gown that night. And look how well that turned out! A duchess, no less!"

"Oh, but you know George wasn't there that night, Cesca. He didn't even see me until two years later."

"And he adored you on sight. Now, do stop worrying so about this silly hunting party. No one is going to eat you, after all. You will do splendidly."

"Well, George thinks I shall, and you know how very smart he is, but I . . ."

"George is absolutely right. And he will be beside you the whole time, you know."

"Yes, thank goodness." She looked at Francesca, letting a smile turn up the corners of her mouth. A tiny dimple appeared. "But I'm afraid George is just the tiniest bit put out with me just now."

Francesca knew that mischievous smile only too well. Many was the time she had shared in the devilment that brought it on. "Oh, Sarah, whatever have you done to the poor man?" she asked.

"Well, I haven't *done* anything. It's rather what I didn't do."

Francesca waited for her to go on, but the mischievous smile only grew. "Well?" she finally prodded. "What didn't you do?"

"I'm afraid I neglected to tell him something rather important until just this morning." Her smile grew even larger. Her nervousness seemed to have left her completely.

Francesca stopped abruptly and looked closely at her friend's face, at the glowing cheeks, the dancing blue eyes, the radiance. The truth dawned. "Sarah! You're not . . ."

"Yes, love. I am. Hockleigh will soon have an heir."

The small Duchess all but disappeared into the embrace of the tall Lady Francesca. "Oh, Sarah, how wonderful! Are you quite certain? How long have you known? How do you feel? When will you be confined?"

"Just before Easter," replied Sarah, choosing the last in this barrage of questions.

"Easter? But that's . . . why, Sarah, that's less than five months. And you have only just told the Duke? No wonder the poor man is put out. Why ever did you wait so long?"

"Well, he was only a very little put out, I assure you. And I did want to be quite certain, of course." She was still smiling her dimply smile, but a look of comical guilt also graced her pink face. One look at Francesca told her that her explanation was insufficient. "Oh, very well. If you must know, I didn't want him to cancel the hunt. You know he would have done, besides making a very great fuss and making me take to my bed. You know I cannot stand to be fussed. George thinks I am a piece of china or something. I just couldn't bear to have my party canceled, Cesca."

"But, dearest, such a houseful of people at such a time! Won't it be too much for you?"

"Pooh! It will be no such thing, and so I told George. Why, I have never felt better in my life, Cesca. I did have to promise George to lie down on my bed every afternoon without fail, which is certain to be a great bore, and not to overtax myself in any way. But he couldn't very well cancel the hunt when the guests will be arriving at almost any moment."

"How wicked you are, Sarah." Francesca laughed. "And how clever, for all your adoration of George's opinions."

"You know I'm not at all clever, Cesca. Not like George. Or like you, for that matter. That's why I have you here to see to all the dreary details that I am certain to be far too fatigued to deal with myself."

"Yes, indeed. Very clever." The two young woman broke into laughter. "Well, I shall like it excessively," said Francesca when she brought her laughter under control. "You know how odiously managing I am, and I have been too much alone of late, boring myself with my own company and having no one at all to manage. This is just the sort of challenge I enjoy."

"Oh, Cesca, you shouldn't be alone. I so long to see you happy, as I am. Will you never marry? I know very well you have had ever so many proposals."

"More than I care to recall, love, and every one of them from some insufferable bore I can scarce bear to converse with for five minutes together. I know that sounds odiously conceited of me, and I will freely admit that modesty is yet another of the womanly virtues, like submissiveness, that seems eternally beyond my grasp. Papa did not educate me to be a simpering miss. I have never cared enough about anyone to even consider giving up my freedom, and I don't suppose I ever shall. I've been lucky enough and smart enough to avoid the curse of Romance for three-and-twenty years."

"But love can come after you are married, Cesca. That's what George said, and he was right, you know. I didn't love George when we married. Well, of course I scarcely knew him, but he talked me into it, and now I really think I would *die* without him."

Francesca looked at her friend lovingly. "I know you would, love, and believe me, I am very happy for you. But we are not the same. Your life would not make me happy."

"How can you know?"

The question caught Francesca unaware, and she stared sightlessly out a nearby window. "How can I know?" she repeated, almost to herself. "How indeed?"

A booming voice interrupted the young Duchess's speculative look and Francesca's reverie. "Sarah! Sarah, where are you?" The two young women had just reached one end of the Long Gallery and turned into its vastness. The source of the bellow was still out of sight around a corner at the far end of the room, but the voice echoed off the picture-hung walls, "Sarah! Look who's arrived. Sarah!"

Francesca smiled. It was impossible not to like the young Duke of Hockleigh. He was so full of goodwill toward the whole world that it constantly spilled out and engulfed everyone around him. His tall round frame now burst into the far end of the gallery, and he was not alone.

"Whoever can that be with George, I wonder," said Sarah in an undertone as they started down the long length of the room. "Do you know him?"

"No," said Francesca. "I've no idea who . . ." She stopped abruptly as she stared at the stranger. She took in his fine features under a deep tan, the breadth of his shoulders, the sheen of his pale gold hair. Memory stirred within her. The room seemed suddenly to be permeated with the smell of honeysuckle and the warmth of a drowsy summer sun.

Richard, Lord Devlin, entered the gallery in the wake of his exuberant friend, nearly shadowed by the Duke's bulk. Walking toward them, as they traversed the room he saw two remarkably handsome young women. The smaller of the two, in fluttering yellow muslin, was favoring George with a look of joy and abject adoration, hurrying to greet him with her arms out before her. Beside her was a taller, more graceful young lady with golden hair. She was smiling. When his eyes met that smile, memory seemed to catch within him. He thought he tasted strawberries.

It was him, she realized, a flood of emotions long forgotten coursing through her. How very dark he has grown. And how handsome. I had forgotten how handsome he is, like some Greek god. Adventuring must have agreed with him. I wonder if he ever married.

He recognized her with a start, like an electric jolt. Her hair is darker, he mused as he approached the two ladies. More like burnished gold than it was then. I wonder what she is doing here at Hockleigh. I wonder if she is here alone. I wonder . . .

"Look, Sarah!" the Duke's deep voice rolled out again. "It's Dev! I've told you about Dev, haven't I?"

The two pairs joined, and the Duchess reached out to shake the hand of the gentleman no longer a stranger. "Of course you have, dear. We are honored, Mr. Devlin. Welcome to Hockleigh."

"But it ain't *Mr.* Devlin, Sarah," corrected the Duke. "Been Lord Devlin for nearly a year now. That's why he's come home. To take up the inheritance, you know."

"Well, that is one reason, at least," said Lord Devlin.

Francesca started at the sound of his voice. She had forgotten how smooth, how musical it was.

"Then it is an even greater honor to welcome you, my lord," said Sarah. "And this is our dear friend Lady Francesca Waringham."

Devlin's eyes twinkled as they slid back to Francesca; a lopsided grin creased his face, a grin of both pleasure and acute embarrassment. "Lady Francesca and I have met." He noticed her blush and found it oddly pleasing.

"Devlin," she said as though to herself. She had all but forgotten his name. Belatedly remembering her manners, she held out her hand to him. "My lord," she said. She felt deeply embarrassed at the memories he stirred, vaguely angry at him still for running off and leaving her, and undeniably happy to see him again.

Their eyes locked. Each began a slow grin. By the time the foursome headed toward the drawing room for a cup of tea, they were able to speak normally, explaining to the Duke and Duchess—though not in its totality—their previous acquaintance.

3

By early afternoon, all the guests had arrived at Hockleigh—no one was likely to turn down an invitation to the greatest ducal mansion in all the north—and had begun to settle in. Introductions had been performed for those few unknown to each other; rooms had been inspected and accepted; tea had been drunk. An army of servants began the unpacking.

Though she would never admit the fact, especially to herself, Lady Francesca had been shocked to her soul at sight of this seeming specter from her past. Memories of a feeling she had not experienced since last seeing Lord Devlin, a lovely, confusing, delicious and very uncomfortable feeling, flooded into her mind and caused that unwonted blush that had claimed her face at sight of him.

For himself, Lord Devlin had been nearly as surprised as was the young lady, and nearly as confused, at their unexpected meeting. His memories of her were a strange mixture which he had not the leisure, nor the inclination, to examine too closely. He was aware of a tinge of amusement at his inexpert fumblings in that garden house so long ago. She had not responded as though he were inexpert, but he had bungled it all the same, he knew. He'd learned a good deal about women since that day; he had had many opportunities to do so.

He wondered idly if she would run away from him

now in such disgust as she had done then if he tried to kiss her again. She was certainly grown beautiful enough for the question to warrant some wondering. She had pricked his pride then. Why, it had been the very next morning that he had left for Southampton and his ship to India. He did not even speak to her again. He could not bear to. He had counted himself lucky to have gotten off so easily. With such a girl as Lady Francesca Waringham he might well have done something unpardonably foolish, like give up his travels. He may as well have given up his life. He was no longer the least bit foolish.

Odd, then, that he felt so like a schoolboy now in her presence. She had turned into such a calm, cool beauty, so obviously sure of herself, in need of nothing from anyone. And running lightly over all his other emotions in her presence was that same rustle of fear that had caused him to run five years ago. He recognized in her still the only woman he had ever known who might have the power to tame his restless spirit.

He had come near to climbing back into his shiny new curricle and beating a retreat south when informed that a large house party was in the offing. True, he was glad to be back in England. Also true that he had plans to settle in, at least for a while, and take up his place in society. But he did not feel quite ready to be put on display and ogled like a monkey in a menagerie. He remembered quite well the tastes of the *ton*.

The Duke and his pretty young wife had implored him to stay. They told him several of his old Oxford friends would soon be arriving. They promised him excellent hunting. They declared that they would feel themselves sorely used if he refused. Still Lord Devlin hedged. Lady Francesca added her quiet entreaties to theirs. Lord Devlin gave in and agreed to stay.

A calm had fallen over the great house, that warm calm that, though refreshing, is pregnant with excitement to come. It was the hour before dinner. The dressing gong had sounded some little while ago, and the entire company had dispersed each to his or her own elegant chamber, there to compose themselves and undertake the serious business of dressing for dinner. The sun had gone down, after all, and one did not appear below stairs of an evening in merino and cambric. Upstairs the starched linen and glossy silk was rustling with abandon.

It, the silk that is, was especially active in Lady Francesca's room. The pink-cheeked maid, a look of speculation in her intelligent eyes, was even now carrying away the third silken creation to grace her mistress's long limbs in the past quarter of an hour. This indecision on the young woman's part was far from normal and might portend important events. Then again, as the maid well knew, it might mean nothing more important than that her mistress was blue-deviled.

Francesca stood before the long cheval glass, an analytical frown on her oval of a face, studying the moss-green lustring gown she had tentatively decided upon. Its low, rounded neck showed off a lovely expanse of creamy bosom, the soft ruchings at the shoulder echoed the amber of her eyes and made them glow.

Had she given the matter much thought, which she had not, she could not have said why she felt so dissatisfied with her appearance this evening. Though far from vain, she knew herself to be a handsome woman. She was confident of her taste in dress, her beautiful posture, and her especially nice hands. But for some reason the total picture could not please her tonight.

As she allowed her frown of concentration to relax, she noticed that the trace of a wrinkle remained behind on her otherwise smooth brow. She stared at it, not in horror really, but in some wonder. Good God! How had she gotten so old?

The first bloom and freshness of youth was not the only thing missing from the lovely face staring back at her. For the first time she realized that the eagerness for life, the reaching out for whatever would come next, that had characterized the young Lady Francesca had been missing for some time now.

She sat and allowed the maid's nimble fingers to work on the heavy golden hair while she stared into the mirror, now with unseeing eyes. How had she looked to Lord Devlin this afternoon? she wondered. She was not the same person she had been five years ago, a green girl full of hopeless plans and silly dreams. She had been restless, enthusiastic, ready for anything then.

And nothing had happened. Or, more rightly, she had failed to make anything happen. Here she was with fully three-and-twenty years in her dish and nothing whatsoever to show for them. Her generosity and loyalty, her powerful intellect and many selfless deeds, were all overlooked at the present moment. Lady Francesca was in a mood to be hard on herself.

She discarded a pair of necklaces before clasping a set of jade and baroque pearls around her neck. She mulled over a drawer full of scarves and shawls before settling on an ocher gauze shot with gold. And she snapped at her maid in a singularly unusual manner.

Well, she was ready, she thought, old maid that she was. Picking up a pierced ivory fan, she turned to her maid. "You must not heed me, Rose," she begged, placing a hand lightly on the girl's arm. "I am being unaccountably grumpy tonight, I know, but it does not signify. You know I should be a complete wreck without you."

"I should hope not, milady," sniffed Rose. No one condemned her mistress in her hearing and got away with it, not even the mistress herself. "You'll take the shine out of the lot of them, you will. You do look a treat."

Francesca gave a rueful smile. "I must find a suitable reward for such blind loyalty," she said lightly. "Go and enjoy your dinner and forget my grumps."

As the maid curtsied her out of the room, the look of speculation came back into the sharp dark eyes. Lady

Francesca might say what she liked about her low spirits, but Rose Steele knew that look of excitement that hovered in her mistress's amber eyes just below the surface of her "grumps." It looked like being an interesting visit after all.

They sat down a full two dozen revelers to dinner that night, and the sounds emanating from the formal dining room were the clearest evidence of the high spirits and good breeding of the elite who were invited to Hockleigh. Laughter bubbled as softly and gently as the champagne. Witticisms accompanied the soft chink of silver on bone china. Clever *bon-mots* were passed around with the buttered lobsters.

It was an impressive company. Even the difficulty of finding one's way to the wilds of Yorkshire was unlikely to dissuade many from accepting an invitation to Hockleigh, most especially this year. Not only was there lavish hospitality and excellent hunting to look forward to—the Hockleigh pack was known as the finest north of the Belvoir—but this year held the added fillip of a new young duchess to be scrutinized and judged on the performance of her awesome new duties.

Lord and Lady Jersey had condescended to make the trip, he for the hunting, she for the society. She was the uncrowned queen of the *ton*, and their presence alone guaranteed that the party would be long talked about. Old Lady Braethon had brought her granddaughter, and the Duke's lovely sister Augusta, Marchioness of Aurelm, had brought her even livelier children. Also, her husband. A sprinkling of older people accompanying their nearly grown children, an assortment of young lords and ladies, Honorable Misters and Misses, and the odd relation completed the guest list.

Most of the young people were old school friends of either the Duke or the Duchess. It was a fun-loving, lively group and augured well for the success Sarah so badly wanted. Still, she was nervous.

She needn't have been. Everyone had settled smoothly into the assigned rooms. Everything was going beautifully. Even the Dowager Lady Braethon had expressed pleasure in her overheated room and was even now attacking with gusto a roasted pigeon in caper sauce and a large dish of stewed mushrooms. And this after commenting that she was certain she could manage nothing more than a little thin gruel and some heated wine in her room after the rigors of her travels. Across the table sat her granddaughter, Miss Jane Magness, pretty as a flower, picking daintily at a matelote of rabbit.

With the unexpected addition of Lord Devlin to the group, the success of Sarah's party was assured. It was clear from the moment that introductions were begun that the dashing traveler and adventurer was destined to be the new pet of the *ton*. It was to Lord Devlin's credit that he had no desire for the position about to be bestowed.

Conversation flitted around the table, touching lightly on many subjects, but by far the bulk of it centered on the surprising return of the wayfarer and his many adventures. He was unknown to most of the company, excepting Francesca and his Oxford friends who were present. His travels of the past five years, most particularly in America, made him a natural subject of curiosity.

Questions both thoughtful and ridiculous came his way in droves, revealing an amazing breadth of imagination and an even greater depth of ignorance among the *haut ton* about the great world and most especially their former colonies.

"I understand all the black slaves believe in voodoo and witchcraft and such," said Lady Jersey. "I shouldn't think I would like having my servants putting hexes on me or sticking pins into some wax doll in my image," she concluded with her famous laugh.

"I've a cousin in Boston," said Graham Symington.

"Name of John Whitney. Or is it Whitby? No matter. Ever meet him?"

"How could you bear it?" put in a distinctively middle-aged Lady Poole, shaking her chins in indignation. "Everyone of every class whatever all jumbled up together like that. Shocking!"

"New Orleans!" breathed Miss Magness. "I have always fancied it such a romantic-sounding place. Pirates and riverboat gamblers and such."

Lady Francesca, like everyone else, sat with her eyes most often on Lord Devlin and listened to his calm, sensible answers to these and other insensible questions. He looked up once and surprised her gaze upon him. He grinned at her in a strangely intimate way. Unthinkingly, she grinned back, and they shared a moment of perfect understanding.

"The United States! Humph!" grumbled Lady Braethon, spooning up a large dish of custard between words. "They may call themselves what they like. *I* shall always refer to them as the colonies, and very ill-behaved colonies at that."

"Hear there's some decent horseflesh coming out of Virginia," bellowed Lord Jersey, horses never far from his mind or his conversation, "and some other outlandish place name of, uh, what was it? Kentuck or some such thing."

"Very decent indeed," confirmed Lord Devlin. "I've brought a few back for my stable. But even finer are some of the wild horses from the Western Territories. They're not always so beautiful as our English stock, but they're all heart and can run most English horses into the ground. Why, I've seen them go at a full gallop for upwards of twenty-five miles and scarcely be winded. But you shall see for yourself. I am having a few of my mustangs sent up from Hull."

"Surely you will not hunt some shaggy wild pony, Devlin!" gasped the Honorable Mr. Dudley Dalton in outraged tones. "Got to keep up the image of the field, y'know."

"Oh, I fancy they won't put me quite to shame," answered Devlin with a twinkle of anticipation. "But you must judge for yourself. In the meantime, George has kindly consented to mount me."

"Haven't forgotten how to hunt, have you, Dev?" asked Sir Algernon Pett. "Used to ride the lot of us into the ground back at Oxford, but daresay you're out of practice."

"Oh, I hope I shall contrive to keep up, Algy. There's some pretty hunting in Virginia and some very hard riding in the West, so I have not been totally deprived."

"Did you spend much time in the Western Territories, my lord?" asked Lady Francesca. "Is it not an extremely wild country?"

"Extremely. But very beautiful, unmatched by anything I have seen anywhere else. I arrived on the Western Coast, you know, from Australia, and then worked my way eastward. It was an awesome experience, I can tell you. Deserts the size of Kent and rock canyons larger than London. And then one comes to the central section of the continent, where one can ride alone for days at a time without seeing anything but an endless stretch of prairie covered with grass high as a man."

Mr. Maltby looked up from his raspberry trifle. "*Euchlaena mexicana*, I imagine. Sometimes grows to ten feet, I have heard. A very hardy perennial," And so saying, he returned to his trifle.

"It sounds like heaven to me," said Francesca, her eyes sparkling with the imagined wonder of it all. "So much space! Such freedom!"

"Yes. The freedom was absolute," agreed Devlin. Then, looking directly into her eyes, he added, "but such freedom has its price, Lady Francesca. It can be very lonely."

She could not hold his gaze, and soon looked down to

the Chantilly basket she had been nibbling. Mr. Dalton broke in in astonishment. "But were you quite alone, Devlin?"

"Why, yes, most of the time," he answered.

"Well! Myself, I shouldn't like to be without my valet. So uncomfortable wearing scuffed boots. But then, I daresay there was no one about to notice."

"No one at all!" replied Devlin in amusement. "Except, of course, my occasional Indian guides. But they didn't seem to mind, or even notice, that I was less than perfectly dressed. I thought they rather admired me in my fur and leathers." Mr. Dalton could not even bring himself to reply to such an astonishing remark, as he could in no wise conjure up an image of a gentleman dressed in furs and running around with redskins.

"Indians!" exclaimed Lady Poole. "You actually allowed them to guide you? But was that quite safe, my lord? Were you not afraid for your scalp?"

"On the contrary. Not only was it safe, it was very necessary. You can have no notion, ma'am, of the wildness of the country through which I was passing."

"No, I am pleased to say that I cannot," she readily agreed.

He ignored this statement with a wry smile and went on. "You may know that Misters Lewis and Clark, on their crossing of the continent a few years back, would have been utterly lost without Sacajewea, their Indian-maiden guide. I found myself in much the same position." He turned his smile back to Francesca. "It is only common sense to be guided through uncharted territory by someone who knows the way."

"Well, *I* for one should not feel safe in my bed *anywhere* in America!" exclaimed Mrs. Pennington. "What with Red Savages running about loose and all. I cannot think why it is allowed. Do they not hate all white men?"

"Some do, of course, and with good reason, you must admit. They have been very badly treated, robbed of their lands, pushed aside, slaughtered as though they were just one more exotic American beast. I have spent considerable time with the various tribes. On more than one occasion I owed them my life. Certainly they are different from us, but I have found that, by and large, they are no better or worse than anyone else. Some are foolish. Some are wise. Most are just very human."

A silence followed while the company digested this. Sarah looked around the table at her guests, then looked at Lord Devlin with obvious satisfaction and gratitude. For the first time in several days she felt herself able to relax. With such an interesting, wise, and thoroughly delightful guest as the unexpected Lord Devlin, her party could not fail.

Francesca found herself surprised at the man's wisdom and obvious understanding of human nature. Such were the benefits of travel, the benefits she had never been able to have. She really must get to know him all over again—to pick his brain, as it were.

"Yes, yes," said Lord Jersey finally. "That's all very well, but what of these horses of yours, man? Mustangs, you called them? What's the stock? High-blooded? How heavy can they carry?"

"What about finesse, Dev?" said Mr. Symington. "Can they take a bullfinch?"

"How about a double oxer?" added Sir Algernon. "Any good at going in and out clever?"

It was clear that the conversation had taken a masculine turn. The young hostess nodded to the ladies and rose. They left the gentlemen to their port and cigars.

4

While talk of horses and hunting and adventuring in general continued in the dining room, cutting through a rapidly building layer of thick, pungent cigar smoke, the ladies's drawing room was filled to overflowing with chatter and speculation about one adventurer in particular.

"He is so excessively handsome," chirped a very young and eager Miss Hollys. "Do you not think so, Mama?"

"He will do, Letty. He will do," answered Lady Poole. "Though I am not at all certain I can wholly approve of him, you know. I am sure I understood him to say that he had actually *lived* among the aborigines. Very odd behavior, that. Very odd indeed!" The exclamation point caused the necessity of reaching up and righting her puce satin turban and its dancing plume.

"But only think, ma'am, what he must have learned about life," said Francesca. "Things one could never learn from books. Things like—"

The older lady cut her off with a severe frown. "Things that young ladies *do not* know about or care about, I am sure."

"He is just like a hero out of a book," continued Miss Hollys, her eyes aglow.

"He'd not thank you to hear himself described as such, I'll warrant," put in Lady Jersey with her irrepressible air of no nonsense. "Looks to me to have no flummery about him." This was high praise from Sally Jersey.

"Pooh, Sally," said Roxanna Gordon, a young, beautiful, and very dashing widow in a low-cut crimson demi-robe gilded with diamonds. "What can you know of the mysterious Lord Devlin? Is he not completely unknown to all us ladies? I adore enigmas. Especially such rich and handsome ones."

"No, I have never met, Lord Devlin," admitted Lady Jersey. "But I hardly think, Roxanna, that a gentleman from an old established family, whose uncle was well-known and admired and who has inherited one of the finest titles in the country, can ever be branded a complete stranger amongst us."

"And besides," said Sarah, "he is not *entirely* unknown to us. Of course many of the gentlemen knew him at Oxford. And Cesca met him on a number of occasions before he left England."

All eyes now turned to Francesca. The young Miss Hollys wore a clearly hopeful face that Francesca could be persuaded to tell them all about his lordship. Mrs. Gordon was just as clearly annoyed that any lady present should have better knowledge of Devlin than she did herself. The others were all curious. "Did you really know him, Cesca?" and "How did you come to meet?" floated across the room to Francesca.

She gave a tiny, disinterested shrug. "It was a very slight acquaintance, I assure you. We had mutual friends, that is all." Only Sarah, who knew her so well, could detect the trace of embarrassment in her voice, and she wondered at it. Cesca was usually the last person on earth to be embarrassed about anything, especially a gentleman.

Roxanna Gordon looked at her with narrowed eyes. She was not a particularly perceptive woman, except when it came to her own interests. But she did just think that something in Francesca's simple statement did not ring true.

Other questions flew at Francesca, but Mrs. Gordon was quick to turn the discussion away from such a prior friendship. "Such a pity, you know, that Lord Byron could not attend your party, Sarah," she said. "I am sure his nose would be put completely out of joint by our dashing new adventurer. And about time, too. He is become odiously top-lofty and full of himself of late. That ridiculous business with Caro Lamb making such a fool of herself over him in public."

"Ah, but Lord Devlin does not write poetry," stated Mrs. Pennington, nodding her feathers in total approval of the fact. "At least I sincerely *hope* he does not!"

"But he might still fit Caro's description of Byron," said Miss Hollys. "You know, 'Mad, bad, and dangerous to know!' " Obviously the idea had great appeal for her.

"Don't be foolish, Letty," said her mother. "He hasn't a trace of the corsair in him. I am sure he is perfectly respectable, which no one could say about Byron!"

"Not so respectable, I hope, that none of us will get the chance to play Caro to his Byron," said Mrs. Gordon with a light laugh. Her eyes glittered with anticipation.

"Poetry, faugh!" exclaimed Lady Braethon, a trifle behind in the conversation. "It is an easy enough matter to write in verse: rhyming is child's play, after all. As for Lord Byron's outlandish ideas, who can say where he gets them? If he were simply *Mister* Byron, no one would so much as glance at his nonsense. But he is a lord, so every silly miss must romanticize him and every town fribble ape him, and everyone who should have better sense hangs on his every word."

"But you must admit, ma'am," said Francesca with a grin, "Byron does seem made for a romantic hero with those wild dark looks and his limp. And while I don't suppose Lord Devlin can do anything about his unfortunate blond hair, I do think he might at least have managed a scar to show for all his travels. I don't quite see how we can make him a hero without one."

Lady Braethon gave a hearty guffaw of laughter. A

few others tittered. Miss Hollys flushed a deep red. "I know you are laughing at me. I must seem very silly and romantical to you."

"On the contrary, Letty," said Francesca in a kind voice. "We are laughing at ourselves."

"I am sure Lord Devlin needs no scar to make him interesting," added Sarah. "He is an exceedingly handsome and polished gentleman, and I am awfully glad to have him at my party."

Mrs. Gordon let out a ripple of laughter. "And no one in possession of forty thousand pounds per annum can ever be *un*interesting," she said, her eyes now shining as brightly as her shower of diamonds. The comment effectively put an end to the conversation. Luckily the gentlemen chose that moment to rejoin their female counterparts, and the tea tray was rolled in after them.

It was immediately evident from their comfortable expressions that the gentlemen had been well entertained during their absence from the ladies. No doubt Lord Devlin had been regaling them with anecdotes of a somewhat warmer nature than those recounted before the ladies, thought Francesca. She was certain he must have a large store of them.

She pondered with annoyance her own lack of adventures. Oh, she had not been an absolute dull dog. In fact, in her earlier years she had come close to scandalizing the whole of the *ton* with her romps. But hampered as she was by her petticoats, so to speak, she had never had Lord Devlin's rich opportunities to really drink of the cup of life. Her attempts at independence she now saw as little more than childish revolts, silly little intrigues that would have been sordid had they not been so innocent, flirtations with empty-headed rascals in the hope of discovering what all the talk of *romance* was about. But her heart had always come up empty.

She had long since thrown in the towel, to use the boxing cant of some of her more sporting beaux, and sunk once again into respectability. She no longer flirted, though the Lord knew the gentlemen still flocked about her. Indeed, she now had little patience with the *ton*'s almost total preoccupation with the mating game, however well she might understand its rules.

Lord Devlin's eyes moved easily to hers almost as soon as he entered the room. He looked at her speculatively a moment, smiled a brief, almost diffident smile, then turned his attention to Mrs. Pennington, who was tapping his arm lightly with her fan—just as though he were a naughty schoolboy, thought Francesca with disgust—and directing his attention to the nondescript daughter at her side.

Poor Pris, thought Francesca, looking at the girl. Such a little mouse of a thing, and here was her mother trying to feed her to the lion of the evening. She wondered idly just what sort of a woman would be able to stand up to his lordship and briefly considered taking him on herself. For all her disdain of fashionable flirtation, she was perfectly versed in the art. Her vanity wondered if she could bring him to heel.

Then she remembered the disastrous results of their last encounter. That had not been flirting, of course, at least not for her. It was something very much stronger that had swept her along—and him too, she had thought at the time. But she had been a fool. He had easily shown her how little his emotions had been engaged. Indeed, she was thankful for it, wasn't she? In a moment of thoughtlessness she might have thrown away all her hopes and dreams of independence. And she had not really wanted him, after all. Not for a moment. Not under her mask of eagerness. Well, perhaps for only a moment. But she had quickly come to her senses.

Luckily for her peace of mind, her attention was claimed at that moment by Graham Symington, who took the chair beside her. He was a longtime favorite of hers, for he never tried to flirt with her. "Well, Graham," she said brightly. "Has our wondrous newcomer been regaling you all with delicious stories of Oriental living dolls and buxom Indian maidens?"

"Naturally," he replied with a grin of easy friendship. "What else do you suppose gentlemen talk of over their port?"

"I have always wondered."

"Dev is far too good a resource to let pass by. The things he has seen!"

"I can well imagine," she answered dryly. "And what he has not seen, he can easily make up. Who is to contradict him, after all?"

"Not Dev. Why, he's the soul of honor, Cesca. If Richard Devlin says a thing happened, then you can bet your life on it."

"Strange!" came her arch answer. "I have never thought of his lordship as particularly honorable. Interesting, surely, and, oh, many other attractive things, but . . ." She let her voice drift off, remembering a young man who had tempted her into folly, and when she had nearly succumbed, had allowed her to run away and had taken himself off without so much as a by-your-leave, much less an apology or an honorable offer.

"What sort of bee have you got in your bonnet, Cesca?" asked Mr. Symington. "Dev wouldn't wound a soul could he help it. Why, at Oxford he was forever calling the rest of us to task for thoughtlessness. Nothing of the rotter about Dev."

She did not reply to this for the simple reason that she didn't know what to say. Instead, she let her eyes rove to where Lord Devlin had just been standing, to see if her imagination could clothe him in the outfit of such a paragon.

But his lordship had moved on, having dexterously managed to pry himself loose from Mrs. Pennington and her dutiful daughter. Francesca could not resist the impulse to look at Priscilla. Surprisingly, she was still in one piece and even allowed her eyes to rise from their habitual focus on the floor to follow his magnificent figure across the room. Then she caught Francesca's gaze upon her and quickly returned her eyes to their usual floor-bound position.

His adventuring lordship now stood listening quietly to the animated conversation of Miss Julia Dalton, an acknowledged Beauty. At twenty, she had been a full two years on the town, and she was not loath to put her vast experience to work to her advantage. Her long-lashed dark eyes sparkled with vivacity, and Francesca could hear her tinkle of laughter ring out at some comment of Devlin's.

"Silly little twit," she muttered to herself.

"What?" asked Mr. Symington, "I say, Cesca! You haven't heard a word I've been saying." He followed her gaze. "I see. It's Dev, of course. I can tell that I shall have to call the fellow out before I'm much older. Uncomfortable when the fellow's a friend of mine. But there's nothing else for it. The bleater's been here less than a day, and he's turned all your heads already. Not surprising, of course, but I shouldn't have thought *you* would fall for his blue eyes,"

"Don't be ridiculous, Graham!" she snapped more hotly than she intended. "I am not so easily cozened. I was merely remarking the ridiculousness of everyone lionizing him so. Why, only look! Now Letty Hollys and Jane Magness are at him. I see they have quite cut Julia out. He shall be much puffed up in his own conceit before the evening is through, I doubt not."

"Not Dev. Best of good fellows, Dev," said Mr. Symington. He did not, however, take his eyes off Lord Devlin or, more particularly, off Miss Hollys.

Very soon, the object of their discussion managed to draw himself away, as though summoned by their talk of him, and presented himself in person before Francesca. "Lord!" he exclaimed, but in a voice only his two listeners could hear. "I've half a mind to get on the next boat back to America. If George hadn't promised me some good hunting, I'd do it, too. I had forgotten how *predatory* English females can be!"

As an English female, Francesca thought it her duty to take public exception to such a generalization, even though she tended to agree with the assessment much of the time. Had he thought her predatory five years ago? Was that why he went away so quickly, no doubt in disgust of her? "Really, my lord—" she began her defense of her sex.

"Oh, you needn't worry. I didn't mean you. I know only too well that *you* have no designs on me, my lady. It is why I have particularly sought you out. I must breathe for a moment before one more young lady tries to flirt with me." And so saying, he threw himself into a chair beside her, or came as close to doing so as a pair of tight-fitting pantaloons, a strict upbringing, and a very elegant drawing room would allow.

"Well, old man," said Mr. Symington, rising to his full lanky six-feet-plus, "if you plan to leave the field open to us lesser mortals for a moment, I'll just go say a word to Miss Hollys. You know, Dev, if you really wanted to give the rest of us fellows a break, you'd adjourn immediately to the billiard room. Out of sight, out of mind, y'know." And sketching a grinning bow to Francesca, he crossed the room to the most current object of his affections.

"Are you so certain that I shall not try to flirt with you, my lord?" asked Francesca. "Such a very *eligible* and *interesting* gentleman must certainly be a temptation," she finished with a nice blend of archness and sweetness and a maidenly flutter of her golden lashes.

"Don't you dare to! I shall not be responsible for my actions if you do," he answered in mock, but only slightly mock, horror. "But I have no fear of it. I know I shall be safe with you." The elaborate casualness with which he spoke struck her as not quite true. Did it hide a note of bitterness? And whatever did he mean, anyway?

It had, after all, been he who had abandoned her five years ago.

"Oh, yes, my lord," she said. "Quite safe."

His blue eyes darkened at her tone. He wondered what he could have said to upset her. "I do wish you would put away all this 'my lord' business. I am quite unused to it—no one lordships anyone in America, you know—and I am finding it wearying in the extreme. My friends call me Devlin."

"Am I to take that as an offer of friendship . . . Devlin?"

"Of course. A friend is merely the opposite of an enemy, and I hope we are not that, my lady."

"I see no reason why we should be," she replied coolly, much more coolly than she felt. "And my name is Francesca."

"It suits you, you know, in its regalness. Makes you sound like some cool Italian beauty sitting on the balcony of her palazzo and gazing placidly down onto a Venetian piazza, wondering at the robust antics of the throngs below."

She could not keep a gasp of surprise from her lips. Was that really how he saw her? She could not know that he had only this evening been told of the nicknames bestowed on her by the unlucky London bucks she had spurned. "The Ice Goddess" and "The Citadel" were two of the more common. They had replaced "Carefree Cesca," which had graced her just three or four years earlier.

"I should hope I am not so far removed from life as that, Devlin. To merely look down upon it like it was a play on a stage." The words rang hollow in her own ears, for was that not precisely how she had been viewing herself of late, the very reason her life had been so empty?

"I should hope so too, Francesca," he said quietly, remembering a bright-eyed, eager girl with a woman's passions, and wondering where she had gone. "I should hope so too."

Eyes may say much, but the gaze of these two locked on each other had time to murmur little more than a word before the ripple of laughter that was the calling card of Roxanna Gordon joined in the conversation. "Naughty Cesca!" she chided. "Monopolizing the only truly interesting man present. I have brought you more tea, Devlin, though I don't imagine you can bear the wishy-washy stuff. I imagine you frontiersmen stick with rum or brandy or some such delightfully masculine drink."

"Whiskey, Mrs. Gordon," he replied, slipping easily into a bantering tone. "And on occasion coffee, but coffee such as you have never tasted, I'm sure. Roasted black as coal and brewed just as strong. It's thick and hot and chewy. A bit of heaven, in fact. I don't advise it for a lady, however," he continued mischievously. "The Americans are fond of saying it will put hair on your chest."

"Oh la!" she cried on a ripple of mirth, and tapped his hand with her busily working fan. "How naughty you are!" She had long since lost the ability to blush on command, to her vast annoyance, and needs must use her sultry smile instead. She gave him one of her best. "And you, Devlin? Can you prove the aphorism a true one? I daresay you can, but how intriguing to wonder in uncertainty."

Disgusted at the woman's forwardness, though she had been rather amused by it in the past, Francesca excused herself and went to where Sarah was pouring out fresh tea. Devlin was left to suffer alone the pointed flirtations of Mrs. Gordon.

Luckily for his lordship, the beginning of hunting on the morrow precluded a late night. Everyone was eager to be well-rested and in good trim for the opening meet. It was not long, therefore, before Sarah led the ladies up the stairs to their bedchambers. The gentlemen followed very shortly.

The stars glittered, and the dew fell. The Stopper-up rode over the fields filling foxholes in preparation for the festivities to come. The dogs snoozed peacefully, as yet unaware of the excitement the morning would bring.

The lights of Hockleigh winked out one by one until the great house lay in darkness, gilded only by the soft glow of the moon as it slid lower in the sky.

Lady Francesca slept.

5

Early-morning dampness best held the scent of the fox on the ground, and the next morning was perfectly calculated to hold high the spirits of the avid sportsmen and women who were out in droves. The day was bright but a bit overcast; everyone looked forward to a brisk ride to warm body and spirit.

The Hockleigh Hunt had such a grand reputation that everyone for miles around, be he peasant, squire, or stable boy, wanted to be on hand. The Duke was well known for the generosity displayed at the opening Lawn Meet, when all the countryside was invited to gather on his great lawns and partake of his largess.

The swirl of color that greeted Francesca as she stepped out of the house was exhilarating. There was a crisp autumn chill in the air, severe enough to keep everyone's blood moving but certainly not enough to keep anyone away from the hunt. Indeed, it would have taken a foot of snow at the least to manage that feat.

Tenants and ostlers, shopgirls and servants, drank warmed ale from giant cauldrons and munched on crusty bread, salty ham, and good country cheese. Over on the main lawn, the gentry, sporting their pink and leathers, put away great quantities of kidneys, beefsteaks, kippers, muffins, and jam. They burned off the chill with coffee and tea and beakers of hot mulled wine. Tiny puffs of steam emitting from hundreds of chattering mouths wafted away on the cold air. Small groups gathered around warmly glowing braziers, their hands wrapped comfortingly around their steaming mugs.

One look at the groaning table that provided the hunt breakfast and one could but pity the poor horses; it would be amazing if each was not called upon to carry an extra stone at the least this day.

Looping the long green velvet skirts of her riding habit over her arm, Francesca began loading a plate with gusto. The first hunt of the season always whetted her healthy appetite. She could hunt with the best of them, and she could certainly eat with the best of them. Her eyes were shining with anticipation, and her cheeks glowed a becoming pink from the chill air. Regardless of her recent lassitude of spirits, it was quite impossible for Lady Francesca Waringham, possibly the finest horse-woman at present in Yorkshire, to feel less than excited about a hunt that promised such good sport.

"Oh, Cesca, how lovely you look this morning!" exclaimed Sarah, herself presenting a very pretty picture in a Circassian dress of deep rose edged in Muscovy sable. "And you are just the person I need. Do be a darling and go speak to old Mr. Nevensby. He is the local squire, you know, all gruff and bluff. He shall set us all by the ears, I fear. But talking to the prettiest woman present always put him back into a genial mood."

"Then you should do the honors yourself, my love," said Francesca. "You look a picture. I declare, if that is what being in the family way does for one's looks, I am half-tempted to try it myself."

"Well, I wish you would," said Sarah matter-of-factly. "After securing a proper husband, of course."

"Of course," said Francesca wryly.

"Well, it would do you a world of good, you know."

"Perhaps your squire would do. Nevensby, is it?"

Her answer was a little choke of laughter. "Thank goodness you are not being serious. The squire is all of eighty and would drive even you to distraction in a week. But do go and talk to him, I beg you. Actually, you needn't talk at all. Only listen and smile and nod occasionally and open your eyes *very* wide in admiration."

"Use all my feminine wiles, you mean," Francesca laughingly returned. "Very well. Where is this ogre in such need of taming?"

"He is over there blustering at poor George," said Sarah, discreetly pointing out the offending personage. "And I fear my poor love is in great need of rescuing."

Francesca, her lack of a white charger notwithstanding, hied herself off to the rescue.

The Duke of Hockleigh was not the only one in the party in need of rescue at that moment. Lord Devlin, however acute his need, saw no hope of it, though. He had been cornered by Mrs. Gordon. By some wonderful trick, he knew not how, she had managed to maneuver him to a stone bench in the topiary garden, where the pair of them were all but hidden from the view of the others.

"*Do* tell me more about these strange American Indians, Devlin. Do they have fanciful mating and fertility rites and all?" she asked as she slowly stroked the deep soft velvet of her riding habit. It was crimson, her best color, and was cut to show off her ample bosom and tiny waist.

"Some tribes do," he answered in a casual tone that hid his discomfort. "They have more need of them than we do, you see. Many of their children die, and a man's status is measured by how many sons he has. But even more respected are their holy men, who choose to remain celibate."

She gave a ripple of laughter, cocking her head to the precise angle to show to best advantage her little red toque with its curled black feather carefully set on her glistening black curls. "One would hope that their numbers are few, for the sake of their women as well as for the future of the race."

"I heard few complaints from their ladies."

"None, I'll wager, whilst you were among them, my lord," she returned with a smile nicely blending coyness with archness.

Fortunately, his answer was drowned out by the horns giving the call to mount. The hunt was about to get under way.

A flurry of activity now began. Prancing horses were led out, fresh and eager, snorting clouds of steam into the air. The yapping of the dogs filled everyone's ears. In the general mêlée, Devlin magically managed to detach himself from Roxanna and blend into the milling throng.

Francesca, just as willing as his lordship to call a halt to a tedious conversation, happily relinquished her empty plate and cup, bade a civil good morning to Squire Nevensby, and strode confidently to Desdemona, her newest hunter, a high-bred and prickly bay mare. A handful of sugar lumps found their way from her skirt pocket to the mare's soft mouth, for which the mistress received an affectionate nudge from a cold wet nose.

"Yes, yes, my darling. I am eager too. We shall show them all today, shan't we? But you really must not draw over the fox and bring me home in disgrace."

"Is it a practice with her?" came Devlin's voice behind her.

"Good morning, Devlin." said Francesca pleasantly. She had to smile at sight of him. She had thought him very fine in his traveling clothes. Last evening she had remarked how well evening clothes became him. But now, in the finely molded leather breeches that showed the entire line of his powerful thighs, in the olive coat that perfectly fitted over his broad expanse of shoulder, with a single shaft of sunlight glinting on his sun-streaked hair, he looked like some sort of a god. She felt a small lurch in the pit of her stomach, a feeling she had not experienced in many years, but she managed to keep her voice calm as she remarked, "Oh, no, Desdemona is the best horse in the world. But she has only recently learned her manners. This will be her first trial in the field. But I have every confidence in Desi." She patted the velvety nose.

"She is a beauty," he replied, "just like her mistress." His eyes glowed the admiration he felt at the sight she presented.

Francesca felt an acute need to change the conversation and gestured to the big raking grey Devlin was leading. "Isn't that the Duke's Odysseus?"

"Yes. George has been kind enough to mount me until my own horses arrive."

"He will give you a superlative ride. I have had him under me once or twice; he shows good spirit."

"Oh, I am sure we shall do fine. May I?" he asked, offering her a lift onto Desdemona's high back.

The horse pranced about as she mounted, and it took all Francesca's attention to calm her. Devlin watched in admiration as the frisky mare was brought easily to heel. Throwing a leg over the broad back of Odysseus, he smiled at her and the pair made their way toward the others.

The swirl of movement had by now organized itself into some semblance of order. The Master blew his horn, and the Whipper-in led the yelping pack toward the first covert. The whole field was off at a gentle trot behind them, trailing a cavalcade of prancing children, holidaying tenants, and ladies in elegant carriages. Most of the ladies could not deal with anything so strenuous as actually hunting themselves, but they must just dress up in their prettiest frocks and drive out to "see hounds" and wave their gentlemen off.

The excitement within the group grew as they neared the covert, until it was almost palpable. The cacophony of sound—the yapping dogs, the clopping horses, the rumbling carriage wheels, and the chattering riders— grew to a crescendo until the children were nearly beside themselves with the excitement of it all. Francesca

looked at Devlin, and they offered each other a smile of
genuine delight.

The hounds were thrown into the covert, and the
group quietened in expectation, nearly holding their
breaths while the hounds searched out their quarry.
Their luck hit almost at once. The barking increased to a
roar. "View-Halloo" was sounded at the very moment
the fox broke covert; the hounds were quickly gathered
and given the scent. The field was off at the gallop.

Francesca felt her heart lurch and her blood begin to
pump at the sound of the View. She dug in her heels,
and Desdemona surged forward. Francesca heard herself
laugh. This was why she hunted, this feeling of exhilaration, of danger, of knowing that she must count only
on herself and her own skill to bring her through.

The mare broke into a long rolling gallop. They flew
past trees, scrubby bushes, and low stone walls. Pebbles
and clots of turf thrown up by the hooves of the horses
ahead whipped past Francesca. There were probably
birds twittering in the trees not far off; she did not hear
them. She heard only the thunderous roar of the hooves
and the thudding of her equally thunderous heart, the
rush of the wind past her ears as she pushed her way
through it, and the strong steady breathing of the mare.
Over it all was the occasional exclamation point of the
huntsman's horn as he tried to keep the field in some sort
of order.

She scarce noticed the other riders, so wrapped up was
she in the exhilaration of the chase. But as one of the
horses began to gain on her just to the left, she let her
eyes glance briefly over. Lord Devlin grinned at her as
he drew even. She grinned back. Then, almost at once,
they found themselves laughing outright, the sound lost
in the rolling thunder below them and carried away on
the rushing wind.

Just ahead lay a gritstone wall, dark with age. They
eyed it at the same moment, glanced at each other, then
spurred their horses to even greater efforts.

Francesca measured the wall with her eye, even as it grew closer. She tried to guess what lay on the other side. Damp glittered on the stones, grey with patches of green where moss had been allowed a hold. A slight change in speed, a minor shift in position. She put down her head. She could feel the heat rising from the neck of the straining mare. Here was the wall. She held her breath and threw her heart over it.

The two horses left the ground at the same moment. They sailed over the wall as if they were of one heart, and touched the soft earth on the other side in absolute unison. Francesca let out her breath with a sigh.

The two young people now dared to look at each other again, this time offering each other a smile of the most perfect understanding.

What a magnificent horseman he is, Francesca told herself, as though it were a surprise. The magnificent horseman himself was having similar thoughts about her, albeit in somewhat more colorful terms. Damme! But that girl can ride! was what his mind was repeating.

Just then the fox was headed, and turned sharp to the right. The pack followed, and Francesca and Devlin were separated.

It was a fabulous opening to the hunt. A run of a full twenty-seven miles, the whole field in at the kill. Francesca was presented with the brush, and everyone returned to Hockleigh very weary and very dirty and very well pleased.

After a hearty luncheon during which they all congratulated themselves profusively on some very good sport, the company retired to their respective chambers. Tonight was, after all, the grand Hunt Ball, and they must make certain repairs to their persons.

6

The new Duchess of Hockleigh had always had excellent taste tinged with a touch of natural whimsy. Until the dramatic change in state brought about by her marriage to the Duke, she had had little opportunity to exercise it. Now she was giving it full rein, and delighting in the freedom to do so. She had decided that her first Hunt Ball was the perfect opportunity to show off her skill.

Until the death of the old Dowager Duchess some two years ago, Hockleigh in general, and the Hunt Ball in particular, had been steeped in tradition. Potted palms in the ballroom had always been the rule. It was past time for a change.

And so Sarah had decided that the ball was not to take place in the ballroom at all but in the Orangery. It was much the prettier room, with its long wall of glass and its bounty of greenery. And it was nearly as large as the ballroom and far less formal. The banana palms and citrus trees in their huge white tubs were pushed into the corners of the room. Among their branches were hung dozens of gilded cages housing brilliantly plumed parrots and cockatoos, fluttery finches, and sweetly singing canaries. Fragrant blooms from the hothouses were banked around the wooden tubs holding the trees. More deep red and golden flowers graced the doorways, windows, and the many mirrors that doubled the images of the swaying dancers.

Beyond the window wall, tiny lights twinkled in the trees along the terrace, and overhead the heavy crystal chandeliers glowed with hundreds of candles, their light mirrored in the highly polished floor.

As the residents filtered in from the dining room, the guests invited from the neighborhood began to arrive and express their awe and pleasure at the sight the Duchess had created. The room quickly began to fill. All the gentry for many miles around were expected. The date had been specifically chosen to coincide with the full moon, to help guide their carriages. And although an autumn chill had set in, there had been no rain for nearly a fortnight. The roads were in excellent shape and the sky free of moon-obscuring clouds. No one was expected to remain at home.

The Duke and Duchess, as was the custom, led off the ball with the highest-ranking lady and gentleman present. This chanced to be the Duke's sister, Lady Aurelm, who had snagged a marquis, and her husband. The Duchess strode into the opening cotillion on the arm of her brother-in-law. The regal manner of both the host and hostess did nothing to hide the fact that both were in high spirits and ready to enjoy their own party.

"Well, little miss," said the Marquis of Aurelm as he led Sarah through the stately moves of the dance. As he had known her since she had been in short skirts, she was unlikely to object greatly to his familiarity. "I hear we are to have a miniature peer added to the realm before many months are up. Good girl!"

Sarah blushed a pretty pink. "I accept your congratulations, Ronald. Naturally we are delighted. But I wish George had not told you. I know you will tease me to pieces, for you always have." She laughed up at his "Who, me?" look of mock surprise. "Well, I warn you, Ronald. I shall have the vapors or faint or do something equally dreadful if you do. You must remember what a delicate state I am in."

"Ho!" he bellowed. "You, delicate, Sarah? You may be built like a twittery little bird, you may even have bamboozled George into thinking you delicate. But I know you. Hardy as a bear. You'll sail through the whole thing. Daresay you would have been on a horse's back today if George hadn't forbidden it."

"Well, I should have been," she admitted. "What a bore it is! And I hear you had a famous run, too. Cesca could hardly stop talking about it, till I was green." She let her eyes wander shortly around the room, checking on the progress of her guests. She saw Cesca dancing with Dudley Dalton, and received from her a a smile of encouragement. "Tell me, Ronald," Sarah chattered on to her partner, "do you really think my party will be a success?"

"What, with Devlin here? Can't miss, m'dear. Famous bit of luck, that. Fancy him turning up here just at the right moment, when no one even knew he was back in England. Your reputation as a hostess is assured."

"Well, I hope you are right." She now saw Lord Devlin, who had just entered the room with Sir Algernon Pett. Nearly every eye in the room noticed his entrance as well and followed his progress as the pair strolled around the room. Sarah happily returned her attention to the dance, her fears for a moment laid to rest.

After having bowed over what he considered an overabundance of trembling female hands, though considerably less than half the room had been covered, Devlin pulled up in a corner with Sir Algernon in tow. He retrieved two glasses of champagne from a passing footman and pushed one into his companion's hand.

"Well, old man," he said grimly. "Let us drink to my return in earnest to English Society. Tonight looks to be a real trial by fire." He downed his champagne in one gulp.

"Oh, it won't be so bad, y'know," said Sir Algernon. "Haven't forgotten how to dance, have you, Dev?"

"Not forgotten, no," replied Devlin, "but I fear the newer dances will have to do without me. The waltz reached America in the last year or so, but this quadrille I've been hearing about is a complete mystery to me."

"Wish it were to me," muttered Sir Algernon. "Dashed ridiculous dance. Bobbing about like a deuced jack-in-the-box! And in French, too! *Grande ronde* and *pas de quatre!* Think I'll head for the card room when they strike it up."

Mr. Symington approached in time to overhear the end of this minor diatribe. "Your only problem, Algy, is a complete lack of grace. The quadrille takes a certain flair. That won't be a problem for Dev here."

"Oh, I think I would prefer to watch you," replied Devlin with a smile for his friend. "I always did like a good farce."

"Ho! I'll show you. I'll get Cesca. She does it superbly."

"Does she, now," answered Devlin, his eyes moving automatically to where Lady Francesca was bowing gracefully to her partner. As she rose from her curtsy, he was struck with the full magnificence of her toilette. A Grecian tunic of celestial-blue tissue fell over a slip of deeper blue satin. French beading adorned the hem, and the whole presented an appearance of classical simplicity and absolute elegance. Her hair was dressed in the Sappho, and the silver cords wrapping it vied unsuccessfully with the burnished gold which nature had bestowed on the young lady. She was far and away the loveliest woman in the room.

The first thought that went through Lord Devlin's mind at sight of her was: What a pair we would have made! And to think that he had lost the chance at her that fate had so kindly thrown into his lap five years ago. Well, of course, "lost" was not really the right word. He had given her up of his own accord, knowing how wrong they would be for each other. It was generosity as much as anything, he had told himself then. He could not bring himself to cage such a magnificent bird. But in retrospect, which usually tends toward a bit more honesty, he admitted that he had been afraid for himself as well. Such a creature could have engulfed him completely, and he, green young man that he was, would have thought the world well lost for her. He had been very young.

And then of course she had rejected him as well. She had never once sought him out after that little scene in the garden, to ask him to stay. Obviously she had not wanted him to do so. The idea still rankled. "Yes," he said at last to his friends. "I am sure Lady Francesca dances the quadrille exceptionally. She is most accomplished."

"Dashed right! Cesca's a trump, y'know. Can always count on her."

Devlin had pulled his eyes away from the vision, only to encounter a much less pleasing sight. Roxanna Gordon had entered the Orangery and was surveying the room with a purposeful stare.

"Well," said Devlin, "they are striking up a waltz, and that I *can* do. And if I don't find a partner double quick, I'll be cornered by Mrs. Gordon. She is eyeing me already. I can feel it."

"Better run, if the Widow's got her cap set for you. It's rumored she always gets her man. Mind, there are plenty who wouldn't mind being got by her. A pretty piece of baggage."

"I'd mind," said Devlin. "I would most definitely mind." Out of a corner of his eye he could see Mrs. Gordon making her way toward him, and he looked wildly around for escape. "I am off, and none too soon. Tell Diana to save me a waltz, Algy." And he beat a hasty retreat toward Mrs. Pennington and her tulle-draped daughter.

Francesca saw his retreat from the Widow and

grinned in amusement. She had been pursued by gentlemen of every stamp ever since her come-out, and more than once she had turned tail and run from the tedious boredom of their repeated entreaties. Only once had her flight been precipitated by fear of the strength of her own emotions.

Before her mind had long to dwell on *that* morbid recollection, her hand was solicited by Colonel Tranch, a decent-looking young officer of a rather woeful expression and not much to say for himself. He would be, she thought, a totally inoffensive partner. She nodded pleasantly, glided into the circle of his arms, and they waltzed off.

When the music ended, Devlin, having safely deposited the silent and furiously blushing Miss Pennington back beside her beaming Mama, and suffering that lady's effusions on everything from the cut of his coat to her daughter's abilities on the harp, continued to do his duty, to the delight of nearly every woman in the room, including his hostess. He moved from one young lady to the next, from a country dance to a boulanger and back to the waltz, carefully avoiding the vicinity of Mrs. Gordon. At one point he and Francesca chanced to be near each other on the floor.

"I trust you are enjoying the evening, Devlin?"

"To be sure," he replied. "I hope you will put me down for the quadrille."

"The quadrille?" she remarked with a raised brow. "If you truly wish it, of course I will."

"I do." He smiled back and turned on to his next partner. Francesca joined a set on Mr. Dalton's arm. She had assumed that Devlin would offer the civility of a dance, but she was frankly surprised at his choice. She had simply assumed he would request a waltz. She refused, however, to recognize the stab of disappointment that went through her for what it was. Instead she turned a dazzling smile on Mr. Dalton as they went down the dance.

He wondered at it, since he had felt quite certain she had not been listening to a word he had been saying.

Devlin felt the evening begin to drag; Francesca thought it an eternity till the quadrille was heard. The moment did, however, arrive at last, as even the most eagerly awaited or anxiously dreaded moments have a habit of doing. Lord Devlin and Mr. Symington reached Francesca at the same moment.

"Well, Dev," said Mr. Symington. "Now you shall see. C'mon, Cesca. We'll show this bleater some dancing!"

She laughed as she replied, "Well, I am sure we might, Graham, but I am engaged to Lord Devlin for this dance."

"Dev? Nonsense! Fellow can't dance the quadrille. He'd be all over your slippers. They don't do it in America, y'know."

"I feel sure Lord Devlin would not have asked me to stand up with him if that were true." She smiled at her promised partner.

"But he's right, you know," said Devlin easily. "Never even seen the silly dance. I wouldn't subject you to my fumblings."

"Then why did you ask me?" she demanded, annoyance beginning to bubble up in her as it so often did in his company, along with other, less easily identified emotions.

"Because I wanted your company," he said truthfully. "Why else does a gentleman ask a lady to save him a dance. If you've no objection, we can sit in that alcove over there and watch Graham and the others trip over their feet."

"Unfair, Dev!" protested Mr. Symington. "Get someone else to natter at. Cesca's the best quadrille dancer in the room. You can sit with her during the waltz!"

"But I shall be dancing then," he explained with a patient smile. "Take yourself off, Graham. Can't you see when you're not wanted?" He took Francesca's elbow and began to turn her away.

"Tell him, Cesca!" demanded Mr. Symington with a laugh.

She looked at her partner, and gave her friend a shrug. "I'm afraid I am promised to him, you know. Go dance with Letty. She told me herself that she has been practicing the quadrille all summer just so that she may dance it with you."

The young man seemed much struck by this information, true or not. "Did she, by God?" His eyes went to Miss Hollys, smiling shyly in his direction from not far away. "Well, I'll do it." And he strode purposefully off in her direction.

Devlin guided Francesca to the relative privacy of the alcove without further ado, their progress followed avidly by several pairs of eyes, both jealous and questioning. Their scrutiny was not lost on Francesca.

"I shouldn't have thought you would wish to be counted one of my flirts, my lord," said Lady Francesca as they gained the alcove. "You are certain to be called one now."

"Oh, I won't mind being called one. Of course, I shouldn't like to *be* one. I am certain you are terribly cruel to your 'flirts.'"

"I am no such thing! Not at all. In fact, I seem to spend an inordinate amount of time trying to discourage them."

"And is not that cruel?" he asked with a teasing lilt.

"I should rather think it a kindness, since I don't mean to have any of them."

"Well, you cannot blame them, you know, for hankering after such an eligible young lady."

"You have put your finger right on the problem, you know. It is my 'eligibility.' I hope I am not vain, but I recognize that I am not a positive antidote."

"Well, not quite," he said with a grin.

"And I am a considerable heiress. I have enough wit to

know that young ladies who command large fortunes and who do not suffer from plainness are not in great supply."

"It is a problem common to our age, I will admit."

"I should have far more respect for my 'flirts,' as you call them, if they simply made it clear that they were looking for a rich and passable wife."

"Well, I hope I am safe from any such suspicions. My fortune must be at least as large as your own, and, more importantly, I know only too well your attitude toward marriage. I believe the words were 'I shall be no man's slave,' and said with great emphasis, if I recall correctly."

"Your memory is remarkable, sir. No doubt they were my very words. And I seem to recall something rather similar from you. Something about 'apron strings,' was it not?"

Lord Devlin laughed heartily, causing several curious heads to turn their way. "Guilty, my lady. I cannot plead otherwise. And my opinion of domineering females has changed not a jot. Age, however, has given me cause to think twice about condemning the entire institution of marriage."

Interest and surprise vied with each other in her eyes. "Has it? Well. I suppose it comes to all of us sooner or later. Perhaps it is what is meant by growing up." Now interest sparkled in his eyes as well. This hardly sounded like the young lady he had known five years ago. She went on. "But do tell me in what way you have altered your opinion, Deviln."

"I fancy a man can never be truly comfortable until he gets him a wife. It isn't the institution of marriage itself that is the culprit I detest, but merely the ramshackle way most of us go about choosing a partner for life."

"I couldn't agree more, my lord. Those who are so foolish as to fall prey to ROMANCE and marry for love I feel deserving of their fate. But then do you favor a return to the old-fashioned method of marriages of convenience?"

"By no means! That is, not what has always been thought of as 'convenient.' I should find it very *in*convenient indeed to be shackled to some harpy whose father's estate just happened to march with mine or one who had inherited several woolen mills and herself had the face of a sheep. By marriage of convenience, I would mean *my* convenience, my comfort. Now, am I not horribly selfish?"

"Most assuredly, but then, I think most of us are when the veneer of elegant manners is stripped away."

He studied her, trying to discover any trace of satire in her face, and could find none. She looked completely sincere, and he once again was struck by how closely her mind matched his own. "So young a cynic, my lady?"

"Oh, I do hope not. I despise cynicism. But I am a realist. I find it no bad thing to acknowledge our basic selfishness. We cannot love the world or help it if we cannot first love ourselves. But we stray from our point, sir. Have you given thought to just what sort of a wife would suit your notion of convenience? Someone sweetly docile, I should think, with never a word to say for herself," she concluded with a very sweet smile.

"Precisely," he agreed with a laugh. "And she must be strong enough to present me with a healthy heir, pretty enough not to embarrass me, wellborn enough to fit into my world, and stupid enough to let me make every decision affecting her life."

"She sounds a hopeless bore to me."

"I'm quite sure she will be. But then, there are ample means outside of marriage for relieving boredom." The twinkle in his eye would have made a lesser maiden blush. As it was, Francesca felt an odd little lurch in her stomach but put it down to the smoked oysters she had consumed at dinner. "Ah, so she must be blind as well as stupid, I see, or at least exceedingly tolerant."

"Of course," he said affably. "Now, the only problem is to find her."

Francesca allowed her eyes to scan the room a short

moment until they alighted on a cloud of pink tulle ruffles. "I think you have just been dancing with her," she said dryly, unable to suppress a grin.

His gaze spun in the direction of hers. The cloud of tulle totally enveloped a young woman with indeterminate brown hair and a permanent blush. She was sitting uncomfortably on a chair and staring at the floor while an older woman beside her lectured her behind her fan.

The older woman caught Lord Devlin's eye on them, smiled brilliantly, fluttered her fan, and nudged her daughter beside her. The young girl glanced up, flushed an even more fiery red, and looked quickly down again.

"Good God!" exclaimed Lord Devlin, a vaguely stricken note in his voice. "You can't mean Miss . . . Miss . . . What the devil is her name?"

"Miss Pennington, Priscilla. She is a sweet little mouse who wouldn't say 'boo' to a goose. She would seem to fit your requirements in every particular, I should think. She is well enough born to be invited to Hockleigh, pretty in a nondescript sort of way, and she is very unlikely to contradict anything you choose to say, be it ever so outrageous. You may be as autocratic and despotic as you like with her, I'm sure."

"I am not a despot!"

"No? Well, then, you may be as indifferent to her as you like. I am certain she will not complain. Yes, I think you must certainly marry Priscilla Pennington."

He forced his gaze back toward the object of this interesting discussion. It was clear from the variety of expressions flitting across his handsome face that he was having some difficulty bridging the gulf between elaborate theories and the reality of putting those theories into practice. Francesca smiled wryly at his discomfort, not even taking herself to task for producing the effect. Mrs. Pennington looked up again, beamed a huge smile, and waved a slightly vulgar little wave.

"No, no," huffed Devlin. "Can't have such a dragon for a mother-in-law."

"Oh, she really isn't so bad," said Francesca. "She is only very anxious to get Pris off her hands. She is a born squire's wife and quite out of her element in the *haut ton*, even though her birth gives her the *entrée*. She wants nothing more than to retire permanently to the country to enjoy her chickens and her vegetable garden and her grandchildren. I feel sure that puffing off her daughters has been a sore trial for her."

"How many of them are there?"

"Only two. And she did manage to snare an earl for Liza, her elder girl, and within a month of her come-out, too. But then, Liza was a real dazzler. Priscilla was always lost in her shadow and didn't 'take' in her first season."

"Which earl?" asked Devlin, harking back to the first part of this discourse.

"Strotwood."

"Strotwood, eh? Not a bad connection, I should think." He looked at the girl with greater interest.

"Yes, such a brother-in-law might prove 'convenient.' "

At this he had the grace to give her a rueful grin. "Well, of course I'm in no hurry to choose a bride. But I shall certainly dance with her again. I don't recall that she stepped on my toes or disgraced herself in any way the last time we stood up together."

"Oh, no. Pris would never call so much attention to herself."

7

By the end of their very interesting discussion, both Lord Devlin and Lady Francesca had much to think about. But a ball offers little time for musings. For the next hour they each moved from partner to partner. Francesca smiled civilly to everyone, but her attention was as often as not following Devlin around the room. She noticed that despite Mrs. Gordon's managing to snare him for a waltz and a quarter-hour's flirtation in the corner, he got away from her to claim two more dances with Priscilla Pennington.

Even were she unaware of his motives, Francesca would have remarked such behavior. For any young lady to stand up more than twice in one evening with the same gentleman was practically tantamount to announcement of a betrothal. Ninety-nine percent of the young ladies at the ball would have been in alt to have been distinguished by Devlin in such a fashion. But Pris would be in agony, Francesca knew, to be made such an obvious focus of everyone's attention. She was shy to a lamentable degree. Francesca knew a moment of misgiving, wondering if she had done the right thing by setting Devlin onto the girl. But she dismissed the thought at once. It was a great piece of luck for Pris, whether she saw it or not, that Devlin was looking for a wife of just her sort. And she could surely not be insensible to the man's charm. What woman could be?

Francesca was not so fully focused on poor Priscilla's sufferings and bright prospects for the future that she had no attention left to notice that Devlin danced very well, at least in the waltz, even if the intricacies of the quadrille were as yet beyond him. She also managed to wonder if he would waltz with her before the evening was out. She surprised herself by realizing that she very much hoped that he would. Well, of course, she did love to dance, and such an accomplished partner always made it doubly enjoyable. They would make a pretty sight, too. There could surely be no other reason she so eagerly awaited his approach.

It came, alas, just as she was about to take the floor with Sir Algernon for the supper dance. "Come waltz with me, Francesca," said Devlin coolly. "I wish to speak with you." He reached to remove her hand from Sir Algernon's arm.

But the young baronet was not so easily routed. "Ho! Don't you think it, Dev. Be off with you," he commanded. "Cesca's engaged to me for supper." He kept firm possession of her long-fingered hand.

Devlin looked at her with a question in his eye. "I'm afraid, Devlin, that I *am* engaged to Algy," she said prettily. "Perhaps after supper?" she added hopefully if a little brazenly.

"No. Now," he answered flatly. "I am engaged to Diana for this dance, so we may very easily switch."

"See here, Dev!" sputtered Sir Algernon. "I don't wish to switch. Don't know how they do these things in America, old boy, but—"

"Oh, give over, Algy!" said Devlin. "You know very well you would much prefer to dance with your own wife, but are only afraid of being thought so unfashionable as to enjoy her company."

"Devlin," said Francesca, "I really cannot—"

"And you know, Algy," Devlin continued as though she had not spoken, "if one of us doesn't show up soon, Diana's like to go eat with that Storeton fellow. Been dangling after her all evening. I can see him heading her way right now."

"Storeton! That commoner?" exclaimed Algernon, totally forgetting that fashion required a man look with equanimity on his wife's cicisbei. "Well, he'll catch cold at that! I shall see to it! Where is Diana?"

"Just there, under that parrot," he pointed out casually.

Sir Algernon belatedly remembered his obligation to his partner, "I say, Cesca, old girl. Don't mind, do you? Dev'll take good care of you."

"Oh, go on, Algy," she replied, laughing in exasperation. "Go dance with your Diana. No one shall laugh at you, you know." And Sir Algernon took himself off after his beloved wife.

"Good," said Devlin matter-of-factly as they watched him go. "They are beginning the waltz." And he reached for her hand again.

She lifted a brow at him and withheld the sought-for hand. Her mind was poised between vexation at his impertinence and admiration for the masterly way in which he had handled Sir Algernon. "I have not as yet agreed to dance with you. Are you always so high-handed, my lord?"

"When it is necessary, yes, but only to my good friends. And besides, no offense to you, but he really does prefer to dance with Diana, you know. I suppose they are In Love."

"I suppose so, poor things," she answered brightly, and finally allowed herself to be led to the floor, where she was swept into a moving embrace that left her almost breathless.

Now, Lady Francesca considered herself quite a sophisticated young lady, perhaps even a bit jaded. She had danced with princes and prime ministers, and turned off importunate suitors by the score. But never in her five years on the town had she ever experienced a dance quite like this one.

She was at a loss to explain it. He danced well, of course, but she had had better partners. He held her close, but not so close as some had done. The mass of twirling couples around them, the gay laughter, the tinkle of the music, all faded away till there seemed to be nothing in the room but a pair of blue eyes smiling down at her and a strong and very masculine hand around her waist, its heat easily permeating the thin silk of her gown and warming her right through as they spun around the large room.

Oblivious as they were, for the moment, of their surroundings, they were very well observed indeed by the other guests in the room. Roxanna Gordon, in the arms of Lord Poole, eyed them with distinct displeasure. Devlin had certainly not looked at *her* in such a way when they had danced. And she had very definite plans for his lordship, plans that had no room for a rival. She could not bring herself to worry overmuch about poor little Priscilla Pennington, even after he had partnered her three times, but she would not put up with Lady Francesca Waringham as a rival. She would put a spike in *that* wheel soon enough!

Mrs. Pennington also observed the waltzing pair with some concern. He could not, of course, be expected to stand up with Priscilla again; she had been just the tiniest bit remiss in her duty to have allowed the girl to stand up with him that third time. But she could wish that Lady Francesca were not quite so lovely. If she meant to set her cap at Devlin—and from the besotted smile on her face, it looked very much as though she did—then Priscilla would stand no chance at all. Now, if it had been her elder daughter, Liza, she would not have worried. But Priscilla was such a disappointment, nothing at all like her lovely, vivacious sister.

Still, his lordship *had* shown a marked degree of attention to the girl, for whatever reason, and Mrs. Pennington was never one to look a gift horse, or rich baron, in the mouth. And she was determined to get Priscilla off her hands this year. She would just have a look through the girl's wardrobe in the morning. Perhaps something a little more daring . . .

Lady Braethon watched Francesca and Devlin with a raised eyebrow. Miss Jane Magness eyed them with chagrin. And the Duchess of Hockleigh smiled after them with satisfaction.

Francesca, blissfully unaware of all the intense attention focused upon her, was yet very much aware of herself and her partner. The prolonged silence between them finally became too much for her. She thrashed about in her mind for something to say. "Well, my lord . . ." she began brightly, not entirely sure what she would say next.

"Devlin," he corrected gently, gratified at her flustered reaction.

"Very well. Devlin. How does your courtship progress?" It was with a mixture of disappointment and relief that she saw his dreamy expression fade, to be replaced by a tiny frown just between his brows. The moment of intimacy had been broken. "I saw you chattering away to her," she continued. "Whatever did you find to say?"

"I'm not sure I can recall the questions I asked. I can tell you her answers, however. They consisted of a series of 'Yes, my lords' and 'No, my lords,' with an occasional 'Thank you, my lord,' thrown in for good measure."

"But, how perfect! Did I not tell you Priscilla was precisely the wife for you?"

"She does seem a very biddable and malleable girl. I think it would take little more than simple kindness to win her. By her reaction to my compliments, I would judge she hears few of them."

"There you are, then," she replied. "You need only get on with it."

"You know, I had not thought of marrying just yet, even though the idea has been in my mind now and then. But you, with your inimitable good sense"—and here he grinned at her—"have jolted me awake and shown me my true needs. I am inclined to think you have chosen well for me. Miss Pennington is precisely the sort of wife I have long had in mind. And now that I am reminded what English Society is like, I shouldn't like to go up to London in the spring still a single man. I should have no peace at all!"

"Rather, you would be eaten alive," she said dryly and with quite a bit of truth. "But as a married man, you shall have every opportunity for romantic dalliance, with no danger of being netted."

"Precisely," he said with a smile. "It is one of the few advantages of being an already landed fish, you know."

"Well, I am gratified that you approve my taste in wives, sir. And me with so little experience!" Her bantering tone successfully masked the emotion rippling through her, an emotion suspiciously like disappointment. "But why tell me about it, sir? Tell Pris. I shouldn't think it would take more than a word and the deed is done."

"The thing is, she's skittish as a colt. I don't wish to scare her off before she's had a chance to learn what a capital fellow I am. I've never tried to woo a miss just out of the schoolroom before," he went on, pushing aside a flash of memory of another young miss and how badly he had mismanaged his handling of her. "I am certain to need advice, and as I would prefer not to broadcast my intentions too widely just yet, the advice will have to come from you."

"It seems to me that you have already announced yourself pretty plainly by dancing with her so often."

"What?" he asked, genuinely puzzled. Then a light of understanding crossed his face. "Oh, Lord! I had completely forgotten *that* particular iron rule. In America they are not quite so niffy, you see. No wonder she was silent as a turtle all through that last dance, and would not even deign to look at me."

"Well, it does seem that you have some lost ground to

make up already. Obviously you shall need help if you are not to botch the whole thing hopelessly. Very well, I shall be pleased to undertake your instruction in how to woo a lady."

"A girl," he corrected. "I am quite adept at the wooing of ladies."

That smile that made her tingle was back in the deep blue eyes, and she could barely get out an answer. "I am sure that you are," she whispered. His hand tightened around her waist. They spun off to finish the dance in silence, wonderful, warm, delicious silence.

When the music ended, they adjourned to the supper room, speaking in commonplaces until they were seated at a small table in the corner. Two plates before them were heaped with cold mousse of salmon, savory pâté, plover's eggs, raspberry cream, and lemon ice. A bottle of champagne was chilling in a silver bucket beside them.

With a slightly devilish grin, Lord Devlin took up the conversation once more. "Well, you seem to have neatly packaged my future for me, Francesca," he said lightly. "Now, what of yourself?"

"Me, sir? I am not sure I understand what you mean," she said, but with a look that said she understood only too well.

"Why, your future, of course. Your marriage. What sort of a mate shall we pick out for you? There are plenty here to chose from."

"But I don't . . . That is, I haven't . . ."

"Let's have no rubbish about your not meaning to marry. That is all very well when one is eighteen or so, and none knows better than I what a fine thing it is to sow one's wild oats before one settles down to respectability." He looked at her with a teasing grin, wondering if she had sown many herself.

Her face scowled at him, but her eyes laughed. "You can undoubtedly feed the whole world by now with your abundantly growing oat fields," she retorted.

"Undoubtedly," he agreed with a laugh. "And from what I understand, you have had a wild lark or two of your own before now. But a steady diet of anything does begin to pall after a while, you know. Surely you have noticed how oats alone, be they never so wild, begin to stick in the throat after a while without a bit of good common home-brewed to wash them down."

She choked on a swallow of the French champagne as an involuntary giggle broke out. Before she could answer, he went on, "Whom have you chosen, then, as your good home-brewed? I can see only two possible types for the likes of you. There is good dark stout, strong enough to give even an experienced tippler a kick in the pants . . ."

"As well as a ghastly head the following morning! No, thank you, my lord."

"Well, then, it shall have to be some bland lager, more water than malt, easily swallowed and just as easily forgotten once the oats are thoroughly washed down. I had a mare once who was quite partial to lager. Seemed to thrive on it. Don't see why you shouldn't do the same."

"This is a ridiculous conversation, Devlin," she said, a testy edge to her voice. "Stout and lager and drunken horses!"

"Oh, yes, she was a quite ridiculous horse. But she did take one for a marvelous ride." She could not ignore the twinkle in his eye, but she tried to make him think she could. She did not answer. "I had to give her the lager. She wouldn't breed without it, you see. And she was such a splendid specimen. It would have been a terrible waste not to pass on some of her spirit."

This time he waited for a response, grinning all the while, and she was forced to speak. "Do we still talk of horses, my lord? I am not one, you know."

"A quite obvious truth," he replied. Admiration was evident in his tone, and as he gazed at her the lightness left his voice. "Though I am sure that that golden hair, when released from its pins, must be a quite glorious mane," he finished, almost, but not quite, to himself. It was all he could do to restrain himself from reaching up and pulling out those pins to prove his point.

A tremor ran up Francesca's spine at the softly murmured words and set her neck tingling. She felt her face grow hot, and prayed that the soft glow of the candlelight suffusing the room and the kind shadows would hide her blush.

She turned abruptly to look around the room and saw Miss Pennington sitting with a young local gentleman, a Mr. Rathnor. They both looked acutely uncomfortable, as neither of them could think of a thing to say to the other. "Let us hope that you have better luck with Miss Pennington than with your mare, sir. She scarce strikes me as the lager type."

"Oh, no. Plain milk, I fancy, will do for her. Or perhaps a glass of ratafia now and then should she prove reluctant."

"I am certain she will not," Francesca replied without thinking. What woman would prove reluctant, after all? Except perhaps herself.

Devlin let her comment pass as though unnoticed, which it most definitely was not. "But we digress, you know, and I shan't let you change the subject. We were talking of your own plans."

"You were. *I* have no plans."

"Have you really no thought of marriage? It would be a great pity, you know. I saw you in the garden this afternoon with Lady Aurelm's children. You have a sort of magic with them. You can enter into their world with a naturalness that is a joy to watch. You were obviously meant to have a dozen of your own."

He was not teasing her now, she could see. His sincerity deserved a like response, and she answered him honestly. "I do find children a particular joy and have longed for some of my own. I did think I might make a fine aunt, but as I have no brothers or sisters, that seems out of the question. I admit that the notion of motherhood has been in my mind of late. I suppose it is being around Gussie's children, who are all dears. And of course there is Sarah. She is so full of the joy of the child she will soon have." It briefly crossed Francesca's mind that she had never found herself talking so freely with anyone before, not even Sarah. She wondered how it had come about. She could not explain it, but it seemed perfectly natural that she should be speaking so to Devlin. She gave a sigh. "I suppose the time is not far off when I shall have to begin looking around me for a mate."

"Of course, strictly speaking, a husband is not a prerequisite for having a family," he said. "Only look at the Duke of Clarence's Mrs. Jordan and her ten little FitzClarences!"

"I prefer not to," she said dryly.

"They are a motley lot, aren't they, or so I'm told."

"And besides, it would not do for me. I thought it might, you know. Even Mrs. Wollstonecraft gave birth to her daughter before she married Mr. Godwin, and I cannot find it in my heart to condemn her. But I have discovered I care too much for the good opinion of Society to follow her example. Is it not horridly missish of me?"

"I hadn't thought you would care so much for that."

"Yes, I surprised myself. It is quite lowering, I assure you," she said, and dropped her head in mock chagrin. "But too true!"

"Well, then, a husband it must be, and the sooner the better. Now, whom can we find to fill the post?" He let his eyes wander about the room.

"Oh, but I haven't yet decided to—" she blurted out, but he would not let her finish.

"Enough! Fair is fair, you know. You have saddled me with Miss Pris, and I have no intention of going through such an ordeal as a courtship quite alone. You must and shall join me in my agony."

"I imagine courting Pris will be a bit of a trial. She is so painfully shy."

"Exactly. Now, who is it to be?"

"I am sure there is no one here who—" she began.

"Now, there is young Hollys. He is enough of a nonentity to at least apply for the post."

"Hollys! Benjamin Hollys? That silly boy?"

"True, he is very young. A scarce licked cub, in fact. And while he may do very well at present, one can never be entirely certain of very young gentlemen. He might grow up to have a mind of his own, and then where would you be?"

"Utterly lost! We must certainly disqualify Mr. Hollys," she said with a laugh, entering into the spirit of the thing despite herself. "Now, I feel certain I could tolerate Colonel Tranch. I had always a fondness for a man in scarlet regimentals. And he does seem to be that strange combination: an officer with no air of command. How do you suppose he gets his troops to follow him?"

"He doesn't. Thank God we are at peace. So, shall it be Colonel Tranch?"

"I'm afraid not. He returns to his regiment in the morning, he tells me, and I feel even I must needs have more than one evening to bring my gentleman up to scratch."

"You underrate yourself, I'm sure," he teased.

"Oh, no. I told you I am a realist."

"Well, then, scratch Tranch from the running," he concluded with an appropriate gesture.

They munched awhile in companionable silence, each very much aware of the other's nearness. Without realizing she did so, Francesca let out a sigh. Devlin turned to look at her; she looked back at him. They just stared at each other a moment, virtually without expression, but their eyes were locked. Then they smiled, a very small, almost sad smile, a smile with more than a trace of resignation, of regret.

Devlin looked away first. "Well," he said with forced

good cheer, "I'm sure there must be someone in all this crowd who . . ." He let his eyes scan the eating, chattering group. They came to rest on a couple a few yards away. "Of course," he exclaimed. "The obvious choice!"

"Who?" said Francesca.

"Maltby. He is the perfect mate for you. A clever fellow, Maltby, in a vague sort of way. Never give you a moment's worry. Probably won't even recall that he is married most of the time, and won't much mind it when he does. You must certainly marry Caspar Maltby."

"Caspar Maltby! Oh, no, I couldn't. I mean . . . Good God! I'd forgotten he was here." She let her eyes find him, no mean task, as Mr. Maltby was prone to blend into the walls.

"Precisely my point," said Devlin. "I feel sure you may just as easily forget him after you are married. He won't mind, you know. Just let him have his gardens and his hothouses, and he will go on like winking. You may bully him all you like; he won't even notice."

"I am not a bully!"

"No? Well, then just don't bother about him at all. If you only compliment him on his hybrid roses now and then, he will think himself very well married."

"Well, even you must admit that he does grow very nice roses."

"I wouldn't know. You forget, I have been away."

"I don't forget," she answered shortly.

He ignored the remark, though it did pique his curiosity. "Perhaps he will even make a name for himself as a famous botanist or something and you may bask in his glory."

"How nonsensical you are! I am sure Mr. Maltby is very well respected, but *really! Me* basking in Caspar Maltby's glory!" She sniffed with more than a touch of wounded vanity.

"I will admit it is an unlikely possibility. Amusing, though."

"You would find it so."

"And of course you needn't worry that he would ride roughshod over you or squander your fortune. It would never occur to him to spend your money, I'm sure. I imagine his valet has to remind him when to buy a coat. If he has a valet,"

"I understand Mr. Maltby's fortune is respectable, and besides, he is next in line to the Viscount Coltraine."

"There you are, then. You need have no fear he is a fortune hunter." He gave her a speculative look. His manner remained elaborately casual. "Of course, there would be the problem of attaching him. That could prove a neat trick."

He had pricked her feminine pride, as he had meant to do. Her eyes flashed magnificently, her smile frozen in place. That she, who had turned down dozens of offers, could fail to bring a man of Caspar Maltby's stamp around her thumb! Unthinkable. "You assume I could not manage it?" she asked in a honey-smooth voice.

"I've really no idea," he replied. "You forget," he added in a voice as smooth as her own and with an embarrassing touch of intimacy, "it has been many years since I have seen you in action."

"Oh, I am better even than I was," she said in that same deceptively sweet voice. "You may recall that back then I was not quite irresistible enough to keep *you* in England."

His facade broke for the briefest moment to reveal a look of pure astonishment. Not only had she not tried to keep him in England, he thought, but she had gone out of her way to show him that she had no desire for him to stay. But he covered his thoughts so quickly with his usual urbane manner that she, though she did notice it, immediately began to think she had imagined it. His next words convinced her of it. "You forget, though, that I was a particularly hardened case. Caspar is like to present a different sort of problem entirely."

"I'll lay you a wager I can bring him up to scratch before you can get Priscilla to accept you!" she challenged rashly. Her pride often led her to make foolish statements.

His crooked grin flashed. "And may I name the stakes of this wager?" There was a pronounced twinkle in his eye. It brought that strange tingle to her neck again.

"V-very well."

He raked her with his glance in a very discomfiting yet strangely satisfying way. "On second thought, I believe I shall name the forfeit at a later time. But I promise it shan't be more than you can afford. Done?"

She hesitated, trusting neither his expression nor her own galloping emotions. But a wager was a wager, and she had brought this one on herself. "Done," she answered, and reached out her hand to seal the bargain.

He took the hand, but rather than shaking it as she expected, he lifted it to his lips. To compound his crime, he did not lightly and chastely kiss it as he might. He turned it gently over and kissed first her palm, then her wrist, then raised his eyes to hers with a wicked grin.

She looked quickly away to see if anyone in the room had observed his outrageous behavior. But she did not pull her hand away. It seemed no longer to be connected to her brain. For though her mind told her to pull it sharply away at once, the hand itself felt an almost overwhelming urge to caress his cheek. Luckily he lowered the hand again before it could do anything so absurd.

"Old Caspar may be getting more than he can handle," he said in a silky voice. Then, even more softly, he added, "Certainly more than he deserves."

8

The four principals in the impending romantic quadrille enjoyed varying degrees of rest that night. Mr. Maltby perhaps fared best. Being sublimely unaware of what was in store for him, and only vaguely curious as to how it had come about that he had waltzed twice that evening with the dashing Lady Francesca Waringham, his sleep was not disturbed by visions of her. He did, however, lie awake some little while pondering the question of marriage, and his own at that.

Left to himself, he would not even have been at this house party, even though he was a cousin to the Duke and was routinely invited. His finest mums were just coming into bloom at home, and he could scarce bear the thought of missing their show.

But he had not been left to himself. His Mama had made a decision: at nine-and-twenty it was past time that her Caspar settle his wife into his home and begin populating the countryside with the elder Mrs. Maltby's grandchildren.

Now, Mr. Maltby felt no particular need for a wife as yet—there was Mama, after all—but he was quite unaccustomed to disobeying his mother. He realized that he was occasionally too abstracted for his own good, and his Mama had so much more sense of the world than did he. If she said it was time he married, she was most probably correct.

And so he had come to Hockleigh with rather strict orders to look over the young ladies present. It was already the end of October, and he had agreed to make his choice before the end of the year.

No one at present at Hockleigh had particularly struck him as right for the post of Mrs. Maltby, but then, he had as yet hardly looked. While the others had been hunting a fox this morning, he had been out hunting specimens of *Onopordon acanthium* near the Home Wood. And the afternoon had been whiled away in touring the Duchess's hothouses. At the ball this evening he had attempted to pay more attention to his duty, and he really was rather proud of himself. He had danced with at least half of the ladies present, had forgotten only one of their names, and had not trodden on a single toe.

He fell asleep at last, basically satisfied with himself, and determined to attend to further matrimonial hunting on the morrow.

Miss Pennington was the next of the quartet to block out the real world with the solace of dreams, but she was not at all satisfied. Before she had been allowed to bury herself under the eiderdown quilt, snuff her candle, and sink into the comforting blackness, she had been treated to one of her Mama's monologues. She had been hearing them all her life, of course, but she was quite sure she would never grow completely used to them.

This particular speech had concerned Lord Devlin, his good looks and address, his estates, his income, his importance, and Priscilla's amazing and undeserved good fortune in attracting his notice. Mrs. Pennington had every good intention of capitalizing on the fact that Devlin had distinguished Pris with *three* dances this night. She told her daughter what to expect.

She must be perfectly turned out on every occasion; much thought must be put into her wardrobe. Every opportunity would be found to bring her to his lordship's notice and keep her there. They must do whatever they could to hold his company on every occasion.

Priscilla could not help but cringe at what she knew the next few days would hold, and she knew she must fail miserably, even had she wanted to succeed. She was convinced that only so much charm, poise, and beauty had been allotted to the Pennington girls, and her sister, Liza, had got it all.

The first step in Mrs. Pennington's campaign to snare the most interesting baron in the country for her least interesting daughter was to inform Pris that she would ride with the hunt on the morrow. With wide eyes, Priscilla so far forgot herself as to begin to protest. She was an indifferent rider at best. Horses made her nervous. "But, Mama," she murmured, "I—".

"You can wear that blue habit, the one we had made in London for the Season. I will add a new plume to your hat myself. I've a lovely cerise one that will do nicely. And those particularly fine yellow gloves of mine . . ."

With a look of misery, Priscilla turned away her wide, blue, remarkably pretty eyes. "Yes, Mama," she wispered, like the dutiful daughter she was, when her mother finally wound down her monologue.

When the older woman left the room and Priscilla had tied her lacy nightcap under her chin, she climbed miserably into the high curtained bed. She had long ago given up crying for her own unhappiness; it never changed anything. So she escaped into sleep, where she could dream of peace and rest, of no Mama, of oblivion.

Farther down the hall were two more bedchambers, not too near each other, but each housing a very restive young person. Francesca pounded her pillow in annoyance, determined to make her mind go blank and allow sleep to overtake it. But no sooner did the words of resolve form in her mind than her thoughts spun off in other directions entirely. What a scrape she had gotten herself into now! She had allowed Devlin to goad her into running after Caspar Maltby, of all unlikely people. She had even recognized what the odious man was doing to her, and had still allowed herself to be drawn in. Why? she wondered.

She must think it through logically, she told herself firmly, or she would never sleep. Was it really such a scrape after all? In the dark room, with only the dying embers giving a faint light to the bed tester over her head, she forced her chattering mind to slow down and look at things rationally. Lord Devlin's taunts had really been like a pitcher of water thrown in the face of a sleeping person—definitely unpleasant, but it *did* awaken one.

Well, she was awake now, in more ways than one. And she had to admit that Devlin was in the right of it, even if for the wrong reasons, just as she had been when she proposed Priscilla Pennington as a suitable wife for him. It was time that she married. Seeing Gussie's children again had made her ache with the realization of her own loneliness. She wanted children of her own, to love and to teach and to be loved by in return. And she could have it.

But she would do it only on her own terms, as she had always done everything. Really, Caspar Maltby was an admirable choice. She had known him vaguely for years. He was not a bad-looking man, and he was possessed of a considerable intelligence beneath his air of abstraction. And although he showed little interest in the doings of the *ton*, as heir to a viscountcy, he was accepted everywhere. He had his own interests and would not be likely to tamper with hers, and he could do very well at providing her with the children she so badly wanted. Really, she considered, she could hardly do better, and she could certainly do a great deal worse.

Very well, then, she told herself, unconsciously nodding her resolve in the dark. She would marry Caspar Maltby and make Richard Devlin laugh out of the other side of his face.

As her mind began to relax at last, she did vaguely wonder why Devlin had pushed her so hard to go after Caspar. What possible reason could he have for wanting to see her married? Unless it was simply for the fun of watching the courtship. He believed she couldn't do it, anyway. She new very well that she could.

When she drifted off into a restless sleep at last, it was to dream of a white lace gown and wedding chimes. She turned to the groom at her side. She could not see his face. But didn't Mr. Maltby have brown hair? A shaft of sunlight through the high arched Gothic windows of the church glinted on this man's hair, and it shone like gold.

In the last bedchamber in the house to show a glimmer of light that night, Richard Devlin was making no pretense of sleeping. He sat wrapped in a simple and comfortable dressing gown, staring gloomily into the fire and mulling over the events of the evening. Damn that chit! he said to himself, and he did not mean Miss Pennington. She had gotten him into something that he was not at all certain he was ready for.

But try as he might, he could come up with no good reasons to prove Francesca had been wrong in her judgment of him. Why not marry, after all? Was it not one reason he had come home? Everyone had to settle down sometime. And this Pennington girl, so conveniently at hand, did seem the perfect choice. She didn't sparkle and shine, she had no conversation or wit, but then, that was exactly what he had decided he required in a wife. If he could only get through the courtship and engagement! Priscilla would make a comfortable wife. Of course, there would be little excitement in such a marriage, but such kind of excitement could always be found elsewhere. Who could tell? Perhaps Lady Francesca herself would soon be a married lady with a boring husband. The situation offered endless possibilities. He smiled for the first time since coming upstairs. She was still the most exciting woman he had ever known, ever held, ever kissed. And she was not now indifferent to him, whatever she might pretend. He had seen it in her eyes, had felt it when she trembled in his arms as they waltzed. His smile grew for a moment as he thought of the extra freedom granted to married ladies.

But the smile disappeared when the image of Caspar Maltby entered the picture beside her, holding her hand, putting his wedding ring on her finger, kissing her. Lord Devlin was scowling into the fire again when his candle guttered and went out.

The group of hunters next morning was inevitably a bit smaller than on the opening day. Farmers and ostlers, who could afford the luxury of only one day off from their labors, went reluctantly back to their fields and their stables. The diminishment of the carnival atmosphere that always prevailed at the Lawn Meet kept many of the onlookers at home as well.

Mr. Maltby, on a neat bay who, though past his hunting prime, was not yet ready for the glue factory, trotted along comfortably enough. He was no neck-or-nothing rider, but he didn't dislike to hunt for a day or so now and then. And he was determined to follow his Mama's strictures not to bury himself in the garden or the woods for the whole of his visit with his cousin. And so off he trotted.

Miss Pennington, to her definite dismay, also joined the field. The Duchess had provided her with a very docile and pretty little mare, and Priscilla was trying hard not to be too nervous. She had much rather be sketching the fox than chasing him—her animal and flower drawings were her major accomplishment and her chief joy—but she had never been able to stand up to her Mama like Liza had always done. Of course, it was easy for Liza; she was beautiful, vivacious, witty, everything Pris was certain *she* was not. And Mama liked Liza and was proud of her. She liked being able to say, "My daughter, the Countess." Pris knew she was a trial to her mother; she tried hard to make up for it by being dutiful.

And so she had joined the hunt, holding on to the pommel of her sidesaddle so hard her knuckles were white under her jonquil-yellow riding gloves and praying that the docile little mare would not run away with her.

To make matters worse, if that were possible, she saw Lord Devlin trot up beside her as they headed out to the covert. Why on earth he was showing her such a marked degree of attention was beyond her thinking. He was much more the sort of gentleman likely to buzz around Liza than around her. He made Priscilla nervous. He was too handsome, too wealthy, and there was so very *much* of him.

"Good morning, Miss Pennington," he said in a hearty voice. "I trust you slept well after the evening's exertions."

"Y-yes, my lord. Thank you, my lord," she stammered, her eyes glued to her horse's mane.

"I am pleased to see you joining the hunt today. I was afraid perhaps you did not care for it." She looked up once, but could not bring herself to speak to him, to admit the truth of his statement, so she looked down again. "If we have the same luck as yesterday, you shall have some famous sport. A bruising ride that was!" He had turned away to look at the overcast sky and so did not see the convulsive shiver of fear that ran through her. "We missed you yesterday." Well, surely one little white lie in a courtship was permissible. He had, in fact, not even noticed her absence yesterday. But a question or two in a few ears at breakfast had offered up the information. He might as well use what he could.

"Thank you, my lord," was the only answer he got.

"How pleased I am that you like to hunt, Miss Pennington. It is one of my favorite pastimes, you know. I should hate to think that we could not share it." Her eyes flew up to meet his at this alarming remark. It was the first time that he had ever really seen them, and he noticed that they were really very pretty eyes, of a deep, almost aquamarine blue. Though he did not read dismay in their depths, he did see surprise, and it occurred to him that perhaps he was moving a little too quickly for his quarry. She was like a young doe, easily scared off. He changed tack, and spent the rest of the trot in endeavoring to elicit more of her monosyllabic opinions on the weather, the crowd, and the beauty of the countryside.

Mrs. Pennington, riding along in a carriage close by, was nearly beside herself with satisfaction at the sight of Lord Devlin and her daughter. What a stroke of luck that Pris should have caught his attention. She couldn't understand it in the least—Pris, though a sweet little mouse, had not Liza's style and looks—but she was not one to let such an opportunity slip through her fingers. If she could get Pris off her hands before the year was out, she need never spend another tedious season in London. And then, Devlin did seem such a nice young man.

While Priscilla rode along in agony, not even seeing the lovely countryside on which she was expected to comment, Mr. Maltby was examining it in detail. On his right grew a particularly fine specimen of *Trifolium incarnatum*—he would return later to collect a sample of it—and off to his left was a field of late-blooming heather of a particularly intense shade of purple. He would very much like to analyze the soil hereabouts. He guessed it would be found to be very high in chalk content, and rich in the minerals lacking near his estate in Somersetshire. And only look at that *Crataegus oxyacantha* over there—

"Good morning, Mr. Maltby," came a feminine voice beside him, pulling him from his botanic reverie. "Is it not a fine morning for hunting?" asked Francesca.

"Good morning, Lady Francesca," he answered civilly, thankful to have remembered her name without thought. But then, she was not a young lady easily forgotten, even by such as Mr. Maltby. "It is a fine morning. That is a very . . . fetching habit, my lady," he added, remembering his manners. He was, in fact, somewhat dazzled by her appearance.

"I thank you, sir," she answered prettily, favoring him with a smile that made him feel slightly giddy. She *did* present quite a picture. She had taken extreme pains with her appearance this morning, and all for Mr. Maltby's sake, as she told herself. Having made the momentous decision, in the dark of the night, to marry the man, she might as well get on with it. She had donned her most dashing habit of a deep wine-red velvet in the Polish style with braidings and froggings in black and gold. Beautiful gold morocco boots rested lightly in her stirrup. Her masses of hair were pulled back into a low, elegant chignon, and a pert little shako was tilted over her right eye, its gold-tipped black feather curling onto her cheek in a beguiling manner. He caught himself wanting to reach up and brush it away from her cheek. Francesca was very well pleased by his reaction.

"Impressed" was not precisely the right word for what Mr. Maltby was feeling. The man was experiencing a sensation remarkably akin to those he experienced when gazing on a perfectly formed orchid. It was something like wonder that so exotic and perfect a specimen could exist, at least in England. Of course, orchids did not speak and ask questions and demand answers of one. He struggled to pay attention to this talking specimen and to make the appropriate responses, and before long they found themselves arrived at the covert. He was saved from further need to talk by the business of the hunt. A business Francesca took very seriously indeed.

They drew a blank in the first covert, and everyone trotted another hundred yards or so to the next. This time Francesca found Devlin beside her as they rode. With a quizzical smile he raked her from head to toe with his eyes before pronouncing, "Very fetching."

The words, though identical to those Mr. Maltby had

used, had an entirely different effect on her. She grew warm, a rush of blood coursing through her. She felt as though she were naked before him, instead of covered from her throat to her toes. As a defense against the strong sensations running through her, she lapsed into brittle civility. "So glad you approve, my lord," she said coldly.

"Oh, I most assuredly do approve, *my lady*," he answered smoothly. "Though I am not so certain Mr. Maltby would do so. Not quite in his style, I should imagine."

"Mr. Maltby was *very* flattering in his compliments, sir. "Unlike you!" she said hotly. He always seemed able to set up her hackles.

"Did you not find my compliment flattering? I am sorry for it. It was sincerely meant." Some of the teasing had left his voice, for he was sorry to have set her off. He was beginning to wonder if he had lost his touch with the ladies. "You look devastatingly pretty, as you very well know."

"Thank you, my lord," was her curt reply. They arrived at the covert, and she rode ahead to watch the dogs at work.

The fox was quickly found this time, and off they all rode at the gallop. But it was a sad run. Less than a quarter of an hour after the View, the fox found an unstopped hole and went to ground. There had barely been time for the blood to begin pumping and the mind to start racing when it was over.

There was much shuffling about at the burrow, the dogs growling and scratching at the ground. Shovels were brought to dig out the fox, who was so recalcitrant as to not wish to be killed just yet. But the burrow was a deep and complex one. Before long it was obvious that the fellow was lying low well beyond their reach or had broken out the other end and was well away.

There was some discussion of trying another covert in the hopes of finding another fox. But the heart seemed to have gone out of the chase for this day. A mostly desultory group headed home.

The disappointment was not universal, however. Priscilla had never been more relieved. She knew it was only a short reprieve, like a condemned man being rescued from the hangman's noose temporarily, only to be returned to a cell overlooking the gallows. Mama would certainly send her out again with the very next hunt. But at least for today the ordeal was over. And perhaps she could manage to slip away for an hour now with her sketchbook. She needed some peace in which to compose herself and sort out the horrifying suspicions Lord Devlin had brought to her mind.

Mr. Maltby was also not terribly upset with his morning's sport. A good fifteen minutes' gallop was just what he liked. He never had cared for the notion of killing the fox. He was just as pleased that the clever fellow had got away. And now there would be time to return to the woods for those soil samples and specimens he wanted.

Francesca and Devlin turned back toward the castle disgusted. What a wasted morning it had been! So great was their disappointment that they had no thought of the progress they might have each made in their courtships. They caught sight of each other. So obvious was their vexation, so perfect a mirror did they make for each other, that they had to laugh in spite of themselves. They were soon in charity with each other once more.

Without a word, with nothing more than a lifted brow and a look of challenge, they agreed to a race. They dug in their heels, and the two horses took off in unison. A few minutes later they were pounding up the long gravel drive and drawing rein before the wide stairs, still in perfect step. Calling a draw, they entered the house laughing and chatting comfortably. The day's sport had not been a total loss after all.

9

If the morning had proved less than perfect, the evening held more promise. For tonight the dual wooing was to begin in earnest. The Duchess had been more than a little surprised when Francesca came to her bedchamber that afternoon and requested that she be seated beside Mr. Maltby at dinner.

Sarah had, on her lordship's orders, been resting on a chaise, a book in her hand and a light shawl draped prettily over her shoulders. She smiled a warm greeting to Francesca but looked puzzled when the request was put to her.

"But whatever for, darling?" she asked. "I am sure Caspar is well enough, but you will find him a dull companion, I fear. He can speak of nothing but his flowers and his grasses and shrubs. You know you don't care a fig for any of them, Cesca."

"Why, Sarah!" exclaimed Francesca, throwing up her hands in mock surprise. "However can you say so? I find I am developing an enormous interest in chrysanthemums. Or is it dahlias? Oh, dear, I must just go into the library and check before dinner."

"Cesca, I know that look of mischief. I've helped plant it there too many times. What *are* you up to?"

"Up to?" replied Francesca with a great air of innocence. But something behind her playfulness made Sarah grow serious.

"Tell me, dearest. Something is wrong, I fear."

Francesca's facade dropped abruptly and she grew very matter-of-fact, with a note of defensiveness in her voice. She sat abruptly on the end of the chaise and faced her friend. "Oh, very well, Sarah. You know how you are always after me to marry and begin my family. Well, I have finally decided that you are right. And I have been persuaded that I could do no better than to marry Mr. Maltby."

"Marry Caspar Maltby!" Sarah burst out in giggles, but one look at Francesca's stonily determined face and she grew quickly sober again. "Cesca, you cannot be serious! You can do *very much* better than Caspar, and well you know it! Whoever put such an absurd notion into your head?"

"Oh, what does it matter?" she said in vexed tones. She should have known that Sarah would take the whole thing badly. "And I know I could do better by worldly criteria. But I will not be ruled by a husband! Or go through the rest of my life declaring what 'George says'!" A shadow passed Sarah's face, and Francesca was immediately contrite. "Oh, darling, forgive me. I know that being married to George makes you ecstatically happy. And for that reason it makes me happy too. But I am made of rather different stuff. I should simply suffocate in a marriage such as yours. Caspar will suit me very well, you know. He is perfectly willing to be agreeable and so totally absorbed in his own life he will not bother about mine. More importantly, he is absolutely incapable of ruling anyone."

"But you do not love him!" cried Sarah with real anguish in her voice. She rose, wringing her hands, and began to pace the room, trailing the skirts of her pretty muslin wrapper behind her.

Francesca reached up and stopped her, took her tenderly by the shoulders, and settled her gently back onto the chaise. "Of course I do not love him. But you know, dearest, it is highly unlikely that I shall ever 'fall in love' as you did. I never have before." She dared not think how close she had once come to doing just that. "And," she went on resolutely, "if I should ever do so, I would certainly not marry the fellow and give him such unequaled power over me. There can be few chains more binding than emotional ones. I will *not* be so bound. Mr. Maltby will have a certain amount of power, of course—the laws of our illustrious land will give it to him—but it is in the highest degree unlikely that he will ever think to exercise any of it. I will be well contented with him and the children he will give me."

She had said the words to herself so many times in the past eighteen hours that she now nearly believed them. The doubts hovering about the corners of her consciousness, she refused to heed.

Sarah could not like the idea—she cared too much for Francesca to see her throw herself away in such a cavalier manner—but she was at last persuaded that her friend was perfectly determined. She agreed to help in any way she could. Francesca left a rather disheartened Duchess, who stared out her windows with a thoughtful frown replacing her usually sunny smile.

So it was that Mr. Maltby found himself once again the object of Lady Francesca's large amber eyes and dizzying smile at dinner. He discovered himself going on at some length about a hybridization of an apple and a pear that he had been working on for some time, and was flattered by her close attention, intelligent questions, and obvious admiration for anyone so clever as to actually *invent* a new fruit.

In fact, the man became unwontedly loquacious, then extraordinarily thirsty, and then, after rather more of the Duke's excellent wine than he was used to drinking, he became very much aware of the whiteness of Lady Francesca's shoulders, the swell of her bosom, the delicacy of her waist. Of a sudden he became rather less loquacious. Lady Francesca smiled all the brighter.

Lord Devlin had also had the forethought to see that the place cards were rearranged to put him next to Miss Pennington. Unfortunately, Mrs. Gordon had had the same idea. His lordship found himself between one young woman who would hardly speak and another who would hardly stop.

"Such a pity we had so little sport today, is it not, my lord?" began Roxanna Gordon.

Devlin, pleased at the relative innocuousness of this conversational sally, replied easily enough. "Yes. But we can hope for better next time. My horses have arrived, I have been informed, and I should like to show them off."

"What? Not your *wild* horses!" She fingered a large ruby dangling provocatively from her throat and drawing attention to a dashing expanse of creamy bosom. She let her eyes grow very wide. "La! How I wish to see them! You must know that I adore *everything* wild and untamed. So much more thrilling. And I'll wager yours are stallions," she finished with an arch smile and a playful pat on his hand. Such a pity that one could not use a fan at the table.

He drew his hand away quickly to call for more wine, then devoted himself a moment to the tiny roasted larks and savory wild rice on his plate. He was certain he could feel the silent and probably shocked Miss Pennington watching him from the corner of her eye. "One is a stallion," he admitted finally, "spirited but scarcely untamed. The other two are a gelding and a mare, both quite well-mannered." He turned to Priscilla, anxious to make up any ground that Roxanna might have lost him. "I feel certain you would like the mare, Miss Pennington. She is velvet-mouthed and playful and would give you a superb ride." He had been so caught up in his own disappointment in this morning's hunt that he had not even noticed whether or not Priscilla could actually ride. But then, it never really occurred to him that there was anyone who could not ride. He had been raised on a horse and assumed that everyone else had been too. "You are very welcome to try her out soon," he finished in a pleading tone, almost as though he were asking a favor of her.

"Oh, no, my lord," she exclaimed. "That is, I . . . Thank you sir, but I . . ."

"It is not the least trouble, I assure you. I would like to think there was some way in which I could serve you." He had lowered his voice and turned his shoulder so that Roxanna, try though she might, could not catch his words. The softness gave them an intimacy which frightened Priscilla. She wanted to cry out that he could serve her very well by ceasing to single her out in such a way. But all she mumbled was, "Th-th-thank you, my lord."

"I wish you would call me Devlin, Miss Pennington. It is so much more . . . friendly."

"Oh, but I couldn't," she began, then looked up. She was alarmed by what she saw. His smile might have been pleasant to anyone else, but it made her feel like a small furry mouse being watched by a circling hawk. She wanted nothing more than to scurry away and burrow into a hole.

"Please," he said gently. His smile grew more kindly, but she did not see it now. She had looked down again and was staring hard at the veal birds in oyster sauce congealing on her plate.

"Very well, my lord . . . D-Devlin."

Just then, Roxanna was successful in claiming his attention once again, and Priscilla was allowed to finish her dinner in peace, nibbling desultorily on a stalk of iced asparagus and nodding occasionally at the inept conversational sallies of Mr. Benjamin Hollys on her other side.

Francesca had not become so engrossed in Mr. Maltby's hybridizations or in her own dinner that she had no chance to watch Devlin's progress in his suit. They were seated directly opposite to each other—instead of beside each other, as Sarah had intended—without so much as an epergne to interrupt the view. She

really must speak to him, Francesca decided. His approach was all wrong. At the rate he was going, he was
apt to scare Priscilla off before morning.

Devlin, too, had been observant during the meal and
decided that Lady Francesca could do with some kindly
advice. She was throwing herself at poor Caspar as
though she were Roxanna Gordon, for God's sake! The
man was dazzled for the moment, it seemed, but when
he woke up, and that would surely be soon enough, he
was like to be disgusted by such behavior. Gentlemen
might dally with the dashers, but they did not marry
them.

And so, as the ladies rose to leave the table, Francesca
and Devlin chanced to catch each other's eyes. Each
wondered why on earth the other was scowling so.

As the ladies entered the drawing room to amuse
themselves as best they could until the gentlemen condescended to join them once more, Francesca caught an
unhappy, worried look from Sarah. A twinge of guilt
tweaked her conscience—she hated to be worrying Sarah
at such a delicate time—but she believed herself to be doing the right thing. She would see that Mr. Maltby had
no cause to repent his marriage to her. She would make
him a very good wife.

Convinced as she was, she could not quite bring herself to face Sarah just yet. She headed for an empty chair
beside Priscilla. She would try to determine for herself
how much headway Devlin was making with the girl
and do what she could to repair his mishandling of her
so far.

Mrs. Pennington had been cornered by Lady Braethon. By the preening of the former and the speculative
looks toward Pris of the latter, it was obvious what and
whom they were discussing. Everyone must have noticed
by now the attentions Devlin was paying to Pris. Even
Roxanna was pouting in the corner of a sofa.

"May I sit with you, Pris?" asked Francesca. The two

girls, though scarcely bosom buddies, had been acquaint-
ed for more than a year.

"Certainly, Lady Francesca," said Priscilla, minding
her manners and trying hard to forget her wretchedness.

"That is a very pretty frock," Francesca lied easily.
Priscilla looked down at the pile of acid green sarcenet
that engulfed her delicate form. It was wrapped around
with ruchings and rufflings, and the bodice was covered
with far too many ribbons and rosettes for one of
Priscilla's size.

She looked at Francesca to see if she were teasing, but
saw only kindness in the lovely face next to hers. With
unwonted courage she replied, "It is a perfectly horrid
frock! You know Liza would not be seen dead in such a
hideous dress." Her voice was thick with misery and a
touch of self-pity as she added, "Mama chose it."

"Does your mother always choose your clothes?"

"Generally. She never did so with Liza, of course—
Liza would not have stood for it—but then, I haven't
Liza's style."

"Of course you haven't," said Francesca, patting the
girl's hand. "You have Priscilla's style. You need only to
find it. We each of us must find our own way, you
know."

The soft kindness in the voice seemed to open some
kind of floodgate in Priscilla. A suggestion of tears began
to well up in the big aquamarine eyes. "But it is so easy
for you! You are beautiful, like Liza. You do not stam-
mer and blush and make a fool of yourself whenever
someone tries to speak to you. And you don't have a
Mama dressing you up like some sort of doll and
throwing you at the heads of gentlemen who try to be
kind but who really only wish you would go away!"

Francesca discreetly offered the girl a handkerchief
and turned her body so as to shield her from the curious
eyes of Lady Braethon. How completely lacking in confidence the poor girl was!

After a moment Priscilla calmed herself and wiped

away a last tear. "There," said Francesca in a nurse-maidish, that's-better sort of tone. "You must not let your Mama distress you so. She is only trying to do what she thinks is best for you, you know."

"I know she is," said Priscilla on a hiccup. "But I do wish she would not."

"Well, of course you would like the freedom to choose your own gowns and your own friends and your own pursuits. It is what everyone wants. But single girls seldom have such freedom." She diplomatically refrained from pointing out that she had always had just such freedom simply because she had always insisted upon it. "But when you are married, you know, you need listen to no one but your husband." She gave a conspiratorial smile and added, "And husbands, I think, are much more easily managed than mothers."

To her dismay, she saw the hunted look had returned to Priscilla's face to replace the recently vented anger. "I do not think so, my lady," she whispered. Why, the girl was truly frightened at the notion, thought Francesca. And it must be Devlin that had made her so afraid. What an absurd idea, she thought, to be frightened of Devlin. But then she recalled her own fears five years ago. But she had been afraid of herself, of the strength of her own feelings, not of the object of those feelings. Priscilla was a different sort of creature entirely.

"You mustn't let Devlin frighten you, you know," she said quietly. Priscilla looked up in alarm, all her suspicions confirmed. Lord Devlin *had* been singling her out, so much so that everyone had noticed. Tears brimmed up once more, and she could not answer. Francesca, realizing too late her gaffe, changed the subject and began chattering away on totally innocuous subjects for the next quarter of an hour.

When the gentlemen finally rejoined them, it was with surprise and a touch of annoyance that Francesca saw Devlin and Caspar enter together, still deep in conversation. No sooner did they step over the threshold than their eyes lifted to where she was sitting. There was a degree of alarm mixed with the admiration in Caspar's look; there was a definite note of amusement in Devlin's. They had obviously been discussing her. Devlin's glance taunted her with the fact. How dare he interfere, she thought with annoyance, entirely dismissing the equally obvious fact that she was sitting beside Priscilla, holding a handkerchief still wet with tears from the girl's red-rimmed eyes.

With a last whispered assurance to Priscilla, Francesca vacated her seat and went to help Sarah with the recently arrived tea tray. She expected Devlin would take advantage of her vacating her place to continue his wooing of Pris, but instead he followed her to the teapot and stood at her elbow while she poured and handed round the cups. Sarah smiled up at them. "What a dear you are, Cesca," she said, "to relieve me of every burden. If you will pour, I will just go speak to Sally. She has the most wonderful nurse to recommend, she says." She rose and gave Devlin her sunniest smile. "Do I not take shameful advantage of my friends, my lord? Do stay and help Cesca with her task. You will relieve my conscience." Neatly kicking her demi-train behind her, she swirled off toward Lady Jersey.

Francesca watched her go with a puzzled frown. What was Sarah up to? And why was Devlin standing there with such an amused grin on his face, the odious man? She picked up the heavy silver teapot and poured the dark brew into a delicate Wedgwood cup, added warm milk, and handed it to him with a cold "My lord."

He only grinned the more. "Oh, do stop looking daggers at me, if you please." he said without preamble. "Just because I have been doing what I could to mend your fences for you. You should be thanking me."

"*My* fences are in no need of mending, my lord," she said coldly. "And if you had been paying closer attention at dinner, you would have seen it quite clearly." She handed two cups to Lord Poole with a pretty smile. He accepted with a compliment, then carried them away.

"I was paying *very* close attention," continued Devlin, "and I agree that your Mr. Maltby is, for the moment, quite dazzled. But I promise you, Caspar Maltby is not the fellow to marry a dazzler. I suggest you tone down your act, old girl, or you will lose your bet."

"Would you take this to Lady Braethon, please?" she said coldly, handing him a cup.

He did, but, to her dismay, returned at once and went on as though without interruption, "That gown, for instance."

She abruptly stopped pouring and looked down at her dress. It was a long elegant fall of amber peau de soie that exactly matched her eyes, trimmed with Brussels lace of a rich deep brown.

"Very *tonnish*," he said. "Very elegant, and well calculated to direct the thoughts of most gentlemen to your undeniable charms." He could not deny that it had just this effect on him when he had first seen her in it. He had thought her quite perfect. She flushed with embarrassed annoyance as his gaze raked those undeniable charms. He went on, "But something a little more demure would better suit your immediate purposes, I think."

"I suppose you would prefer me to dress like Priscilla!"

He looked toward his would-be wife. "Well, you needn't go so far as that," he conceded. He took in the girl's still-tearful eyes and added, "And by the by, what have you been saying to her? She looks all in a dither."

"What have *you* been saying to her? The poor thing is nearly beside herself. She is terrified at the thought of you, Devlin."

"Terrified? Nonsense! Why ever should she be frightened of me of all people? I am the best of good fellows. I have treated her with nothing but respect and kindness."

"You may think you have. But I might suggest that Pris is a rather nervous little animal. If you want to catch her, you had best use an invisible trap. You have been going after her with beak and talons bared."

"I have only—" he began his defense, but was cut off by what he saw approaching. "Oh Lord! Here comes the Widow!"

"I shall leave you to your *tête-à-tête* with her, then," Francesca replied, and picked up a cup to carry to Lady Aurelm.

He stopped her with an iron hand on her arm and spoke through his teeth. "If you desert me, I shall tell Maltby what a baggage you really are. *And* I shall never speak to you again."

Her eyes laughed at him. "*Such* a temptation!" she said softly, but remained seated. "As you wish, then."

"And don't think I am through with you! We will continue this conversation at a later time!"

Roxanna Gordon fluttered up in a wisp of red chiffon that scarcely covered enough of her alluring form to deserve the title of gown. Her eyes were glittering as brightly as her rubies. "Devlin," she murmured, taking a cup of tea from Francesca rather as if she were a servant, then completely ignoring her. She turned her powerful allure on Devlin. "You must just settle a question for me. Lord Jersey and I have been discussing the mating and breeding of dogs . . ."

The evening ebbed slowly away. Jane Magness performed with much virtuosity and little emotion on the pianoforte. Priscilla was made to tackle the harp, which she did with an overabundance of feeling—her nervous agitation and embarrassment were evident to all except her Mama—and only a modicum of skill. Devlin was called upon to partner Lady Braethon at whist, much to Roxanna's annoyance, and Francesca went to work once more on Mr. Maltby.

Whatever Devlin had said to him after dinner, Caspar seemed less bemused by Francesca than he had been. She began to find it uphill work to amuse him and keep him enthralled. Her questions about his flowers and his shrubs still kept him talking, but a look behind his not unintelligent eyes now and then clearly wondered if she were truly interested or only tolerating his company for some obscure motive of her own. He knew very well that he was not the sort of fellow to usually attract such as she. Also, he had known Francesca for some time, and she had never paid him the least attention before now. It was a puzzle.

"Yes, Sarah's gardens are particularly fine," said Francesca in response to some comment from him. "I do hope you will tour them with me. Sarah has been promising to do so for ages, but I am certain that *you*, Mr. Maltby, would make a far better guide. You could explain the characteristics of the various species so much more thoroughly than Sarah."

"I should be glad to do so, of course," he answered, "if you do not think the Duchess would mind."

"Not at all. She loves her gardens, of course, but she would be the first to tell you that she knows very little about how they grow. I know she is considering adding more color to the beds in the lower terraces. The old Duchess had a penchant for nothing but white blooms."

"Oh, but she must not!" exclaimed Caspar. "The White Garden is superb just as it is. Quite unique, in fact. Of course, the rose garden would be improved with a little more variety. I've a nice cinnamon-red Persian the Duchess might favor."

"Cinnamon! But how intriguing. I am certain she will love it. Perhaps we could visit the rose garden one afternoon. After the hunt, of course," she added, almost as an afterthought. To Lady Francesca, looking at rosebushes, especially bare autumn rosebushes, when one could be riding to hounds, galloping over fields and fences, was scarcely imaginable. "I should so like to see it with *you*, Mr. Maltby," she concluded, laying a hand lightly on his sleeve.

His eyes flitted to her hand in surprise, then to her face, which was smiling a brilliant but strangely intimate smile. He felt his neck begin to grow warm and his head to grow a little dizzy. He really had drunk a great deal of wine, he concluded. It must have been the wine that made him reach out to cover her hand with his own.

"I should be honored to escort you, my lady." He spoke in a voice that came out a sort of croak.

"Francesca," she said softly, and squeezed his hand. When she looked out into the room once again, it was to meet Devlin's glare upon her with a smile of triumph. She would show him that she did not need his advice. Nor would she take it.

10

The party did, at length, break up and the guests retired to their bedchambers. As Francesca sat before her mirror, a pretty peach nightdress gathered at her bosom, and her abigail, Rose, brushing out her rippling golden hair, she mused on the progress of the evening. She felt sure now she could bring Caspar up to scratch, and had, in fact, already gone halfway to doing just that. She would be a married lady before the spring, maybe even sooner. Perhaps, by this time next year, she would find herself in Sarah's condition. She looked down at her firm breasts and flat stomach just covered by the silk shift. How would it feel to be with child? she wondered. Caspar's child. She shivered. Rose handed her an airy peignoir that matched the shift. She wrapped it around her shoulders.

It occurred to her that, for one contemplating such a momentous change in her life, she was strangely dispassionate about the whole thing. It was as though she were observing someone else, a good friend, whose best interests she had at heart, but for whom she felt little emotional involvement.

Of course, Caspar Maltby was not the sort of gentleman to arouse intense emotion. It was precisely why she had settled on him. A husband whom she could like well enough, even respect a bit, was what she required. Not one who would wield emotional power over her. Such affection would be saved for her children.

That thought did bring a smile to her lips. The poor little things were likely to be smothered by her if she wasn't careful. She would cherish them and care for them and bring them up to be strong and bright and free. They would be her world.

She dismissed her abigail, but she was not in the least sleepy. Her mind was too jumbled with thoughts to be able to rest just yet. After a languid stretch she settled herself into a comfortable chair before the fire, her bare feet tucked up beneath her, to read herself into a more composed state. Mr. Gibbon's *The History of the Decline and Fall of the Roman Empire* seemed perfectly suited to the task.

But hardly had she transported herself to the ancient world than a tap at her door jolted her back to the present. It must be Rose returning with some message or other, she guessed. "Come in," she called, and was surprised when the only response was another polite tap.

She walked to the door, her airy peignoir billowing from the movement and her long hair draped over her shoulders. But the angelic picture she presented jarred with the amazed look on her face at the sight of her caller.

Devlin, still perfectly and completely dressed, stared back with equal amazement. Had he given the matter any thought, he would have expected to see her already dressed for bed. But the truth was that he had given the matter no thought at all. His reaction, therefore, was a compound of embarrassment at finding her thus and awe at her striking beauty. The candlelight behind her glowed through the thin silk, perfectly outlining her long thighs, her tiny waist, her elegant arms. Her golden hair looked as if it was on fire, a halo hanging over it.

Francesca was the first to find her voice. "My lord?" she asked softly.

"Forgive me, my lady," he replied, giving himself a

mental shake. "I had not thought you would be so quick." He knew he was making little sense, but didn't know how to remedy the situation.

Suddenly the absurdity of their grave formality while she stood there in her nightdress struck them both, and they smiled.

"Well, Devlin," she said in a more relaxed voice, "what can I do for you?"

"I had thought we might continue our earlier conversation and perhaps map out a little strategy together. But it can wait for another time." He made as if to leave, although with obvious reluctance.

Quickly, and almost involuntarily, she reached out to stop him. "Nonsense, Devlin. Now you are here, there is no reason you should not stay." She looked down at her charming *deshabille*. "I am as thoroughly covered as I would be in a ball gown, you know." He said nothing to disabuse her of her misapprehension. "And with such a house full of guests, it is unlikely we will find many opportunities to be private together." With a smile and with very little reluctance, he came in, and the door was shut behind him. "And I *would* like to know what you said to Caspar after dinner. I had to spend the rest of the evening beguiling him again."

She moved so that the candlelight was no longer behind her; thus she appeared clothed again, and he came back to his senses. "What? Scales beginning to drop from his eyes already, are they?"

"No, they are not!" she retorted, then calmed herself. "I believe you observed how the evening ended. He is scarce indifferent to me."

"Too bad he can't see you now. It would clinch the matter. You look like an angel."

His gaze made her feel hot with embarrassment and something else she could not yet name. She retreated into anger. "Perhaps I shall invite him to do so! Unlike you, he will most assuredly not come without such an invitation."

"No, poor fellow, I am certain he wouldn't. Doesn't know what he's missing. But I shouldn't do it if I were you. He wouldn't come, you know, and you are like to give him a disgust of you if you don't moderate your behavior."

"If you do not give him a disgust of me first. Whatever did you say to him? Are you so very anxious to win your paltry bet?"

"On the contrary. I hope you will win. Married ladies are so much more interesting than single ones." After a pause he added, "And so much more available." She was too amazed at his audacity and at the lurch that went through her at his words to answer. "And besides," he continued, "I rather think I shall win my prize even if I lose."

For a puzzled moment she tried to recall what forfeit he had named should she lose the bet. Then it came to her. He had named none in words, but his look, his manner, had quite clearly demanded *her*, just as they did now.

Even more confusing was the fact that a part of her seemed quite willing that he should have her. He had reached out a tender hand to her shoulder, fingering the long golden hair that lay there so enticingly. A shock went through her at his touch; something within her seemed to melt. Her education had provided her with no compelling moral reason to resist him. She leaned toward him.

But just as he would have kissed her, she remembered, and she knew that once she gave herself to him, she would be forever lost to herself. There would be no going back. She turned quickly away and walked to the fire. "And how goes the battle for your fair Priscilla?" she asked in a brightly brittle voice that sounded on the edge of hysteria even in her own ears.

In turning away, she could not see the look on his face. Had she done so, she would have been very much surprised. There was neither the anger nor the disappointment that she might have reasonably thought to see there. Instead, he seemed strangely relieved, and when he looked at the hand that had touched her hair and saw that it was trembling, a bit surprised. Lord Devlin could scarce be called a novice where the wooing of women was concerned. But he had never been touched in this strange way by any other woman in the whole wide world. It made him distinctly uncomfortable. He stuck the trembling hand into his pocket with deliberation. When he spoke at last, his voice was as falsely casual as her own. "Priscilla? Oh, we progress," he said.

"I was afraid Pris would send you running with her harp this evening," said Francesca, seating herself in the wing chair once more and tucking her bare feet up under her in a beguiling way. The moment of tension was broken.

"She nearly did so, I can tell you," he confessed as he stirred up the dying embers. "But then I saw that the poor girl was suffering as much in the playing as we were in the listening. As soon as we are betrothed, I shall promise her that she need never play again, and she may promise me that I need never listen."

"I begin to think you will suit even better than I at first expected."

"How well you understand my needs." He intended nothing more than the words meant, but as soon as they were out he could have bitten his tongue. "I meant only that you have chosen perfectly for me," he hastened to add.

"Well, you had best take care not to send her running, then. You were looking at her all evening like a wolf at a lamb."

Despite his best intentions, he could not resist such an opening. He grinned at her. "Oh, no, Francesca. It is *you* I look at like a wolf, though I know very well you are no lamb. It is why I have not attacked. I cannot be certain of coming out of the encounter unscathed."

"You wouldn't!" she said quickly, and pulled her feet closer under her.

"Now, Miss Pennington is most definitely a lamb, but I see myself rather more in the role of shepherd than of predator."

"But does not the shepherd have the best interests of his sheep at heart?"

"On the contrary. He has his own best interests at heart. Was it not you who told me how inherently selfish we all are? The shepherd cares well for his sheep because he needs them to earn his livelihood. Luckily, that is also good for the sheep. My lamb will be content, I promise you. I shall take very good care of Miss Pennington because I need her to be my wife."

"I cannot think she would like to hear herself discussed so cynically."

"But she won't. She will hear nothing but kindness and gentleness from me, I assure you."

"Then you had better start, sir. For regardless of your intentions, it is clear that at present you are dealing with a very frightened lamb. The girl is terrified of you."

"Nonsense. Why should she be?"

"*I* have no idea. Have you been so blockheaded as to mention marriage to her already?"

"Of course not! What sort of a noddy do you take me for?" He did not give her time to answer. "But I'll wager her mother has," he concluded honestly.

"And did you not tell Pris how much she would like Kent and how sadly your house stood in need of a woman's touch, and what was *her* favorite color for wall coverings?"

"No, I did not!" he said hotly, then recalled his actual, not so very different, conversations with the girl. "Well, not in those very words," he amended, beginning to see his mistake.

"So I thought," she said dryly. "I can see that you were correct when you said you knew nothing about winning a tender young girl. I suggest you leave her quite alone tomorrow."

"How will that advance my cause?"

"It will give her a chance to calm her fears. And to view you more objectively. She has scarce had a chance to *think* about you; she is far too busy *fearing* you. Give her a little space. In the evening you may speak to her but *only* on the most general of subjects."

"You may be right," he admitted, though reluctantly, staring thoughtfully into the fire. "I do seem to have bungled it a bit so far."

"So glad you admit it."

"Too bad you cannot do the same."

"*I* have not bungled it!"

"Oh, give over, Cesca." She flushed to hear the pet name on his lips. "You've been moving like one of those newfangled steam engines. But you are about to run out of track. And you are like to flatten the poor fellow under such an assault."

"Well, it is working," she reminded him.

"For the moment," he admitted. "But Caspar is no dunce. It will not take him long, certainly not long enough, to come to his senses. He is far too levelheaded to allow himself to remain bemused for long."

"Well, I haven't much time, you know. Just what do you suggest?"

"Well, you are playing for fairly high stakes, and a true gambler never shows his hand too clearly. Your clothes, for instance. That is the reason I came to your room."

"My clothes!" she sputtered in indignation. But he was not listening. He had crossed to the great wardrobe and thrown open the door. "You must have something 'sweet-maidenish' in here." He began flipping through gown after gown, tossing one or two onto the bed and making a great to-do. "No, no, too low . . . too dashing . . . not sweet enough . . ." he muttered as he rummaged.

She ran to the wardrobe to stop him. "For God's sake,

Dev! Do be quiet. Lady Braethon is on the other side of that wall."

"I thought I recognized the snoring," he said with a grin.

"And Roxanna Gordon is just across the hall," she continued to somewhat better effect.

"Oh, Lord!"

"Exactly."

"No matter," he said softly after a moment. "We shall work quietly." He pulled out a blue sprig muslin with long fitted sleeves. "Now, this has possibilities."

She looked at the dress with a frown. "I cannot think why I brought it," she said pettishly. Actually, it was one of her favorite gowns, but she was not ready to give him an inch.

"Of course, the neck is a bit low. Have you got a handkerchief or something you could fill it in with?"

"Don't be ridiculous!" she said, snatching the dress from him and hanging it back in the wardrobe.

"And here is another!" He pulled out a cherry striped toilinette walking dress with a high-necked rose velvet bodice. "You have been holding out on me, Cesca."

"Oh, go to bed, do, Devlin. I promise you I shall look appropriately demure tomorrow." He grinned and looked toward the big bed, then back at her, gratified by her blush. She crossed to the door, opened it, and said in a very regal whisper, "Good night, Lord Devlin."

He came to her and stood a moment, causing her to look up into his blue, blue eyes. "Good night, Lady Francesca," he whispered back; then he leaned down and very lightly kissed her, a kiss like a butterfly's wings that left her breathless.

Closing the door softly behind him, Francesca leaned against it a moment, thankful for its support, and willed her tumbling thoughts and pounding heart to be still.

Devlin, tiptoeing down the hall with a warm smile on his face, was also subject to thought, so much so that he did not hear the soft click of a latch nearby.

Roxanna Gordon stepped back into her room just in time to avoid his lordship's notice. And she was not smiling. She had decided that she would be the next Baroness Devlin. She had thought she had only poor little Priscilla Pennington to deal with, scarce a fair opponent for her formidable powers of seduction.

But Francesca Waringham was a bird of a very different feather. If Devlin was secretly visiting her bedchamber at night, things between them had gone entirely too far. Roxanna would have to see to doing away with such formidable competition.

11

Despite a very late night of intense thinking—or one might more properly say scheming—Roxanna Gordon arose early next morning. The beginning of a plan had begun taking shape in her mind, and she was anxious to begin carrying it out. She sat at a delicate Pembroke table near the window. Strongly angled shafts of sunlight filtered through the grey clouds to light her blue-black hair. Birds were chirping in a tree just outside, and the garden below glowed prettily. But all this went unremarked as her quill flew across the paper.

For a lady of quality, Roxanna Gordon had an odd assortment of friends and acquaintances. Born into the *ton*, she had been married at an early age to the infamous Johnny Gordon. He was a close crony of "Cripplegate" Barrymore, the most notorious rake and debauchee in all England. Everyone had been thoroughly shocked at the marriage. Roxanna's father, Sir Alfred Blythe, had been excoriated for selling a tender young girl off to such a skirter.

But the condemnation was quite unfair, for Gordon had been very much Roxanna's own choice. Her father had agreed to the marriage against his better judgment, and only then because he knew his headstrong daughter would simply run off with the fellow should he refuse the match.

In fact, the infamous Gordon and Roxanna Blythe had

suited each other to the ground. She was a lady of quality with the soul of a courtesan and found herself very well married. He had often invited her along on his riotous rounds, much to her delight. She even attended a few "meetings" of the notorious "Hellfire Club" of which her husband was a founding member. She spent lavishly of his money, with his ungrudging acquiescence, as she spent liberally of her favors, also with his complete agreement. He had, in fact, seemed quite proud of her skill with the gentlemen and occasionally arranged some of her most private parties for her.

Despite all this sordid living, she had always been jealous of her reputation within the *ton*. She had managed to retain at least a facade of respectability within the upper echelons of Society. The more riotous of her adventures with her husband were limited to dark corners of the town unfrequented by the *ton*, and her *innamorati* were always from the lower orders, whom no one was likely to believe, should they decide to make public the liaisons.

The starchier matrons around town thought her too fast by far to be totally respectable, but she was still accepted everywhere. Most of her *tonnish* friends had always felt a sort of pity for her, assuming as they did that she was stuck in a miserable marriage. They forgave her high spirits and open flirtations as a desperate reach for some warmth and affection.

When John Gordon was killed in a tavern brawl, Roxanna's grief had been genuine. She knew she would be utterly bored without him. A full year in blacks to retain her respectability had certainly not improved matters. But the years of her marriage had enlarged her circle of friends to a useful extent. Although there were no *ton* parties, no theatre or opera, there were men of a less nice disposition who were not loath to escort a plucky lady to cockfights and bull baitings, on outings to Bartholomew Fair and on riotous evening romps that were, truth to tell, much more to her taste than fancy balls and routs. She had even attended the annual Cyprian's Ball at Covent Garden, well-masked of course, since many gentlemen of the *ton* always attended. After amusing herself flirting with a string of earls, viscounts, and other "respectable" gentlemen, all of them well known to her, she had allowed a visiting Austrian, due to return to his own country in the morning, to escort her home.

She had now been out of blacks for a year, and was taking full advantage of the even greater freedom that widowhood gave her. She was more jealous than ever of her position in the *ton*. Even the most riotous living must begin to pall after a while. She had felt her position slipping, and she knew only one sure way to retrieve and ensure it. She needed to remarry and to marry well. Lord Devlin had all the cachet she needed. Also, he was just enough of an adventurer to appeal to her taste. He would not bore her to death as most respectable men would do. She decided to have him.

Her marriage had left her with a useful acquaintance of scoundrels and rascals and other assorted blackguards. Many of her former friends owed her in one form or another. Now seemed a good moment to collect on one or two of those debts, and her quill scribbled her needs concisely and unhesitatingly in a firm hand.

With no hunting that day—the horses and dogs needed a rest even if the most avid hunters did not—it looked to be a quiet day at Hockleigh. Quiet, that is, upstairs. In the nether quarters things went on much as usual, which is to say that every servant on the estate was up to his elbows in chores.

It had come on to rain, one of those grey, drizzly mornings, confining all those inmates with any choice in the matter to the dry, well-heated rooms. In the front parlor, the ladies chatted, read, or stitched over their morning coffee. In the billiard room, the gentlemen exchanged stories over their cue sticks of recent pugilistic battles and famous hunts, or commented on various articles in the current issues of *The Gentlemen's Magazine* or *Gray's Sporting Journal.*

Lord Devlin had been unable to stifle a grin on first seeing Lady Francesca that morning. Despite her indignation of the night before, she had donned the cherry striped gown. With a red ribbon simply tying back her long golden waves, she looked as fresh and young as a schoolgirl. The effect, he also noted, had not been lost on Caspar, whose eyes widened in appreciation at sight of her.

For her part, Francesca was also pleased to note that Devlin all but ignored Priscilla at breakfast, much to that maiden's obvious relief. He merely commented on the grey weather and hoped it woud turn fine later—what did Miss Pennington think?

Francesca, in the parlor with the other ladies, was absentminded; inactivity always made her restless. Her eyes wandered frequently to the window, streaked with rivulets of the chilly rain, while she listened halfheartedly to the conversations of the ladies around her.

"Well, miss," said Lady Braethon in a schoolmistress voice, claiming a more direct share of her attention, "just when do you propose to stop all this independent nonsense and settle down with a husband and babies? You are not getting any younger, my girl."

Francesca smiled at the impertinent question. Lady Braethon had known her and bullied her all her life. And although she had always been somewhat in awe of the old woman, she held her in considerable affection. "Quite soon perhaps," she said serenely. "I have nearly decided to gratify your so often voiced desire. I should rather like to start a family, I think. Only look at what it is doing for Sarah. How would you like another godchild?"

Lady Braethon's sharp gaze grew sharper still, and gratification as well as curiosity gleamed behind her sharp black eyes. "Good girl!" she said. "But I'll not have just anyone siring my godchildren. Who's it to be?"

"As to that, I am not perfectly decided," Francesca lied with an air of total unconcern. "I just thought to begin looking around me for a likely candidate."

"Humph!" grunted the old lady. "All very calculating. I thought all you modern misses were holding out for love matches."

"Oh, I am far *too* modern for that, ma'am," she said with a teasing grin.

"Well, you *do* mean to marry the fellow, I hope," said Lady Braethon, suddenly realizing that the word "marriage" had not yet figured in the conversation. She was well aware of Francesca's unorthodox education, and although she liked a girl with a bit of spirit, she could not wholly approve.

"Oh, yes, ma'am," she was reassured. "When I find him."

Francesca had thought she was speaking in a low tone, but Roxanna Gordon, desultorily pretending to read a novel on a nearby sofa, had missed not a single word of the conversation. She was not deceived by the young woman's air of nonchalance: it was far too cool, too self-confident. Clearly things had gone much further between Francesca and Lord Devlin even than she had feared. She thought of the express letter she had sent off that very morning and willed it to sprout wings. She had immediate need of assistance in her campaign to oust Lady Francesca.

A few of the other ladies also heard snatches of the conversation, just enough to lead them into a general discussion of matrimony. It very nearly made Francesca change her mind about the whole thing. Did she really wish to enter into an institution so fraught with trickery and deceit and the use of all sorts of low feminine wiles to get her way? But then, was she not already sunk to just that state? Was she not using those very wiles to capture Mr. Maltby? It all seemed so sordid, and she felt another pang of guilt. Then came an even stronger pang of anger. Not for the first time, or even the hundredth, did she wish she were a man, with all a man's freedom of action and independence. She would not then be in this pickle.

But Francesca was a realist. As she was a woman, and a very pretty and wealthy one in the bargain, she must use the weapons she had to fight for the right to be herself. And being married to Caspar Maltby could be a very powerful weapon in that ongoing battle.

Francesca was not the only person in the room who was set to serious thinking by this discussion of marriage. Priscilla was made miserable by it. She feared that she would never marry, almost as much as she feared that she would. She could not bear the thought of spending the rest of her life under the thumb of her Mama. But neither did she see any escape for herself in being married. There was not a trace of deceit in Pris's soul, and she knew very well that she had no feminine wiles at all. She was so timid and so used to bending to authority, so afraid of offending and so loath to express even the smallest desire of her own, that she could not imagine herself being able to stand up to a husband any better than she had ever been able to stand up to her mother.

She had not given the matter deep thought in the past, being convinced as she was that no man would ever wish to marry her. But now that Lord Devlin was making such alarming overtures, the idea of being a wife—and more particularly wife to *such* a man—struck her most forcibly and set her to trembling.

"Oh, yes," Mrs. Pennington was saying, breaking into her daughter's disturbing thoughts. "I believe there lives not the man who cannot be brought round a clever woman's thumb. Even so strong a gentleman as our interesting Lord Devlin." The significance of the remark was not lost on Priscilla. She had been stitching absently and ineptly on a ragged piece of embroidery and gave a little cry of pain as she stabbed her needle into her finger.

Roxanna, though she could not but agree with Mrs. Pennington's statement, disliked hearing it in connection with the gentleman she fully intended wrapping around her own thumb. Still, she could hardly bother to worry herself over the Pennington chit. That was rather like a snake worrying about a worm that lay in its path. With a delicate yawn, she turned her eyes, if not her attention, back to her book.

Francesca also reacted rather strongly to the mention of Lord Devlin. Recalling her advice to that gentleman on the previous evening—and she blushed to recall any of that scene in her bedchamber—she thought it prudent to keep him as far from Priscilla's thoughts as possible. And that could only mean getting her away from her mother.

"It seems to have stopped raining," she commented as though without purpose. Casually laying aside the fashion magazine she had been languidly perusing, she rose and gave a delicate stretch. "Would you care to go for a stroll in the shrubbery with me, Priscilla? I cannot bear to be cooped up inside a moment longer."

The younger girl shot her a grateful look. "Oh, yes. Yes, I should like that," she said quickly. "I will just get my shawl," she added, and ran from the room before her mother could stop her or find some magical way of getting Lord Devlin to accompany them.

Once the two girls had gained the relative privacy of the shrubbery, Priscilla began to relax visibly, no longer looking back over her shoulder constantly like a hunted animal to see if they had been followed. They walked some little while in silence except for the soft crunch of their feet on the damp gravel. The sun had managed to wriggle through the grey clouds and glistened on the droplets still clinging to the hedges. A spider's web still wet with the rain shone like silver lace in the sun, and they stopped to examine it.

At length they began to chat, talking of the most mundane of matters, until Priscilla became almost comfortable. Francesca wanted to learn something about the girl if she could, as well as give her a much-needed boost in self-confidence.

"Priscilla," she finally said in a serious tone, "may I ask your advice about something?"

This took the younger girl by surprise. "Advice, my lady? From me?"

"Yes. You perhaps heard me mention to Lady Braethon that I have been thinking the time has come to look around me for a husband. But you know, I rather think that our world has grown so sophisticated that we have forgotten what is important in a mate, what has real value, you know. But you are so unspoiled still. I very much admire that in you."

Priscilla blushed to the roots of her hair. "You are too kind, my lady," she whispered. "But no one could admire such clumsiness, such total lack of polish."

"You are wrong, you know," said Francesca. "There are those who admire you very much indeed. You have not allowed your values to become distorted like so much of the *ton*. I think perhaps you can see people more clearly than many of us can. I would greatly appreciate your opinion. . . ."

"I could not presume, my lady—" she began.

"Please," replied Francesca. "Tell me. What do you admire in a gentleman? What would *you* look for in a prospective husband?"

The girl looked up with intent eyes, reading her companion's face. She saw no insincerity there. She looked away again, apparently giving the question some thought. She did not think to mention love as a requirement of marriage, as she had long ago given up the thought that anyone would ever love her. What else, then, was important? Finally she spoke. "Kindness," she said simply. "He must be kind."

There seemed to be little to add to such a simple truth. The two girls walked along in silence, each lost in her own thoughts, until a chill breeze sprang up to drive them back into the house.

The gentlemen, though perhaps a bit restive from the grey weather that kept them indoors, were managing to amuse themselves tolerably well. They had most of them been at school together. Consequently they were used to the teasing and jests of each other and found themselves in comfortable company. Even Devlin, once the novelty of his unexpected reappearance had worn off, was one of a congenial group.

Casper, though seldom in town and therefore not a regular crony of the group, knew them all quite well and was generally liked by them all. He had elected not to join in the billiard game that was now going forward, and sat instead with his attention turned to a botanical journal he had discovered in the library.

"You know, Maltby," said the fastidious Dudley Dalton, who was seated nearby awaiting his turn at the table. "If you intend being a viscount, you really oughtn't to wear brown boots with a black coat." Casper looked down at his brown Hessians, well made but worn and comfortable. When he looked up again, there was a vaguely puzzled look on his face.

Graham Symington completed his shot with a crack of the balls, then looked up from his stick. "What you need is a good valet, old man."

"Or a good wife," added Devlin in an offhand manner.

"Yes, I suppose I do," said Casper with a sigh.

Surprise registered on Devlin's face along with puzzlement as to whether the man referred to the valet or the wife. This might be promising. "Yes, nothing like a wife, I've heard, to make a man comfortable," he said, turning back to his newspaper with an elaborately casual air. "May even come to it myself before long. Of course, not just any woman would do, would she?"

"I suppose not," said Casper. "Not if she were to become a baroness." Recalling his own prospects, he added, "Or a viscountess." He had never much relished the idea of coming into the title. He was not really *ton* material, as he well knew. "How does one go about finding her, though?" he asked the room in general.

"Only one way," said Sir Algernon, leaving them in suspense as to the answer to this great mystery while he lined up his shot. The balls cracked again, and the point was scored. Algy looked up in satisfaction. "Got to go up to London for the Season. Do the pretty, y'know. Almack's, the Opera. All that. A bore, but there it is. It's what they expect. That's the Marriage Mart."

At the image conjured up by these innocent words, Lord Devlin and Mr. Maltby experienced quite similar feelings of horror, if for differing reasons. Devlin saw himself being pursued by the Widow and others of her ilk, or sought out by an endless string of schoolroom misses with fluttering eyelashes and matchmaking mamas with matrimonial gleams in their eyes.

Casper tried to imagine himself in evening clothes and uncomfortable shoes night after night while his prize-winning tulips bloomed at home without him. Unthinkable!

"Good Lord!" muttered Devlin.

"Shouldn't like that," muttered Caspar.

At that moment, their individual resolves to marry before the spring took on even greater significance. The pair of them sank back into thought, even Caspar's botanical journal forgotten in his lap.

Thus it was that when Caspar appeared before Francesca for the promised tour of the rose garden, the question of marriage—his marriage—was more than ever in the forefront of his mind. And here was a very eligible and desirable young lady hanging lightly on to his arm and smiling up at him and making him feel ever so bright.

She looked somehow different today, he noted. Younger and softer. More like she might need a man to lean on. They strolled casually through the nearly denuded garden, with Caspar examining every cut-back bush and thorn variation and explaining them all in excruciating detail. Francesca thought her jaw would crack with smiling, and her eyes ached from so much widening in maidenly appreciation of his superior knowledge.

Soon they had covered the entire rose garden and headed for the hothouses. Francesca sighed with relief. Here at least there were some actual living flowers to exclaim over and admire, to smell and to wonder at. Hundred-leaved cabbage roses from Holland, chestnut roses from India, delicate damask and tea roses, and the sweetbriers that made the air smell of fresh green apples grew here in abundance.

Francesca had asked Sarah's permission to gather a basket full for the drawing rooms. Catching sight of her reflection in the glass wall, she could not forbear smiling at the picture she presented. With a pair of shears in her hand and a basket of flowers over her arm, she looked the veriest country maid, milk-fed and fresh-scrubbed. Reluctantly she had to admit that Devlin had given her good advice. This was much the better tack.

Dimpling up at her companion, she chose a small white Chinese rose from her basket. With a pin from her pocket—she was nothing if not prepared—she attached the flower to the collar of his coat.

Caspar seemed much struck by her action, looked around for the finest specimen within reach, a large perfect doubleheaded Persian rose of a deep amber yellow nearly the shade of her eyes, and with something of a flourish—especially for Caspar Maltby—presented it to her.

She gave a gurgle of pleasure and a flutter of her eyelashes. After breathing in the heady scent of the bloom, she rose on tiptoe to give her swain a feathery kiss on the cheek. He blushed as red as the reddest rose in her basket.

She knew she had scored an important point in the game. She was also shrewd enough to know when to stop. After one wide-eyed look at him, she turned toward the house and ran off, the still-blushing Caspar trailing behind her.

Another pang of guilt went through Francesca as she ran up the stairs to her room. She detested flirtation in others, and here she was wallowing in it. Really, she should have been an actress on the stage! And Caspar was really such a very nice young man, and not at all an equal foe. It was too unfair of her.

But she pushed the uncomfortable thought aside. She would make Caspar a good enough wife. She would give him superlative children and a very comfortable home. What more could any husband expect, or even want, from a wife?

She did just chance to wonder how long she could keep up this elaborate charade that seemed to be working so well. Could she ever just relax and be comfortable with the man who was to be her husband? As she was comfortable with Devlin? She pushed that thought from her mind even before it had a chance to become completely formed.

The evening passed away uneventfully over cards and conversation, with a sprinkling of music thrown in to lighten the mix. Devlin did speak to Priscilla, but only for a short while and only on the most innocuous of subjects, as instructed. The anxiety he could still read behind her eyes said quite clearly that Francesca had been right. He must back off.

Roxanna Gordon made a careful observation of both Francesca and Devlin, smiling slyly now and then and hugging a very comforting secret to her bosom.

The fact of the next morning's hunt sent the company early to their beds, to sleep, to scheme, or to fret, as their various personalities and predicaments dictated.

12

There were few sluggards in the house next morning. A day off from hunting had whetted the riders' appetites for a good chase. The teakettles whistled early in the kitchens. Abigails and valets began laying out habits and breeches, and chambermaids and footmen trudged up and down staircases with great copper pitchers of steaming water. Down in the kennels the dogs were yapping in expectation; in the stables horses frisked in anticipation of a good hard run.

The breakfast room offered up without demur its bounty of sirloin and ham in thick slices, toast and muffins oozing butter, and tea and coffee filling the air with their fragrant steam. No one dabbled there, however, and soon ladies in merino and velvet and gentlemen in Melton and leather spilled down the wide stone steps of the porch toward their waiting mounts.

Once again, Lord Devlin was the center of everyone's attention. His strange American horses had arrived.

"Say, Dev," exclaimed Sir Algernon, looking over a sleek but small and tightly muscled black stallion. "You'll not hunt that runt, will you? Scarce looks up to your weight."

"Oh, Arapaho is up to it, Algy. He's pulled me through more than one pretty tight corner before this."

"He's not even fifteen hands," said Dudley Dalton in

derision. "Can't expect a slug like that to keep up with a field of pure bloods."

"Keep up!" exclaimed Devlin, laughing. "Lead is more like."

"A hundred guineas says I don't believe it," said Lord Jersey flatly. He eyed the horse critically, a trace of a smirk on his face. The horse didn't much seem to like his lordship's looks either. He offered the gentleman a kick that sat the Earl right on his noble backside.

A general round of laughter at Lord Jersey's expense was punctuated by further offers of wagers against the frisky black horse's speed and staying power. Devlin accepted them one and all with an amused grin.

As the others drifted off to their own mounts, Devlin turned to discover Lady Francesca running a practiced hand lightly and knowledgeably over the stallion's powerful withers. "You stand to make quite a sum today, Devlin. He'll stick," she said with perfect confidence.

"Yes, he will," Devlin replied, somehow pleased at her perceptiveness. "But I am surprised that you should see it. Jersey couldn't, and he is said to be one of the finest judges of horseflesh in all England."

"Lord Jersey doesn't want to see it. An American horse outrunning an English one? God forbid!"

"Oh, dear, I hope I am not to be branded a traitor."

"You needn't worry. Your standing with this group is so high you're in no danger."

"How fortunate," he answered wryly. He received a grin from her in return.

"But what of your other horses, Devlin? Did you not bring several with you? If they are all like this handsome little fellow, I must see them."

"I have brought three. The gelding is in need of a day off, but I have promised the mare to Miss Pennington today." A murmur arose from the crowd at that moment, drawing their attention. Issac, Devlin's servant-of-all-work, was leading out another horse. "Ah, here she is," said Devlin. Francesca looked at the horse, and her eyes grew wide.

The mare was small, like the stallion, and compactly built. But the thing that was causing such a stir among the group was her unusual and altogether beautiful coloring. She was as golden as a newly minted guinea and shone just as brightly. Her mane and tail were the pale yellow-white of sun-bleached straw. With her pretty head held high, she glowed in the morning sunlight.

The horse pranced gaily as the huge black servant led her out, and she tossed her silken mane as if well aware that she was the cynosure of every eye.

"I say!" exclaimed one amazed voice, and "Good God!" came another. Francesca smiled her appreciation of the sight and turned to Devlin.

"Priscilla is a lucky girl," she said.

He grinned back. "So glad you think so."

Questions came flying at Devlin from several directions. "She is called a palomino in America," he answered. "It is a not uncommon coloring among mustangs. Very highly prized by the Indians." He took the horse's rein and led her toward where Priscilla waited cowering at the edge of the group. She was trembling inside her habit and wishing she could sink down and hide behind the mounting block.

"Miss Pennington," said Devlin, "may I present Morning-Sun-on-the-Water?" He grinned. "Rather a mouthful, I know. She was named by the Indian from whom I bought her, you see. But if you just call her Sunrise she will understand."

"She . . . she is very pretty," Priscilla managed to blurt out.

"Yes. She is my beauty." He patted the warm nose that nudged his shoulder, and smiled warmly at Priscilla. "Until now, she was quite my favorite lady." She could scarce pretend to misunderstand either his words or his look. "I shall like to see you on her," he concluded, then reached out a hand to her. Priscilla reluctantly allowed herself to be led to the golden animal. The next thing she knew, his lordship's hands were under her boot and up she went onto the horse's back.

The movement caused the animal to prance playfully. Priscilla went dead white and gripped the pommel. She did however, manage to keep her seat while Devlin quieted the horse.

He chuckled. "She is itching for a good run, as I am sure you are. She is playful but really a quite well-mannered little lady. Just keep a firm hand on the rein and let her know you are in control, and you will go on delightfully."

Priscilla tried to make some answer, but her teeth were clenched so tightly shut that she could not speak. Devlin moved away and mounted the stallion. The field trotted off.

The run was a good one, promising to outdo even the opening day. Devlin, on the compact little stallion, easily led the field. The horse was incredibly agile, would jump anything without hesitation, and could turn so suddenly and without a check as to take one's breath away.

Despite her solid intention of staying back beside Caspar all morning, Francesca allowed herself to be swept up in the excitement of the chase and took off after Devlin, leaving Mr. Maltby in her dust. It took every bit of her skill as a horsewoman to stay anywhere near Devlin, but she would not have missed the sight of that magnificent horse for anything.

Priscilla would clearly have chosen to remain far back in the group, somewhere back by Mr. Maltby and the other sluggards. But she was given no choice in the matter. Morning-Sun-on-the-Water did not much like tasting another horse's dust. Moreover, she and Arapaho had run together ever since they had roamed the Great Plains free and wild. There was no reining her in, and Priscilla, terrified, could only concentrate her attention on simply holding on.

Apparently, however, her concentration was not

enough. It was a rather low gritstone wall that was her downfall, quite literally. The golden horse sailed over easily enough. Priscilla held her breath and held on. They landed together and Pris opened one eye in relief and relaxed her vigilance. But the horse, agile as her mate, turned quickly to the right after him. The girl, her attention slackened, flew just as quickly to the left, her habit sketching a perfect blue arc through the air before she landed with a thud. She rolled a little way and came to rest at the base of the wall.

Devlin saw her fall and immediately turned Arapaho in a quick turnabout that would have been impossible for any other horse in the field. The rest of the group was pounding along at such speed that none of the riders could stop. Priscilla had lost consciousness momentarily, but she came quickly to again and shook her head as if to clear it. She was beginning to rise just as the first horses headed into the jump.

"Don't move!" shouted Devlin over the thunder of the approaching hooves. He sprang from his horse and dived for the base of the wall, pulling Priscilla flat down onto the grass and covering her with his body. Clods of earth flew onto them as the horses cleared the wall and landed only inches from their heads. The sound of hooves crashed beside them, outroared only by their own rushing blood.

It had all happened so quickly that few of the riders were at first aware of just what had occured. Francesca, however, had been riding close behind Devlin and had seen the whole. She could only marvel at the man's quick thinking and courage. And thank goodness for the speed and agility of Arapaho. What a horse!

When a relative silence had descended again, Devlin slowly raised his head, then allowed Priscilla to do the same. "Are you hurt?" he asked, real concern in his voice.

"I . . . I don't think so," she managed to answer, turning her pretty eyes up to his. "I . . . I am so sorry, my lord," she added as the blue of those eyes became washed with a film of tears. "I tried to hold on."

"Of course you did," he answered gently. "But are you truly all right?"

By now most of the rest of the field had turned back, abandoning the chase. The fox was to be allowed a day's reprieve. While Priscilla tested her limbs, Francesca slid lightly to the ground. "Of course she is not all right, Devlin!" she exclaimed, moving to the prostrate girl. "That was very well done of you, I grant you. But you would have done better not to practically force an obviously inexperienced rider onto such a horse! It is a marvel the girl wasn't killed."

"Well, how the devil was I to know?" he exclaimed, and turned back to Pris. She looked so woebegone that he could not be angry with her. He took her trembling hands in his. "Forgive me, Miss Pennington. I ought to have known better."

"Oh, no, my lord!" she cried. "I mean . . . my fault . . . so stupid . . . so sorry." The tears had begun to roll down her cheeks now as she gulped out her apology.

"Oh, go away, do, Devlin," said Francesca impatiently. "You are only making the poor thing feel worse." She sat beside the girl and brushed a wisp of hair from her face. Priscilla's hat, thrown off in the fall, lay some yards away, and Devlin, feeling very much out of his element, went to retrieve it.

"Now, Pris," said Francesca in bracing tones. "Do you think you can walk? Shall I send for a carriage to carry you back to the house?"

"Oh, no! Please," said Priscilla, hating to have such a public fuss made over her. If given the choice, she would simply have sunk into the ground under the wall and stayed there. "I am all right. Truly I am." She looked over at the palomino mare, placidly nibbling at some clover a few feet away. "It is only that . . ."

"Of course. You need not get back onto the horse. I

am sure Lord Devlin will be more than happy to take you up with him. If you feel up to it, that is."

Priscilla glanced at him, standing there looking so worried with her hat in his hands. "He saved my life," she said softly and with more than a trace of wonder in her voice.

The tone and the expression were not lost on Francesca. Since it turned out that Pris was not seriously injured, this accident might prove to be exactly what Devlin needed to finally win the girl. There was no worship, exactly, in Pris's face, but there was considerable awe.

"That he did," said Francesca, forbearing to mention that there would have been no need for such heroics had his lordship been a little more perceptive to begin with.

And so it was arranged. Pris was boosted up onto Arapaho's back, with lord Devlin's strong arms firmly around her, to be carried back to Hockleigh. "So kind," she muttered as they trotted away.

The great to-do made on their return can well be imagined and need not be described in detail. Suffice it to say that the placid atmosphere of Hockleigh erupted into a minor uproar. Sarah, in superb manner, took things efficiently in hand. The doctor was sent for at once, Mrs. Pennington fluttered her gratitude all over Lord Devlin until he thought he would scream. Pris was tucked up in bed, thoroughly wretched at being the cause of such commotion.

At last Mrs. Pennington gave over her grateful effusions to go upstairs with the doctor, accompanied by Sarah and Francesca, and Devlin was able to escape. But he got only as far as the crowd still milling about in the great entry hall. Here he was accosted again.

"Quick thinking that was, Dev. Probably saved the girl's life!" exclaimed Graham Symington.

"Shows what happens when you let women join the field," muttered Dudley Dalton with a purist's scowl.

"Remarkable horse, that, Devlin. Never saw such a

turn in my life," put in Lord Jersey. "You've won my bet, even if the fox did get off."

"And mine," added Lord Poole and several others.

"Thinking of putting him out to sire, are you, Dev?" asked Sir Algernon. "Got a promising mare I'd like to see mated with that one."

"Demned fine horses, the both of them," conceded Lady Braethon, sitting magisterially in a straight-back chair. She had been a notable horsewoman in her younger years. "But that's not to say you should have put the Pennington chit on that filly, Devlin. Any fool could see she's not a horsewoman, never will be."

"But then, Lord Devlin is *not* a fool," cooed Roxanna Gordon. "So he could not have known it. I'll wager the girl fell on purpose just so that she could be so dramatically rescued by his lordship. No doubt that mother of hers put her up to it, poor thing." She laughed her fluty laugh, working her crop as if it were a fan, and laid a hand on Devlin's arm in a possessive fashion. "Only imagine! A silly miss like Priscilla Pennington setting her cap at *you*, Devlin! She would do much better to put her sights a bit lower. Such a sophisticated gentleman as yourself will have quite other ideas of what he requires in a wife."

Roxanna conjured up an image of Francesca Waringham and studied it intently, the face, the clothes, the manner. Obviously that was what Lord Devlin did appreciate in a woman—enough to steal into her bedchamber late at night—and Roxanna would be happy to oblige him in his tastes. Except that she would be far more clever about it than Francesca had been. When she drew him to *her* bedchamber—as she had no doubt she could do—he would not leave without an offer of marriage being made, and accepted.

Though unaware of her thoughts, Devlin could not help but understand her words. He sprang to Priscilla's defense. "Miss Pennington would never think to act so deviously, ma'am, I am sure. It is all my fault for not noting her inexperience with horses. I shall undertake to teach her to handle them better in the future."

No one could mistake the intention of a future and rather prolonged relationship with the young lady that his words implied. No one except Roxanna. So deeply convinced was she of his intentions toward Francesca, and with good reason as she thought, that she only half—heard him.

In a moment, Francesca herself appeared on the stairs, and a babble of voices began inquiring into the condition of the young invalid.

"The doctor is convinced that there has been no permanent damage. Priscilla should be perfectly restored to health after a good night's sleep and a day or two of inactivity," she said to a general chorus of "Thank Gods." "Thanks to Lord Devlin's quick action," she added with a smile for him. He was the only person in the group that saw the cynical glint behind the amber eyes.

For the benefit of the others, he nodded his appreciation of the compliment, adding a wry smile just for her.

Thus relieved of worry, the company filed into the drawing room for a much-needed restorative cup of tea. But Devlin thought he would scream if he had to spend another moment with any of them. Any except one.

"Let's get out of here," he murmured to Francesca as he headed for the door.

She watched his retreating back a moment, smiled, and followed him out the door and across the lawns. They did not speak until they reached the White Garden, now blooming with the last dahlias and some hardy carnations. Francesca seated herself on a gleaming marble bench, her habit of celestial-blue velvet a vivid counterpoint to the snowy blooms and the dark green foliage.

"Is she truly all right, Cesca?" he asked at length. "You must tell me."

Once again she felt her heart leap at sound of the affectionate nickname on his lips. In defense against the emotion it conjured up, she answered more briskly than she intended. "She is quite all right. Don't worry, Devlin. You have not killed her."

He finally sat, dropping his hands between his knees and hanging his head and looking very much like an errant schoolboy. "But I have certainly killed my chances with her. I've botched it good and proper now, haven't I?"

"On the contrary. Since she is unhurt, I rather think you could have found no better way to win her regard. Priscilla has a romantic nature, I think, beneath all that shyness. You are now beginning to look very like a knight in shining armor to her. If she is not yet in love with you, at least you are no longer the dragon. She will accept you out of simple gratitude."

"You think so?" His tone was an odd mixture of hope and despair.

"Undoubtedly. I would advise you to waste no time in offering, once she is up and about again. What is the old adage about striking while the iron is hot?"

"You know, the Orientals have a notion that if someone saves your life, you then belong to him forever. I might just mention it to her."

She laughed a sad little laugh. "Then your fate is sealed! I shall dance at your wedding before the year is out."

"And I at yours, I imagine. By the by, what has become of Maltby? I haven't seen him since we rode back."

"Good God! I am supposed to be touring the succession houses or some such thing with him. I had quite forgotten him!"

He looked at her with a slowly growing smile. "I hope," he said in a soft, seductive voice, "that I can as easily make you forget him after you are married."

A thrill went through her, but this time she did not blush. Instead, she smiled back at him. A realization stole into her mind: she very much hoped that he would do just that.

13

Despite a great deal of rather furious thinking and planning, outwardly the next pair of days passed in relative calm. The dual wooing moved onto another level, but progressed apace.

Lord Devlin was, by circumstance, forced to limit his contacts with Priscilla, as she was still recovering from her accident. The first day she kept to her room until dinnertime, came down to eat, and retired again after but a short interlude in the drawing room. Devlin, to Francesca's amused satisfaction, was all solicitous kindness yet without crushing the poor girl with his concern for her well-being. She even smiled shyly up at him once or twice. She was as good as won, thought Francesca, no longer smiling.

The second day found Pris even less reclusive—she came down to breakfast at her mother's insistence—but still so unwell as to be allowed to skip the hunt, much to her relief.

Her presence in the field was scarce missed. The hunting was good, the riding hard, and everyone was in excellent spirits. Everyone, that is, except Lady Francesca. She had realized and accepted that she really must restrain herself enough to ride beside Caspar in the hunt. But what a sluggard the fellow was! It had been Devlin's suggestion, of course, delivered with a distinctly malicious grin. He had casually mentioned that constantly outstripping the object of one's supposed affections in the field was perhaps not the very best of strategies. Odious man! Why must he always be in the right of it?

The result was a very irritable Francesca, deprived of her chief joy and exercise and forced to smile constantly at Caspar's increasingly annoying inanities. The day's run was a particularly good one. Consequently, Francesca was particularly vexed to have missed the best part of the sport.

So preoccupied was she with her annoyance, and so wrapped up was everyone else in the thrill of the chase, that no one noticed the disappearance of Roxanna Gordon from the field. She had taken off from the covert with the rest of them. But after a few minutes' run, she was nowhere to be seen if anyone had been looking, which no one was.

She turned her horse unobtrusively into a stand of trees just as the others were setting themselves for a jump over a low hedge. She reined in under the almost bare branches and waited quietly until everyone was well away, then spurred her horse into a trot in the opposite direction.

A quarter-hour's ride brought her to a seldom-used road. This she followed for some time, making several turns and following the directions she had received in a letter that morning. Soon a small overgrown lane branched off from the road. She made the turn and rode another pair of miles before emerging at last into a small clearing graced by an even smaller structure, a tiny stone cottage with boards nailed over the windows.

The clearing seemed as deserted as the house. Silence hung about it except for the soft wind high in the treetops.

"Jerry," she called softly. No answer came. She slid silently to the ground, reins in hand, and started walking toward the cottage. "Jerry," she called again, louder this time. Still no answer. Her horse whinnied gently, breaking the heavy silence. There came an echo of the sound, another horse, very close behind her. Roxanna jumped and spun around to face the sound.

Behind her the door to the cottage was flung open and a pair of rough strong arms encircled her tightly, nearly taking her breath away. She opened her mouth to scream, but before any sound could escape, she was spun around. Her protest was stopped by her assailant's mouth coming roughly down onto hers.

She tried to break free; her eyes flew to his. Then she saw that his were not full of fear or contempt or danger, but held only amusement. When he finally released his grip on her, he was laughing.

"Hallo, Roxie, love," he said with a grin.

"Oh!" she exclaimed indignantly, and stamped her foot—rather ineffectively, as it happened, since there was nothing beneath it but dead ferns and dry leaves. "You nearly scared the life out of me, Jerry. I could kill you."

"Ah, but then, you always was prettier when you was mad, Roxie." He looked her over appreciatively, grinning as her annoyance melted away under his obvious admiration. "Widowhood don't seem to have done you no harm, girl. You be pretty as ever was."

Her good humor was soon completely restored, and she gave him a deep curtsy. "I thank you, sir," she said elegantly, then grinned. "Ain't so bad yourself, you know."

Indeed he was not. In fact, he was quite the handsomest lover Roxanna had ever had. Gordon had found him for her in some cockpit or other. He'd polished the fellow up a bit with some decent clothes and presented him as a birthday gift. Quite the nicest present she'd ever had, was Jerry.

There must have been a bit of the Gypsy in Jerry Parsons, for his hair was black as midnight, blacker even than Roxanna's own. Jet-black eyes glittered in his bronzed face, and perfect teeth flashed snowy white whenever he laughed. Jerry laughed a lot.

"Actually," Roxanna continued, "widowhood has

very nearly done me in. If one can actually die of boredom, I am close to breathing my last."

"Naturally," he said. "You got no Jerry around to amuse you." He offered another of his insouciant grins. The day was mild, and he wore no coat, no waistcoat, no cravat. His linen shirt was open halfway to his waist, showing off the thickly curling blanket of black hair that lay beneath it.

Roxanna's appreciation of the sight he offered was as obvious as his had been for her. "Damned right," she muttered, and moved toward him. "Now, give me a proper kiss hello." She pulled him down to meet her lips; he gave no resistance.

The silence of the clearing was broken only by the soft moans of pleasure that escaped her. It was some time before he pulled away. With hands on her shoulders, he held her at arm's length. "Now, then, Roxie girl. Pretty as I am, I know you got some other reason for getting me here. I'll hear it now."

She was having difficulty breathing. Her skin felt on fire. She had been far too long without a man. "Later," she murmured from deep in her throat, and made as if to pull his lips back to hers.

But he held her off. "Now, Roxie—" he began.

"I told you later!" She moved out of his arms and walked purposefully toward the door of the cottage. With a shrug and a smile, he followed her, kicking the door shut behind him.

Lord Devlin was riding his pinto gelding that day, another of his magnificent mustangs. Everyone in the field was duly impressed. As usual, he rode in the lead.

Francesca, chafing at the bit, as it were, to let her horse out of its full stride, could finally stand it no more. Caspar would just have to do without her for the time being. She broke away from him and charged ahead just before the dogs caught up with their hapless quarry.

She was at least in at the kill. And then the hunt was over for the day.

They were several miles from Hockleigh, and the trip back was far more leisurely than the ride out. Francesca, greatly in need of a respite from her flirtations, came up to ride beside Devlin. "Really, you know," she said, "I begin to wonder if all this is worth it. What a perfectly ridiculous day I have had!"

"Poor sweet," he said with a smile of real sympathy. "I suppose I must be grateful that Priscilla cannot hunt just yet, else I'd be in the same position. The girl simply cannot ride." His voice was edged with disgust.

"Of course she cannot. But you needn't let it worry you. She will be far too busy having your babies anyway."

"I can hope."

"Well, I cannot hope that Caspar will be so occupied!"

"I suppose it would prove a bit difficult. Been uphill work, has it?" For answer he got only a grimace. "You will just have to bring him up to scratch, then. Once the fish is netted, the fisherman can relax, you know."

"Don't be vulgar!" she snapped irritably. But Francesca was nothing if not fair, and she quickly retreated into a self-conscious smile. "The truth is often vulgar, is it not?"

"Too often."

"And speaking of coming up to scratch, when do you plan to speak to Pris? You are like to lose your reputation as a man of action if you delay much longer."

"Well, really, you know," he began, "I scarce know the girl, and I—"

"Oh, give over, Dev! I shouldn't have thought such hedging was in your nature."

"Well, she might refuse, you know."

"Don't be ridiculous. Why ever should she?" she said, asking herself what girl in her right mind would refuse such an offer. "Priscilla couldn't say 'Boo!' to a goose.

She is certainly not going to say no to you. Just tell the girl she is to marry you, and there's an end to it."

"How odiously high-handed you make me sound."

"Well, you are," she replied, but she was grinning. "Really, Dev, I do think you are missing your best chance if you don't get on with it soon."

"I suppose so." He looked glum.

"Come on, man. The deed is always worse in the worrying about than in the doing. She will accept, you know."

"I know she will." He still looked glum. They rode on to the house in silence.

"So you shouldn't have the least trouble," Roxanna was explaining as she buttoned up the jacket of her forest-green habit. "No one will have reason to expect such a thing, and no one knows anything at all about you or your presence here."

"And the girl?" asked Jerry Parsons. "What's she like to offer me?"

Roxanna smiled an admiring smile, taking in his magnificent physique with her eyes. "No more than you can handle." He was stretched out on a pile of straw in one corner of the one-room cottage, his hands clasped casually behind his head, entirely at his ease. Unable to restrain herself, Roxanna leaned over and kissed his bare chest. "I am almost inclined to be jealous of the girl," she murmured.

"What's she like? Pretty?"

She abruptly stopped kissing and nibbling him, straightened up, and set about arranging her disheveled hair. "I suppose if one were partial to blonds, one might call her pretty in a washed-out sort of way."

"I got nothing against blonds," he replied with his usual grin.

"She will offer you no sport!" Roxanna snapped. "They call her the Ice Goddess."

His grin grew. "Ice melts pretty fast when the thaw hits. The thawing's half the sport."

She flounced her shoulder in his direction, looking around for her hat. "Well, you are welcome to try your luck with her. Just so that you don't let her get away."

"How long you want me to keep her?"

"Long enough so that she will be thoroughly ruined in the eyes of Society, so that she may not hold up her head among us again. Long enough so that she will never make a fit wife for a baron!"

"More like she won't want no baron, not after the likes of Jerry Parsons."

"Your handsomeness and virility, my dear Jerry, are exceeded only by your arrogance," she cooed, watching him lace up his breeches.

"Say, Rox, how comes it you ain't never been 'ruined' like that? Don't no one know about you?"

"No!" she snapped. "And they never will. Because I am far too clever for them all."

"Won't let a real toff touch you, eh?" he asked astutely. He shrugged his linen shirt over his head and stuffed it casually into his pants. "Too bad for the toffs."

"And lucky for you," she said, pulling a fat roll of bills from her pocket. She caused it to follow his shirttails, allowed her hand to linger there a moment, then, with a laugh, patted the bulge the money made in the front of his breeches.

His returning laugh echoed around the tiny cottage as he pulled her to him for another long kiss. But when he looked at her again, his laugh was gone. There was earnestness in his black eyes. "Give it up, girl," he said simply. Roxanna only looked puzzled. "What do you want with a baron? Come off with me, Rox. We're good together."

"Don't be ridiculous!" was the only answer he got. She pulled out of his arms and turned away, brushing straw from her heavy skirts. She did not see the hard look that glittered in his black eyes, hard and very cold.

She fussed with her hair and tried to arrange her Hussar hat with its gay orange-tipped yellow plumes on her head. "I look a mess," she complained. Even before she could finish the words, Jerry was handing her a comb and a small piece of mirror that he pulled from a saddle-bag flung into a corner.

"Y'see how well I know you, Rox," he said, his easy smile back in place. But there was less warmth, less joy than usual behind it. "Tomorrow soon enough for you?" he asked as she adjusted her hat before the inadequate mirror.

"Tomorrow is perfect." She gathered up her crop and her lemon-yellow gloves and quickly outlined once again the plan they had been discussing. She wanted no detail to go wrong. She took a small flat parcel wrapped in white paper from Jerry and tucked it carefully into her pocket. "I shall do my part. But remember, *no one* is to connect my name with any of this." She walked from the cottage, her skirt making a whooshing sound on the straw.

Jerry tossed her up onto her horse. She smiled down at him, her most seductive smile. "It's been good to see you again, Jerry. When this is over, I think I shall have to find a place for you in London." She reached down and touched his black hair. "And then you will forget that Lady Francesca Waringham ever existed."

He flashed his snowy smile and offered her a salute as she turned up the path. But as she rode away, his brilliant smile faded and his eyes narrowed. He stood there a long while in thought.

There was to be no formal entertainment that evening, but the young Duchess had arranged for there to be music after dinner for those of the young people who felt inclined to "sport a toe." It was not a ball or anything like, but the younger guests stood up with each other for a few country dances and a waltz or two while the oldsters, Lady Braethon and her ilk, settled down to cards in the adjoining room.

Priscilla was allowed—or perhaps "forced" is a more accurate word—to join the group of dancers. Tonight she had been dressed up in a mound up puce tulle, a color far too old for a girl of her youth and a design far too fussy for anyone.

As the number of dances was limited, there was nothing odd in a gentleman standing up with the same young lady for several dances. It was a very informal affair. But Lord Devlin outdid himself. He danced three times with Priscilla and three times with Lady Francesca, more or less alternately. Roxanna barely noticed the dances he bestowed on Pris and casually dismissed them as of no importance when she did. But his dances with Francesca were noted, recorded, and tucked away in a dark corner of her mind to feed her growing resentment of her supposed rival.

Lord Devlin was having an uncomfortable evening. Reluctantly accepting Francesca's advice, he had decided to make his offer this night. But he was having a deal of trouble getting on with it.

"Miss Pennington . . ." he began during a country dance. "Priscilla . . ." he corrected himself. "You . . . you are looking very pretty tonight."

She looked down at the inappropriate mass of netting encircling her. He was being kind again. "Thank you, my lord," she said quietly, looking down as though wondering whether her feet were perhaps making incorrect moves and needed checking up on.

"We have missed you in the field," he went on. "Will you be feeling well enough to join us tomorrow?"

No one could miss the despair that attacked her at the very thought. "I . . . I don't know, my lord. I suppose so."

The movements of the dance separated them. Watching her as she moved, not ungracefully, through the steps of the dance, he tried, for the first time really, to put himself in her skin. And he thought he came to know something of her. In a moment they were beside each other again. "You do not wish to ride, do you, Priscilla?" he said gently.

She did not look up, and answered so softly he had to bend his head down to hear her. "No, my lord," she said.

"Then you must not."

"Mama will make me," she said even more softly. He looked about for Mrs. Pennington. She would indeed try to force the girl. Such a mother-in-law was going to take some dealing with. He would have to take a firm hand from the outset.

"You need not ride anymore, Priscilla," he said. She looked at him in puzzled surprise. "*I* will tell your mother that you need not."

"Oh, but, my lord, she—"

"I think she will listen to me. Do not you?"

Relief mingled with the wretchedness still in her face. "Oh, yes, my lord. She will listen to you."

"Good. I hope she will have cause to listen to me many times in the future. . . ." The dance took them apart again, and the next thing he knew, it was over. Mr. Hollys appeared as if out of nowhere to carry her off for the next dance.

This was a waltz, and Devlin swooped down upon Francesca and carried her onto the floor without so much as a by-your-leave. "Really, Dev!" she protested. "I was to have had this dance with Caspar."

"You may dance with him after you are married," he muttered.

"Now, what has got you in the boughs? Never say she refused you!"

"I haven't asked her yet. I am not at all sure, Cesca, that I can stand the thought of such a mother-in-law."

"Stuff! You are making excuses. She will not bother you in the least once you are married, I promise you."

"What is Caspar's mother like?"

"I haven't a notion. She never comes to town. But I am sure I shall have no trouble with her."

"I wish you luck of it," he answered, and they finished the dance in silence, forgetting their difficulties with their soon-to-be spouses and giving themselves up to the pleasure of having a partner so perfectly in tune with oneself. They drew apart reluctantly when the music at last crescendoed and came to an end.

Devlin's next attempt with Pris was no more successful than the first. Oh, there were hints and innuendos aplenty from him. He talked around the notion of marriage so thoroughly that no girl could escape his meaning. But, much to Priscilla's relief, the final fatal question was left unspoken. She was left with a great deal to think about as she danced off with Sir Algernon for the next set. And Devlin was left to wonder why he could not simply ask her and get it over with.

He was cornered for the waltz by Roxanna. She had been giving serious thought for days to how best to capture and hold his interest. A thorough study of Francesca had convinced her that she would have to modify her usual style a bit.

The change in Cesca the past few days had not escaped Roxanna, nor had the smiles and admiring glances of Lord Devlin whenever he chanced to look at her. She looked simpler, sweeter somehow. She must have reason to believe that her new look was more to his lordship's taste. And if so, then it would be Roxanna's taste as well.

And so she had raised an eyebrow or two when she made her entrance that evening, but not for the usual reasons. A thorough search of her wardrobe, together with a quick plying of her abigail's needle, had come up with a muslin dinner gown of soft rose with a prettily filled-in *décolletage*, short puffed sleeves of point lace and velvet ribbons trimming the hem in a deeper rose. Her hair had been arranged *à la Méduse*, which was softly flattering to her piquant face, and she had limited her jewelry to a cameo brooch and a carved ivory bracelet.

Her appearance could not have been called maidenly —she was far past that stage—but she looked fresher and younger and really very appealing. Only the slightly brittle glint in her eyes remained to give her away to anyone who looked closely, along with a certain determined set to her jaw whenever she looked at Devlin and Francesca.

She spoke nothing but generalities and inoffensive witticisms as they danced. But she used her flashing eyes and the natural seductiveness of her fluty voice to advantage. She was light on her feet, had a quick mind, and was an excellent partner. Devlin surprised himself by enjoying the dance.

"I see the Widow is still after you," said Francesca when next he partnered her.

"Yes. But you know, she can be a pleasant-enough companion when she manages to tone down her flirtation a bit. She's a devilish pretty piece of baggage, you must admit."

"Stunning," she answered dryly. "With Priscilla for a wife, I daresay you will need to seek more exciting diversion elsewhere. Perhaps Roxanna would care to apply for the post."

"I doubt it. With some other gentleman, perhaps, or after she is safely remarried. But not yet. I have seen the light of matrimony glittering in too many feminine eyes not to recognize it. She is holding out for a ring at present." He looked down at her with that intimate smile that he saved only for her. "And besides, I have a rather more interesting candidate in mind for that job."

She felt herself flushing deeply, a circumstance that had grown deplorably frequent of late. She was vastly relieved when the figures of the dance separated them. She found it increasingly difficult to think when he was looking at her just so.

There was no mistaking the intent of his comment. She realized that she had no desire to mistake it. Just how she would feel about such an "arrangement" after she was married to Caspar, she had no idea. Perhaps her husband, and later her children, would be enough for her. Perhaps they would give her all the warmth and affection she could want. But when she looked at Devlin, she had to doubt it. And what would she do about that? She thought perhaps she had better try to discover just what she could feel with Caspar, her soon-to-be husband.

She moved back toward Devlin, but the rest of their conversation was desultory, as each was wrapped up in his own thoughts.

The final waltz of the evening came, Devlin's last chance to make his offer that night. He was determined to do it.

But he had shown his hand a bit too clearly. Priscilla had been frightened into talkativeness. He had more words from her in the next twenty minutes—a vertitable torrent of them, and all of them nonsense—than he had had in the previous week. All the while blushing an unattractive beet red, she chattered on this and that and the other subject, making little sense and leaving him little chance to say anything more than yes and no. She felt a complete fool, but she did not care. Anything was better than to allow him to say what he was so obviously about to say.

Francesca had saved the final waltz for Caspar, and she now beckoned him with her eyes. To her satisfaction, he promptly answered the summons, came to her side, and danced her onto the floor. That was good. He was falling nicely into the habit of bowing to her wishes. She put all her formidable powers of charm into play, until the poor man was completely bemused.

"It is so dreadfully hot in here, is it not, Caspar?" she said with a flutter of her lashes and with a brave disregard for the truth.

"What?" he said, pulling himself from his reverie. "Oh. Oh, yes, Francesca. Hot."

"Could we not just stroll out onto the terrace for a moment? I feel I shall faint if I do not get some fresh air." She steered him through a nearby French door and outside, trying to suppress a shiver as a blast of cold air hit her.

Devlin watched her leave the room. He was not smiling.

"Ah, that is better," said Francesca leaning on a low marble wall overlooking the White Garden. Before Caspar knew what was happening or how, he was behind her with his arms lightly encircling her. She leaned back against his chest, chatting inconsequentially. He had no idea what she said. He was conscious only of her closeness, her warmth, and the heat rising in his own head.

And then somehow he was kissing her. Once she had brought on his embrace, Francesca stood very still, waiting for something. Something that never came. There was no flood of warmth coursing through her, no tingle at the back of her neck, no trembling in her limbs except for that caused by the chill autumn air. Only one man had ever brought on such feeling in her. Now there was nothing at all. She had been silly to expect that there would be.

When the embrace was broken, a blushing, stammering Caspar spoke. "I am sorry, my lady. I don't . . ."

"Let us return to finish our dance, shall we?" she said. And that is what they did.

A thoughtful, vaguely depressed Lady Francesca and a frustrated, vaguely relieved Lord Devlin made their separate ways upstairs a short while later.

14

The steps of the quadrille are complex and require a certain amount of practice and a degree of expertise to perform with grace and without stepping on the toes of the other dancers. This foursome was learning, but none were yet perfect in the art. They began to confuse their partners.

Devlin, true to his word, convinced Mrs. Pennington to agree that Priscilla need no longer ride in the hunt. He, therefore, enjoyed a happy morning's sport.

Francesca was also set free from her vigilant attention to her swain. Caspar had not been able to forgo a chance to collect some cuttings from the Duchess's greenhouses. Francesca was left to enjoy the morning in the company of her coconspirator.

In fact, she enjoyed it very much. She could no longer deny, even to herself, how much she truly liked him and how strongly he stirred her emotions. But Francesca was a very self-protective animal, and she had grown a rather sturdy shell over the years. The acknowledgment of her reactions to Lord Devlin served only to strengthen her resolve to marry someone else, and that quickly. She would remove herself from temptation. She wanted no emotional strings binding her and limiting her freedom of movement.

As the group rode back to the house after a good day's hunt—Francesca by the merest chance riding beside

Devlin—they happened to observe Priscilla, sketchbook in hand, coming from the direction of the rose garden. She was not alone. Mr. Maltby was beside her, talking animatedly, no doubt on some botanical marvel. They seemed perfectly at ease in each other's company.

"That will never do," Francesca muttered as she espied the pair.

"No, indeed," replied Devlin. And they both turned to intercept the oblivious couple.

"Mr. Maltby," said Francesca, sliding from her horse to land at his feet. "How pleasant to run into you here."

"My lady," he stammered as a blush spread up from his collar. He had not forgotten the scene of the previous evening. He could not imagine how he could have so far forgotten himself as to actually kiss her.

"Miss Pennington," his lordship greeted. "I am glad to see you taking advantage of the sunshine."

"My lord," she whispered, all sign of her recent animation gone.

"You have been sketching, I see," said Devlin. "May I be allowed to see your work?"

"Oh, no, my lord! That is, I do not . . . I mean, I am not . . ."

"Please," he said, taking the book gently from her nerveless fingers. He flipped it casually open, preparing in his mind the platitudes he would utter. But his expression soon changed to one of earnestness. He said not a word as he looked at one drawing after another. "Good God!" he said at last. Priscilla blushed.

Francesca came to look over his shoulder, then stared at Priscilla in surprised admiration. "Why, Pris! They are superb!"

"Yes," said Caspar. "Miss Pennington has a gift. She is quite the finest botanical artist that I have ever come across. Notice the detailing of the anther, here, and the clarity and depth of the calyx and corolla. Extraordinary!"

"Talented as well as charming, my dear," said Devlin. " 'Twill be a lucky man who wins you."

Paris took the sketchbook from him and closed it, rooted to the ground with embarrassment. Francesca took pity on her. "I wish you will come back to the house with me, Pris. I particularly wanted your opinion on a piece of fringe I have been knotting."

A grateful Priscilla walked off beside her, steering well clear of the very large horse that trailed behind them.

At dinner that night each of the four seemed to see the inevitable. They knew that tonight was to be the night. Cesca could feel Caspar's eyes on her all through dinner, a thoughtful, speculative look replacing his more usual abstracted mien. She could easily get him to offer tonight. After last evening, he would feel it his duty, the silly noddy. One did not go about kissing young ladies to whom one was not affianced. Her knowledge gave her little pleasure. In fact, she felt the headache coming on.

Priscilla scarce took her eyes from Lord Devlin. She had come to a decision. Now she was trying to see the positive side of it. She had suffered another of her Mama's dreadful monologues that afternoon on the desirability of having a baron for a husband. The tone and vehemence, if not the words, had turned the trick. The girl was willing to do almost anything to get away from her mother and her constant scolds. She could become mistress of her own fate, at least to a limited extent, by marrying. The fact that the means of her freedom coincided with her Mama's loudly stated wishes offered a bonus of sorts. She would marry Lord Devlin.

Two of the four involved in this tangle were being intently observed from yet another quarter. Roxanna Gordon missed little in their expressions, but misread much of what she saw there. She noted the glances they occasionally shot each other and read restrained passion into what was really absolute sympathy. The small nod they exchanged as the ladies rose to leave the room she read as a signal, a secret agreement, perhaps to meet later in the evening. It was as well that Jerry had other plans for Lady Francesca tonight.

When the gentlemen reentered the drawing room, Francesca was desultorily fingering the keys on the pianoforte. She saw Caspar hesitate, then start in her direction. Oh, how her head ached! She simply could not deal with him and his proposals just yet. She crossed quickly to where the Duchess was pouring out the tea.

"Let me help you, Sarah," she said, taking the pot from her friend. "You must be fatigued to death."

"Pooh! I have never felt better. And I hope I do not look half so fatigued as yourself, Cesca. Why, you are positively white, my love. Do sit down."

"It is nothing. I just have the headache a little. Nothing that a cup of your excellent tea will not put to rights."

Roxanna, overhearing this conversation, rejoiced inwardly. Things were falling out better than she had dared to hope. She picked up her reticule, opened it quickly to remove a small white-wrapped parcel, and snapped it shut again. She went to the tea cart. "You do look pale, Francesca," she said. "Sit here, and let me pour."

Gratefully, Francesca did as she was bid. It was but a moment till Roxanna had poured her a cup of tea, carefully added sugar, and stirred it very well. She handed it to Francesca with a sympathetic smile.

Soon Francesca was sipping at the scalding brew, burning her tongue, and not minding in the least, so comforting was the taste of the favorite English cure-all. She did not even notice that the sweet, pungent tea had an odd, slightly bitter aftertaste. She drained her cup. Roxanna smiled and moved away.

Lord Devlin soon found the Widow at his side. She attacked him with her eyes and her smile and all her other powers of seduction. Strangely enough, he made no attempt to leave her. He knew he should go and speak to

Pris, knew he should make his offer. And he knew she would accept. He chastised himself for acting like a green schoolboy. He ordered himself to go to her. But he remained with Roxanna, returning her flirtation to an unusual degree.

To her surprised delight, he paid her extravagant compliments, told her vaguely risqué jokes at which she laughed delightedly, all the while scolding him for a naughty boy. She was much pleased with the evening.

Francesca felt her headache growing worse, as though a clamp was being tightened over her temples. Her eyelids began to sting as well, and she had the most unaccountable desire to let them sink over her eyes, giving way to sleep. Perhaps another cup of tea would help, she thought.

Caspar, unable to approach Francesca while she was surrounded by Sarah and a few others, moved to a seat beside Priscilla. Mrs. Pennington scowled. The seat had been purposely left vacant for quite another gentleman, but she couldn't very well ask him outright to move away. The two young people spoke of flowers and ferns and such fascinating things.

Francesca drank her tea; it did not help. She was sleepier than she could ever remember being before. It would not do to topple over snoring in the drawing room. She excused herself as best she could and dragged herself up the stairs. She donned a nightdress, dismissed her maid, and crawled under the inviting bedclothes. She was asleep almost before her head touched the pillow.

Some hours later, Devlin, slightly befuddled from too much brandy, was surprised to discover that he, Mr. Dalton, and Roxanna were the only guests remaining downstairs. Mr. Dalton rose to go, giving Devlin a very "man-of-the-world" wink. Devlin, well aware of the danger looming just ahead, quickly did the same. Roxanna could only follow.

At the top of the stairs, the two gentlemen turned to

the left. "Devlin," said Roxanna in an apologetic voice. "So stupid of me, unbelievable really, but I have forgotten my candle. Would you be so kind as to see me to my door? I should hate to trip over a suit of armor or some such thing and rouse the whole household." With a shrug, he followed her.

At her door, out of the hearing of Dalton, she was yet more direct in her attack. "The Duke's brandy is excellent, is it not?" He had good reason to know the answer. He nodded. "Would you care for just one more glass of it? I have had the forethought to order a bottle sent to my room." Her voice dropped even more. "Widowhood can be so lonely, you see. It helps me to sleep when I cannot bear to be alone."

A more direct invitation could scarce be imagined. Devlin was not so drunk that he could not see the abyss that loomed before him. He stepped deftly, or at least effectively, aside. "I thank you, ma'am, but I have had more than enough to send me to sleep for many hours. I trust you will have no trouble doing the same."

An angry glare followed him as he wove down the hall. Roxanna Gordon had met with very few rebuffs in her life. She did not suffer them lightly. After a moment, her door slammed shut with a vehemence unseemly for the hour.

Devlin gained his room and slumped into a chair before the fire, brooding awhile on his uncharacteristic lack of resolve with Priscilla. Damme! Why could he not simply ask the girl and get it over with? He had thought the brandy, of which he had admittedly had a good deal, might do the trick. Instead, it had only seemed to make matters worse. Obviously he needed a dose of something stronger than mere spirits.

The thought turned him suddenly sober. He knew just what he needed. He needed Francesca. He had, almost unconsciously, come to depend on her badgering, her advice, her mere presence, to give him courage. It was as though he was performing some elaborate dance strictly for her benefit, wanting only her admiration.

And tonight she had not been there to watch the performance. She had looked distinctly unwell just after dinner, pale and tired, and when she had gone early to bed, all the flavor had gone out of the evening for him. It struck him suddenly and strongly that he was dangerously near to being in love with Lady Francesca Waringham.

Once such a radical thought had been admitted to his conscious mind, he could not let it go. He sat there examining it from all sides, extracting its juices, as it were, like a cow chewing its cud.

In love with Francesca. What did that mean to him? He was certain she would never marry him, even if that was what he wanted, which of course it was not. She had been quite specific about her requirements in a husband, just as he had been about a wife. He was the antithesis of everything she wanted.

But he knew, deep in some unexplored corner of his soul, that he would never be completely happy again without her near. He had reason to suspect that beneath that icy exterior she had developed over the past few years lay a warm, eager, even passionate woman. She was the only woman he had ever wanted to possess so completely that it frightened him.

A thought squeezed into his mind, and he smiled for the first time since coming upstairs. Caspar Maltby would never be man enough for such a woman. And it would not take Francesca very long after her marriage to discover the fact. There would be an empty part of her life that needed filling, as there had always been in Devlin's. He would be there to fill it.

Suddenly he felt an overpowering need to see her, to hear her voice, to have her boost his courage once more in her own inimitable way. But it was now after midnight, and she had been in bed for hours. It would just have to wait till morning.

Perhaps it was the brandy so copiously imbibed that made him raise and leave the room, almost against his conscious will, made him walk softly down the hall, made him try the knob on Francesca's door. It was unlocked. He would not wake her, he told himself. He just wanted to look at her.

The room felt unusually cold, and he could feel a sharp breeze hit his cheek as he entered. The fire had died; the room was in darkness. But a full moon gave it a silvery glow.

He realized that the large double windows stood wide open, their curtains fluttering and billowing into the room from the autumn wind. Odd, he thought. They must have blown open.

The draperies were pulled close around the bed—he would not have guessed that she would care for such stuffiness—and he gently pulled back one edge to see that she was all right. Within their dark confines he could make out nothing. He pulled the draperies farther back until a shaft of moonlight fell across the pillow.

The bed was empty. The clothes were rumpled, and there was a depression in the pillow where her head had lain. He reached down and touched it; it was warm with the warmth of her.

But where was Francesca? She had come upstairs early and had missed the late supper that had been served in the drawing room. She might have awoken hungry and made her way to the kitchen for something to eat. Or perhaps she had not been able to sleep at all and thought a good book would take her mind off her headache and make her sleepy. She might now be in the library making her choice.

Or perhaps, to complete her victory over Caspar Maltby, she had gone to him. Perhaps she was even now in his room, in his arms, even in his bed.

Devlin shivered convulsively and went to the window, slamming it shut with a resounding bang. He stood looking out over the velvety lawns and the glassy surface of the lake, glowing and shimmering in the moonlight. He did not even see them.

You are a fool, Richard Devlin, he chastised himself. She did not want you five years ago; she does not want you now. Caspar and her children will be enough for her.

But, his unruly mind continued questioning, will Priscilla Pennington ever be enough for you?

He walked, less softly this time, back to his room and threw himself into the chair by the now dying fire. He picked up a decanter of brandy and poured himself a tumbler full. He downed it practically in one gulp. Another just like it followed.

The sound of the slammed window was heard by more than one pair of ears in the neighboring bedchambers. Only one, however, was curious enough, or suspicious enough, to investigate it. Roxanna had just snuffed her candle and eased open her door when Devlin emerged from Francesca's room. Triumph and worry mingled in her mind. She had been right! They had signaled each other about a meeting tonight. What must he now be thinking to find her gone? If the search for her was started too soon, all her plans, and even Roxanna herself, could be ruined.

But Lord Devlin, she was happy to see, did not look like a worried man. He looked angry. He was muttering as he made his way down the hall; she could not make out his words. He returned to his own room, and the door closed firmly behind him.

She must know more, or she could never sleep this night. She walked silently down the hall, her slippers making no sound on the thick carpet, her red silk negligee billowing behind her. She stopped before his room and listened. There came none of the sounds of a man preparing to take up the search, a man readying himself for a gallant rescue mission. All she heard was the soft chink of a decanter hitting the rim of a glass.

She smiled. Bending her knees, she tried to see through

the keyhole. She could make out the bed, empty, and a table set not far from the fire. On the table stood a cut-glass decanter filled with a liquid whose rich amber color proclaimed it to be some of the Duke's famous brandy. That was all that came within her field of vision.

She was just about to rise when a strong, masculine, and perfectly recognizable hand, with a heavy gold signet ring, reached out for the decanter. She heard the chink of glass on glass again, and the hand returned the decanter to the table.

Roxanna Gordon's triumphant smile now wholly claimed her face. She was chuckling softly as she made her way back to her room.

After the second brandy in as many minutes, Devlin's melancholy began to turn to anger. Damn the chit!—and he was not thinking of Miss Pennington—for invading his mind so strongly. What the devil did he care, anyway, whom she married? Or whom she spent the night with, for that matter. There were plenty of pretty women in the world who were not loath to spend the night with him. Roxanna Gordon had proved the point this very evening with her unsubtle invitation.

He could still take her up on that invitation. And why not, after all? No woman had a claim on him. Not yet.

He downed a last large brandy, picked up the decanter, and headed out the door. This time he did not think to tiptoe. He did not pause outside Francesca's door, but went straight to Roxanna's and knocked lightly.

It opened almost at once—almost as though she had been expecting him, he thought—and she beckoned him silently in with her most sultry of smiles.

15

When Francesca's mind began to swim slowly into wakefulness, she wondered idly why it was grown so cold in her room. It must be very early still. Obviously Rose had not been up to light the fire yet. She turned over and started to snuggle down under the covers. Her head felt heavy; she would just sleep a bit longer.

But how had her smooth lined sheets come to feel so rough? And what was that odd, pungent smell?

She opened her eyes, but the room was dark. Through the windows moonlight showed through a small crack. But they were not her windows. Something was terribly wrong.

She sat up with a start, now fully awake. She even shook her head to make certain she was not dreaming. She could feel quite clearly now that she was lying on a pile of straw, a rough woolen blanket tossed carelessly over her. She still wore her nightdress; her lace nightcap was still tied beneath her chin.

She could make out a little more of the room as she came more fully awake. That bit of moonlight was filtering in through a small crack between boards carelessly nailed over the windows. In one corner of the room stood a tiny iron stove with the remains of a fire glowing inside. It added no light and very little heat to the place.

"Morning," came a deep masculine voice from a dark corner near the stove.

She jumped at the sound and forced her eyes to seek out its source. Jerry Parsons emerged from the gloom, a wide smile flashing in his dark face, to stand beside her makeshift bed. "Who are you?" she asked.

"Now, you don't think I'm like to tell you that, do you, love? Leastways, not the whole of it. Just call me Jerry." He sketched her an elaborate bow, grinning all the while. "At your service, ma'am."

This was insane, thought Francesca. The last thing she remembered was snuffing out her candle and burrowing under Sarah's fine sheets.

"Where am I?" she asked. She was beginning to feel very much afraid.

"Why, you be right here, love. Where'd you think?" He grinned even more.

She stared back at his smiling face, then realized he was shirtless. She became acutely aware of her own state of undress. She must try to make some sense of this. But her head was so fuzzy, like it was stuffed with cotton wool. She shivered from the cold, or something else, and pulled the rough blanket closer about her. What have you done to me?" she asked, frightened of what his answer might be.

"Why, nothing, love. Not yet, anyway. Never did fancy messing with a sleeping woman. Where's the fun in that?" He picked up a lantern from the floor and lighted it at the stove. The beam fell on his face; his expression made her more afraid. "Let's have a look at you, then," he said, and plucked the blanket from her hands. Her instinct was to grab for it, to scramble after it. But her innate dignity would not let her show her dismay so clearly before him. She sat up very straight and gave him back look for look. He laughed. "Spirit," he said almost to himself. "Good."

"How did I get here?" she demanded, going onto the offensive to keep herself from collapsing into tears.

"I carried you."

"But how could you do that and not awaken me?"

"You wasn't meant to wake." She digested this information a moment, but he spoke again before she could make sense of it. "It's simple, love. You been kidnapped."

The shock of the words cleared her mind all at once. Quite rationally, she thought: Ah, yes, I have been kidnapped. How obvious. Oh, dear.

Jerry walked back to the little stove. He had somehow managed to coax enough heat from it to boil water in a kettle. "Tea?" he asked pleasantly enough as he threw a handful of leaves into the boiling water.

"Oh, yes. please," she answered quickly. She could scarce feel her fingers, so numb with cold were they. But wait! What had he said? She was not meant to awaken. Why, she must have been drugged! But why ... who ...? "No!" she corrected. She would not be so duped again.

"Oh, it's all right," he said with a laugh, as though he could read her thoughts. "Nothing in it." He poured the dark brew into a pair of chipped mugs. He sipped from one of them. "See?" then he handed it to her. "Don't want you asleep no more." She took the mug and gratefully wrapped her icy fingers around it "Like I said, what's the fun in that?"

His black eyes were glittering over the white smile. She imagined he must look exactly like a Bedouin chief who has just successfully completed a bargain for a white slave. Trembling, she gulped at the tea. She *must* keep her presence of mind.

He came and sat beside her, very close beside her. Before she knew what he was doing, he had untied her lace nightcap and pulled it from her head. "Stop that!" she cried, a mixture of fright and indignation in her voice. She batted him away, spilling some of the scalding tea onto her hand. "Now see what you have done!" An ugly red welt rose where the tea had hit, and she raised it to her mouth to cool it.

Her hair was braided thickly in a single plait down her back. Her movement made it fall forward over one shoulder. He reached up and touched it, causing her to pull away. He just laughed. "Never could make out why you women have to tie your hair up in knots and cover it up at night. Bet that's something when it's hanging down your back."

His voice had lowered. Francesca grew alarmed. He said he had done nothing to her. *Not yet!* His intention of doing that something now was growing alarmingly clear.

She jumped up and walked to the stove. Change his thinking, confuse him, do anything. . . . "It is freezing in here. Can you build up the fire, at least?"

"No more wood," he said simply. " 'Sides, I know a better way."

She ignored this remark. "No wood? Well, here then. This will burn." Before he could stop her, she plucked up his shirt and coat from the floor nearby and threw them into the stove, slamming the iron door shut on them.

He dived for the handle of the door and wrenched it open, but it was too late. The dry fabric of both garments had caught at once and burst into flames. "Damme!" he cried, swinging the door shut hard enough to loosen its hinges. He glared at her, and she felt a tremor of fear. But he could not be any more dangerous to her angry than he was amorous. And she felt somehow better prepared to deal with the former.

Suddenly he laughed. "You shouldn'ta done that, love. 'Tis a long wait you'll have, and a cold one. and now I'll be wearing the cloak I brought along for you."

She shivered. Too bad. She would just have to be cold. There were worse things that could happen. And would happen unless she was very clever. It occured to her to wonder where she was, how far from Hockleigh he had brought her. It didn't matter. If only she could get away, she would find her way to safety. She must.

Was there any chance that she could be rescued? she wondered. Certainly a search would be mounted when she was found to be missing. Devlin, she felt sure, would not stop till she was found. But how long might that take? And what might happen to her in the meantime? No. She must not depend on rescue. She must depend on herself, on her wits and her courage.

"Tell me," she said in a conversational tone, "just why is it you have kidnapped me?"

"Now, love, you don't look stupid. You're a rich woman. I'm a poor man. Seems fair to spread some of that coin of yours about a bit."

Ransom, of course. "How much do you want?" Her tone had grown very business like.

"Way I see it, twenty-five thousand pounds ain't too much for return of such a valuable piece of goods."

"Twenty-five thousand! Impossible! My funds are all tied up in trust. It would take my man-of-business days, weeks even, to put together such a sum, if he could manage it at all."

"I got days. Weeks even."

"Well, I do not!"

"Don't you, now? Well, I figure there must be others who got the blunt who think you're worth it. This Devlin fellow, for instance."

She stared. "What the devil do you know about Lord Devlin?"

"Not so much as I'd like. Like what you all see in him," he answered, a certain grimness touching the edge of his smile. "But enough to know he's like to pay up to get you back. Way I hear it, you're about to marry him."

Francesca could not have been more surprised if he had said she was about to marry an elephant. "Me, marry Devlin?" She laughed a mirthless laugh and wondered why it hurt so. "You, my friend, have been sadly misinformed. I assure you, Lord Devlin is the very last person I am likely to marry."

His dark eyes narrowed. "Here, what game are you playing? She said you was . . ." He cut himself off abruptly.

Francesca seemed not to notice any slip on his part. "No game at all, I promise you. Why, Devlin himself would laugh to hear you say such a thing." She believed this to be a true statement, but enunciating it proved far more difficult than it should have been.

He seemed to find the idea almost as uncomfortable as she did, and he looked at her suspiciously for a moment, as if he didn't believe her. She glared back. "You'll have to come up with someone else, then," he finally said. "Woman pretty as you, someone'll pay for you." The fire had all but died out now, and gooseflesh began to appear on his bare chest. "Damme, it's cold." He peered out the crack at the windows, where the moonlight was slowly being replaced by the first grey light of dawn. He stirred up the coals, but they gave up little heat. "Have to get some wood."

He was not about to leave his captive sitting there quite alone and unbound. She was his ticket either to a fortune or to Roxanna. He had decided that either would do. He picked up some strips of linen lying ready in a corner and bound her hands and feet firmly, but not so tightly as to pain her. Throwing a definitely feminine cloak about his bare shoulders and grinning at the sight he must present, he bowed to her again and left the cottage.

Left alone in the gradually lightening room, Francesca knew she must take advantage of the opportunity to explore her prison. She managed to inch her way to one window and stand up. She could just see through the crack between the boards. Jerry was gathering loose bits of wood nearby, his cloak a definite impediment.

Her hands were bound before her, and she reached up to push at the boards. They did not budge. She half-hobbled, half-hopped to the other windows. All were secure against escape.

Exhausted from her efforts, she sank onto the straw again. The gloom was dissipating from the room. She looked about her to see if any weapon was close to hand.

There was the kettle. And the lantern. She might make something of them, given half a chance. But she must be unbound before she could even try. She needed more time to think, to plan. Jerry would be back any moment.

As the light grew brighter and she sat there in thought, something colorful just at the edge of her field of vision caught her attention. She reached out for the spot of color. Something bright yellow was just peeking out from under the edge of the straw mattress. She pulled out a long ostrich plume of a very good quality. It was full and feathery, and its end was tipped a vivid orange. Now, where on earth had she seen that particular plume before?

With her attention on this mystery, she almost did not hear Jerry's foot kicking out at the door. More by instinct than by design, she shoved the plume back under the straw with her two bound-together hands, throwing herself off balance in the process. When he entered the cottage, she was lying back on the makeshift bed.

The fact made him smile. "That's more like," he said. "Might as well be comfortable." He threw some kindling and a pair of logs into the stove. She had assumed he would unbind her immediately on his return, but he made no move to do so. He simply stood with his backside to the quickly roaring fire and gazed at her admiringly. "She said you was pretty. You're not," he said, smiling even more. "You're beautiful." Maybe not so beautiful as my Roxie, he added to himself, but not bad. Not bad at all. She did not answer.

He let the cloak fall from his shoulders and came to sit beside her. He began unplaiting her heavy golden hair. This time, with her hands still bound, she could not bat him away. She could do nothing.

"Let's see what we got here, then," he said in a frighteningly seductive tone as he ran his fingers through the mass of hair, spreading it out over her shoulders like a fan. "My, my, my," he muttered, struck by her beauty.

As he looked into her eyes, a bit afraid but still full of

pride and her innate dignity, it occured to him that this young woman, with her high cheekbones and her strong jaw, had something that Roxanna didn't. It was Quality, real and true. Funny he'd never noticed the lack of it in Roxie before now. But then, the likes of Jerry Parsons didn't often see real Quality in his life.

He loosened the top button of her nightdress. He stroked the creamy skin of her throat. Francesca trembled; she was growing very frightened, but she would not let it show. She put a challenge into her eyes and her voice. "You said you had no interest in sleeping females. Are bound ones more to your taste?"

He only smiled. "Don't know. Never tried that particular trick before." He looked her over. It was true that making love to a woman whose ankles were bound together was like to prove difficult. He undid the linen strips from them.

"Thank you, Jerry, she said slowly, carefully. She smiled at him—a coquettish smile, she hoped.

When he leaned over to kiss her, she let him do it, though every instinct rebelled and shouted at her to beat him off with her fists. It was not a long kiss. Not yet. But she knew that would come if she was not very clever. He flashed his toothy smile, stood, and began unlacing his breeches.

"Jerry," she said quickly, "these bands hurt my poor hands so. See? They are rubbing just where the tea burned me. Could you not just loosen them? Only a little, please?"

Not for nothing had Lady Francesca Waringham trained in the *ton* school of flirtation. Even as experienced a man as Jerry Parsons was not proof against those eyes when she turned their full power on him. His self-confidence, his unequaled arrogance, betrayed him. He untied her hands.

She rubbed them together. "Oh, thank you, Jerry. That is ever so much better. They are so cold, poor things. Like ice. May I have a little more tea?"

Just like a woman to ask for tea at such a moment, he thought. But even so quickly had he got into the habit of doing as she asked. He refilled the mugs with the tea, now very black and boiling hot from the fresh flames. He gave it to her, then sat beside her, fingering her long hair.

As she raised the cup to her lips, she scanned the room with her eyes. The door was no more than ten feet away; nothing stood between her and it. He bent to kiss her.

Now! her mind screamed, and she threw the scalding tea at him. It hit him square in the face and ran down onto his bare chest.

She was on her feet even before his scream of pain erupted. Instinctively she grabbed the yellow feather from under the straw. Then she dashed for the door.

It would not open.

He was on his feet too now, blinded by the boiling tea but lunging after her, groping wildly. "Open, dammit!" she shouted at the door, and pulled harder. He grabbed at the fabric of her nightdress and threw himself at her. She twisted deftly to the side. The rip of the cotton sounded very loud in her ears as it came away in his hands. He was groping for her again. It was like some frantic, evil game of blindman's buff. *Why would the door not open?*

She forced herself to look down at it, willed her mind to think rationally. The latch, a crude one with a simple bar across. She had not lifted it. Of course. She skirted the thrashing man and made for the door again. She lifted the bar, and it opened at once.

But he had heard her movement and turned to lunge at her again. Throwing himself to the floor, he caught her ankle. Her foot slid out from under her, backward, and she fell onto the damp leaves just outside the door. He tried to pull her back into the room. He was very strong.

She kicked once, hard. She loosened his grip on her

ankle and scrambled out of reach. She made it to her feet. And then she was running, running harder than she had ever run in her life.

There was a horse not far from the door. She gasped with relief. She looked like a wraith, and the horse's nostrils flared in alarm. It raised up on its hind legs, pawing at the air, its dangerous hooves only inches from her head. She could feel its hot breath on her face. The loosely knotted reins fell from the tree where the horse had been tethered, and it took off into the woods. "Damme!" she cried in terrified frustration, and began to run again.

Before long she was under the trees. Without checking her forward progress, she looked back over her shoulder. Jerry had emerged from the cottage, still thrashing about like a wounded animal, still screaming. As she watched, he ran into a tree and fell to his knees. It sounded as though he cried out a name, but she could not be sure.

She did not dare to stop till she had run nearly half a mile—in what direction, she had no idea. She stumbled and fell, splashing in a puddle of mud. She stayed there a moment trying to catch her breath, listening. She could hear no sounds of pursuit. She could hear no sound at all except a lone bird chattering far over her head.

She crawled to a tree, leaning against it for support. And then she wept.

16

A glow of dawn fell on Lord Devlin's sleeping face and teased him awake. He was in his own room, seated in an uncomfortable position in the chair before the dead fire. He was wearing no coat, no waistcoat, no cravat, but was otherwise fully clothed. What the devil was he doing here in this chair? he wondered as he struggled toward wakefulness. He gave a stretch and tried to think. Most of the previous evening was a blank.

The attempt at thought made him dizzy. He had the devil's own head this morning! The backs of his eyelids felt like inverted hedgehogs, and his mouth felt as though he had been chewing cotton wool. Moreover, his dreams had not been calculated to put him in an optimistic frame of mind. In short, Lord Devlin woke in a foul humor.

Where the deuce was Isaac, his servant? He needed a shave. He needed some coffee. He arose slowly, his muscles stiff from sleeping in such an unaccustomed position, and reached for the bell pull. His eye chanced to fall on the mantel clock. It was just gone six. No one in the house would be stirring yet except the lowliest of the lowly servants. Isaac would quite properly not expect him to be up for another two hours at the least.

Perhaps a walk in the morning air would help to clear his head and return some semblance of normality to his thinking processes. In any case, he could not stand to remain in this room a moment longer, alone with his thick head and his black thoughts.

He shrugged himself into a comfortable and well-worn buckskin jacket, disregarding the need for a cravat or even a Belcher handkerchief, and left the room.

The cold air hit him full in the face with a jolt as he unlatched the heavy front door and stepped out onto the terrace. He breathed deeply several times. Better already. Hands thrust into his pockets and head down, he strode off, neither knowing nor caring where he was headed, just needing to move.

His head began to clear perceptibly as his blood began circulating faster. Bits and pieces of his previous evening's activities began to come to mind. He remembered going to Francesca's room to talk. And he remembered finding it empty. He scowled at the recollection. Yes, that was when he had decided to get thoroughly and disgustingly drunk. Judging by the head he had this morning, he had succeeded.

But that had not been all, had it? He struggled with memory. Then it came to him. Ah, yes. The Widow. He had gone to see Roxanna.

She had not been surprised to see him, he was sure. Her room had been bathed in the softest of candlelight. She had been wearing something red, he recalled, something wispy and soft and transparent that almost wasn't there at all.

And pretty quickly it wasn't there. It had gone the way of his coat and his neckcloth. She was really a very beautiful and desirable woman.

Why, then, had he awakened in his own room, fully dressed? He could distinctly remember holding her, kissing her. But he could not remember wanting her, not like he wanted Francesca. In fact, he now remembered clearly that he had *not* wanted her. He had been vaguely repelled, not really by her so much as by himself. He had apologized as gently as he could manage in so undignified a position—though not gently enough, if her stormy face had been a true gauge—and returned to his own room with his brandy. He had locked the door behind him.

Not a very edifying recollection, that. It would be uncomfortable having to face the woman over the breakfast table this morning. Well, it couldn't be helped. He had suffered worse consequences from his own folly before this. And probably would again.

There was no one about on the grounds so early, not even a gardener. He cut across the velvety lawns. His boots were soon damp with dew, blades of fresh-cut grass clinging to their surface. He wandered at will, thinking, eventually heading toward the stables and beyond, without a soul to interrupt his black thoughts. He did pass within five feet of a young stableboy as he neared the tack room. The boy tugged at his forelock in greeting and would have spoken. But the black, closed look on his lordship's face brought him up short with his mouth hanging open. Devlin walked on without noticing him.

Having brought Roxanna to mind, and having called up that sordid little scene in her bedchamber, he promptly dismissed her from further thought. There was room in his mind for only one woman, one person. Francesca. She had so firmly embedded herself in his soul that he thought he should never be rid of her.

He set himself the task of bringing Priscilla's image before his mind's eye. He tried to see her pretty blue eyes to hear her soft, not unmusical voice. But he could not seem to hold the image. He concentrated harder. Her hair? Brown. Yes, it was a sort of brown. Not curly, not straight. Just . . . well, sort of brown hair. Her face was round, but sort of oblong as well. Well, not too square at any rate. And pink. Well, a sort of pink. More of a red, actually, from her perpetual blush in his company.

Now, what had she been wearing last evening? He had complimented her on it at dinner, he was sure, so he ought to remember. A sort of yellow, fluffy thing. Or was it pink? Well, definitely fluffy, frilly, overwhelming. Not at all like Francesca's gown. That had been a smooth almond green, with darker highlights shimmering within it, a soft straight fall of silk *crepe de Chine* from a high waist. Deep brown velvet ribbons had trimmed the neck and hem, and there had been brown silk roses at her waist, just to one side. She had looked wonderful. She always looked wonderful.

Perhaps Francesca would be willing to assist Priscilla in choosing a new wardrobe, he thought. Her taste was so exquisite. In return, he could teach Caspar to . . . to what? The thought stopped him cold. He could teach Caspar Maltby nothing that would please Francesca. He had nothing she wanted or needed in a husband. She had made that quite clear. Caspar did.

He was well beyond the stables and park now, following a footpath that skirted a field of hay already baled for the winter. "Miss Pennington. Priscilla. Lady Devlin." He said the words aloud and stopped to give them a chance to sink in.

A wood edged the far side of the field. He was staring at it, not seeing it. Lady Devlin. He gave an involuntary sigh.

Something moving near the edge of the wood drew his attention, and he focused on it. Standing there, across the field about fifty yards from where he stood, he saw Francesca. "Damme!" he exclaimed aloud, ordering his brain to behave and to cease conjuring up fantastical images. He defiantly turned his face away from the vision and began walking.

He went no more than a dozen steps, however, when his eyes turned back against his will to the wood. She was still there, stumbling out from under the trees. As he stared at her, she cried out in a high, nearly hysterical voice.

"Devlin!" she cried. "Thank God! Thank God."

The vision was real. Francesca was here! He hurdled

over the low wall separating him from the field and began running toward her. It was hardly more than a moment until he reached her. She was on the verge of collapse, and he scooped her up into his arms.

Neither of them spoke for a moment. Francesca sobbed with relief. Everything was all right now. Now that Devlin was here. He was so confused by seeing her here, and by the feeling of holding her in his arms, that he could put no words together. He murmured soothing sounds and stroked her hair until she could quiet her sobs.

When she finally looked up at him and gave him a watery smile, he really saw her for the first time. Good God! She looked horrid! No, that was not precisely true. Francesca could never look horrid. But she did look as though she had been through an ordeal, and a distinctly unpleasant one at that.

Her hair flowed about her in swirls and tangles, with leaves and bits of twig stuck to it. Her face and hands were badly scratched from her headlong rush through the trees. She was dressed only in a nightdress, half torn away and covered in mud. Her bare feet were blue with cold, cut and bleeding.

"What has happened to you?" he asked, wild anger rising inside him at whoever or whatever could bring her to this. "Cesca! Tell me!"

She could manage a tiny smile now that he was here, now that she was safe. "It's quite simple, really," she said in a small voice. "I was kidnapped."

"Kidnapped? Who the devil . . . ?" She let his explosion wear itself out, then told him, in a surprisingly rational voice, the entire story of her night's adventures.

"Where is the blackguard?" he stormed. "I will kill him! How dare he touch you?" He rose as though he would go at once in search of the miscreant. There was murder in his face.

"Devlin," said Francesca, a touch of impatience creeping into her voice now that her story was out, "I am freezing. My feet are bleeding, and my head hurts abominably. I should really like very much to go home."

This caused him to stop his ranting; a contrite smile warmed his face. She really had been through a good deal. "Poor sweet," he said, smoothing back her tangled hair. He removed his leather jacket and laid it gently over her shoulders. He tenderly touched a vicious scratch on her temple and kissed the fingertips of her hand with its cracked and broken nails. "My poor love," he murmured.

Somehow, in the next moment, he was kissing her. Quite thoroughly kissing her. And she was allowing it. His unshaved face scratched against the softness of hers. She hardly seemed to feel its roughness. As her hands slid up around his neck, the jacket fell away from her shoulders. It hit the carpet of dead leaves with a rustle that neither heard. His hands moved down to encircle her waist, then up again until they rested just under her breasts. She was sure he could feel the pounding of her heart; it felt like a rapidly recurring earthquake within her. Her knees felt weak, and she held on to him all the tighter for support.

He wanted to possess her, to meld with her and become a part of her. He knew she wanted the same. He could feel it in her.

She kissed him back in a manner that proved the truth of his thoughts. She could feel her control slipping away. She could feel herself slipping away, slipping into him, disappearing.

With the last vestiges of her self-control, she pulled away from him, gasping for breath. He stared at her with burning eyes, as though he would devour her with a look. She could not stand the power of that look. She broke into an embarrassed laugh and pulled out of his arms.

"Really, Dev," she said lightly, looking everywhere but into those burning blue eyes. "You might at least have the grace to wait until I am married."

"Married?"

"Yes. You have implied often enough your hope to make a cuckold of Caspar. But as he is not yet my husband, you might at least wait before making the attempt."

She had intended it as a joke, an attempt to break the emotional intensity of the moment. Devlin did not laugh. "Is he going to be your husband?" he asked very quietly.

She knew absolutely in that moment that she had not the slightest desire to marry Caspar Maltby, to let him touch her as Dev had just touched her. But what future was there for her if she did not? Devlin would never marry her. He was as good as promised to Pris. And he had made it quite clear to Francesca that he saw her in a very different role from that of wife. What had he said that evening so long ago? Gentlemen might dally with the dashers; they did not marry them. He had meant her. The memory galled her.

"Well, of course he is going to be my husband!" she snapped. "Why else have I been working on him all this time? He would have offered for me last night if I had not gone to bed with that dreadful headache."

The mere mention of Caspar's name had cooled Devlin's ardor completely. The fire faded from his eyes. "He will have other chances," he said offhandedly.

"I will see that he does! Now, do you suppose we might manage to discover a way to get me home? I am not particularly comfortable."

He picked up the jacket and threw it over her shoulders again, less gentle this time. "What do we do about that fellow Jerry? We can't just let him slip away."

"I am sure he has done so already. He is not a total fool. I have been wandering about for hours, and I'm sure I couldn't find that cottage again in any case. And if I did, he would be long gone." She considered this a moment, then added, "Unless I have permanently blinded him. Do you suppose I have?"

"I certainly hope so."

"Well, I don't," she said truthfully. "He was an unpleasant fellow, to be sure, but I don't think any of this was his idea. I feel certain he was merely a hireling."

"What makes you think so?"

She sighed. It was almost a sigh of regret. "Because I think I know who hired him. I think I even know why."

"Who? Who would dare?"

For answer she showed him the yellow plume, now sadly mangled, very muddy, and barely recognizable. It had tugged at her memory when she first saw it; she had had plenty of time to think about it as she wandered through the woods. Finally she remembered where she had seen it before. Roxanna Gordon had worn a quartet of just such feathers on her riding hat the other morning. They were distinctly designed to remain in the memory. This one had done just that.

Francesca could not at first imagine why Roxanna would be involved in such a stunt. She suffered no lack of money; Francesca was no threat to her position. In fact, she had no need of anything Francesca had. There was only one thing in the world she clearly wanted, and that was Devlin.

Francesca was clever, and it was not long before the whole scheme came clear to her. She remembered Roxanna's glittering eyes on her whenever she had talked to Devlin, walked with him, danced with him. Jealousy had been written all over the woman's face. Francesca had to laugh at the irony of it all. Roxanna obviously thought that Francesca was after Devlin. She saw her as a real obstacle to her own plans for the man. And so she had gotten her out of the way. Very neat.

As Francesca shared her conclusions with Devlin, he saw the truth of them at once. They were confirmed by Roxanna's behavior of the night before, though he did not share the story of the scene with Francesca. He exploded. He stamped about, oaths and promises of vengeance filling the air. When the diatribe finally began to run down, he slumped and added, "It's my fault."

"How nonsensical," she said. "How could it possibly be considered your fault?"

"If I'd had the bottom to offer for Priscilla the other night when I intended to, that woman would have had no reason to have you carried off."

"That is perfectly true. And then she would have had Pris kidnapped instead. I hope I am not vain, Dev, but I do think that Pris would not have handled Jerry half so well as I did."

"God no," he readily agreed.

"And then we really would have been in the suds. But now, since I am so neatly escaped, we have the means to remove Roxanna entirely from the scene. And you can offer for Pris this very day with no danger."

All her life Francesca had had a habit of retreating into briskness and matter-of-factness when what she really wanted most in the world was to be held and comforted like a child and have all decisions removed from her head. She had done just that now. Devlin reacted accordingly.

"I will do so, I assure you," he said coolly. "Without delay. And now, shall we return to the house?" he asked, holding his arm out to her as though he had just asked her to dance. "I am anxious to send for the constable."

"You will do nothing of the sort!" she snapped. "I have no intention of exposing Roxanna's behavior to the world. I could not do so without exposing the whole. Whatever the circumstances, I did spend the night in that cottage with that man, and if you care nothing about my reputation, I assure you that I do. If Caspar hears of this, I may as well whistle him down the wind, along with any other gentlemen who might be inclined to offer for me."

"I hadn't thought of that."

"Obviously."

"Well, what do you propose? We cannot simply pretend it never happened."

"Yes we can. And we shall. To everyone except

Roxanna. I am certain that between the two of us we can convince her that her presence at Hockleigh is *de trop*. In fact, I rather think we can scare her sufficiently to keep her from coming to London for a very long time. I believe she has some relations in France. Perhaps it is time she paid them a long visit. Now, if you will just settle down and act sensibly, no one will guess that anything untoward has happened." A breeze came up, and she shivered.

"Well, we cannot stand about here. You are blue with cold. Come on."

She glared at him, hands on hips. "I never took you for an idiot, Richard Devlin! Look at me. It would be rather obvious to anyone seeing me that I did not spend the night peacefully in my bed. It must be after eight. Do you propose we simply saunter up to the front door and bid the company a good morning?"

"Oh," he muttered.

"Quite," she agreed. "But I have a plan whereby no one will be the wiser. Only listen." She proceeded to give him exact instructions to convey to her maid, the only other person to be made privy to the whole. Francesca would trust Rose with her life, and rightly so. She added an instruction or two for Devlin himself, who wondered how she could be so calm and sensible after what she had been through in the past few hours.

"I do hope I can get my feet into a pair of boots," she said, looking down at her bloody toes. "You might just bring along a roll of lint so I can bandage them." She looked up and smiled at him, her first smile for a while. "And you might manage a shave for yourself. You look perfectly horrid. Whatever have you been doing all night?" He did not deign to answer.

Having finished the litany of her needs, she settled herself against a large oak tree out of the wind to wait for him, wrapping his leather jacket closely about her. "And do hurry, Dev," she called after him. "If Rose finds my room empty, she is like to rouse the entire household to look for me."

And so it happened that just as the guests were sitting down to their breakfast, Lady Francesca and Lord Devlin drove up the wide drive together in his curricle, for all the world as though they had been out for an early-morning pleasure drive. She was perfectly outfitted in a toilinette morning-dress topped with a warm pelisse of slate grey edged in marten. Her golden hair was neatly tucked up under a close-fitting fur toque in the Russian style, and her feet were shod in half-boots of black jean. A delicate application of rouge and rice powder hid most of the scratches on her face, and a fierce clenching of her teeth covered the pain in her feet.

When he lifted her down from the carriage before the house, she winced, and she leaned heavily on his arm as they came up the steps. But when the front door was opened to them, she was smiling.

"Cesca!" cried Sarah in greeting. "How pleased I am to see you up and about. Your headache is quite gone?"

"Oh, yes," said Francesca lightly. "I awoke feeling quite the thing. And Lord Devlin was kind enough to take me out for a drive in the fresh air. Is it not a beautiful morning?"

"Yes, but so chilly. Come and warm yourself with a cup of tea." They made their way to the breakfast room, Francesca trying hard not to hobble and thankful for the continued support of Devlin's strong arm.

Chatter was floating about the room as they entered to the usual chorus of "good mornings." But one person at the table grew deadly silent at sight of them. Roxanna Gordon dropped her fork with a loud clatter and went dead white. She was seated near the door, and they had to pass her as they made their way to their own seats.

Devlin retrieved her fork from the floor and set it with deliberation beside her plate, meeting her wide eyes with his own hard, narrow ones. In a voice dripping with menace, but so quiet only she could hear, he said, "Quite, Mrs. Gordon."

The gentlemen had made plans to go out shooting that morning as a change of pace from the hunt, so Francesca was free to retire to her room shortly after breakfast on the pretext of having some letters to write. She collapsed onto the bed as soon as her maid managed to pry off her boots. In minutes—nay seconds—she was fast asleep.

Devlin, before taking a gun out to join the others, invited Roxanna for a stroll in the shrubbery. The invitation was polite, almost casual, but his steely grip on her elbow gave her no chance to refuse. She went.

17

The afternoon turned grey, the gentlemen returned from their shooting thoroughly chilled, and the entire group retreated to the Green Salon for tea. Francesca's nap had helped her to recover from her ordeal to appear very like herself. She was a bit pale and quieter than usual, but no one noticed anything much amiss.

One of several topics of conversation was the suddenness of Roxanna Gordon's departure that morning. A letter had come, they had been told. Something about a sick relation in Devonshire.

"It must be someone she cares a great deal about," speculated Lady Aurelm. "I have never known Roxanna to take less than two full days to pack. I doubt she took two hours today."

"She will have a long trip," said Lady Poole, not overly concerned.

"It is a shame that she will miss the fancy-dress ball tomorrow," said Lady Jersey with a wry smile. "You know Roxanna is always at her most vivid when she is masked."

"What are you wearing to the ball, Sally?" The conversation thus neatly turned, no one thought to mention Roxanna Gordon again.

Devlin watched Francesca from the corner of his eye. A little stiffness remained from her unorthodox morning, but she really was carrying the thing off rather well. He marveled at it; he would have bungled it for sure on his own. He saw red at the thought of that blackguard so much as touching her, and the thought of both the scoundrels getting off scot-free enraged him. But her solution had obviously been the correct one.

She felt his gaze on her. She turned her most brilliant smile on Caspar, and he promptly came and sat beside her. Devlin frowned, rose, and went to join Priscilla on the other side of the room. "Would you care to come for a stroll with me in the gallery, Priscilla?" he asked very pointedly and loud enough for the entire company to hear. He looked to see if Francesca was watching him. She was, but she looked quickly away, fluttering her eyes mightily at Caspar. Devlin took Pris's hand. "As you are an artist, I would like to hear your comments on one or two of the paintings."

Priscilla's eyes grew wide. She looked at her mother beside her, who beamed her acquiescence and gave her daughter a little push. With the look of one on her way to the guillotine, Priscilla took his arm and the two of them left the room together. Every eye in the group followed them out.

Francesca felt herself grow cold and rigid. "Mr. Maltby," she said suddenly, her voice louder and harsher than she had intended. "Caspar," she modified, "I have discovered the most fascinating tract on soil supplementation in the library. But it is so extremely advanced. Would you come and explain it to me, please?" She rose, and he could do nothing but follow. With a hand placed lightly on his arm, she led him magisterially from the room, all the time gritting her teeth against the pain that still throbbed in her poor feet.

As Devlin and Priscilla entered the Long Gallery, it occured to him that he might have chosen a more intimate setting for a marriage proposal. The Gallery, with its rows of Hockleigh ancestors scowling down from the walls, was more than a little intimidating in its vastness. It was too big, too dark, even a bit forbidding.

Odd that Devlin had not found it the least bit moribund that first afternoon at Hockleigh when he had encountered Lady Francesca here. Then it had been full of sunlight and promise.

He commented idly on one or two of the portraits whose eyes seemed to follow their progress down the long room, their footsteps on the hardwood floor echoing off the walls.

He could never say afterward just what his first words had been. He took Priscilla's elbow and steered her toward a sofa halfway down the room, near the fire.

Neither did Priscilla have any idea what he was saying or what she answered, if anything. She was trembling and was thankful when she was allowed to sink onto the sofa. The smooth satin of its upholstery was cold to the touch, and she shivered.

She did not know where to look. And so, as usual, she looked at the floor. But even this reliable support seemed to be in danger of sliding out from under her, leaving her suspended over the abyss of her future. The moment she had dreaded had come. She had known it would, had even persuaded herself that it was for the best, but she had nevertheless prayed that it would not.

"And so you see, my dear," Devlin was saying as he sat beside her, holding her hand, "I find myself in need of a wife. And while it is true that we have not known each other long, I have come to greatly admire you in these past days."

He really was doing the thing rather well, he reflected, for one so lacking in experience at proposals of marriage. The nervous tension so obvious in the girl had brought out his innate kindness and made the whole thing much easier. He did just wonder why this well-rehearsed little scene that was going so well was not making him feel happier. He was, after all, about to be granted a long-held desire.

"Yes, my lord," whispered Priscilla when he had finished his speech.

"I cannot hear you," he said gently, lifting her chin so he could see her face.

She swallowed hard, took a deep breath, and said, "I will be happy to marry you, Lord Devlin." There! It was done, she told herself. And she need never worry about it again.

"I am pleased," he said. He knew he should kiss her. No doubt she was expecting it. She was, after all, sitting there with her eyes closed and her face up to his. But he had not the slightest desire to do his duty at that moment. He would do much more than kiss her in due course, of course. It was the prime reason for marrying her, naturally. But he knew it would mean nothing to him. No woman would ever again mean anything to him in that way. Not unless he could have Francesca.

He patted the hand he still held in his. "Shall we rejoin the others?" he asked.

Pris opened her eyes in surprise. Obviously he was not going to kiss her. She didn't know if she was disappointed or relieved. They rose and left the room. Neither spoke.

Things were progressing along somewhat similar lines in the library. Francesca had chosen her territory a bit better than had Devlin. It was a very cozy, very comfortable room. The settee before the fire was inviting.

"I am honored, Caspar," said Francesca. "I should be very pleased to be your wife."

He blinked and looked down at the hand he was holding. Lady Francesca's hand. He had just asked Lady Francesca Waringham to be his wife. She had accepted. He was not at all certain how it happened. He had quite thought he was explaining the difference between genus *Amaryllidaceae* and genus *Asclepiadaceae*. And he was not at all certain how he felt about the whole thing.

Francesca knew very well how she felt about it. She felt perfectly horrid. She knew she was using this very nice, very simple man for her own ends. She felt guilty. She felt also that she had just said good-bye forever to something beautiful, something few people ever have even a taste of in this life, something she would never have again.

She knew now that whatever she felt for Devlin—and she would no longer deny that she did feel something, and it was called love—she would remain faithful to Caspar Maltby. She had forced him into this proposal. She owed him at least that much.

"I think we should announce it at the ball tomorrow, do not you?" she said, pulling herself from her black thoughts and forcing a smile onto her face.

"What? Tomorrow? Oh . . . oh, yes. All right," replied Caspar.

There didn't seem to be anything more to say at the moment, so they returned to the Green Salon and the others.

The fact that Lord Devlin was still holding Priscilla's hand when the pair of them rejoined the others was not lost on the girl's mother. She let out a squeak of pleasure and bounced in her chair. But she could hardly come right out and ask, in front of the entire company, whether or not her daughter was at last betrothed.

Devlin was conscious of his duty to his future mother-in-law, however unpleasant that duty was likely to be. He must speak to her. Strictly speaking, in the absence of Mr. Pennington, he should have applied to her for permission to make his offer before speaking to Pris. The unlikelihood that the woman would refuse to allow the marriage, however, was so great as to be ludicrous. It was just a matter now of informing her that her dearest wish was about to come true.

He led Priscilla to a chair beside her mother, then bent to the older woman. "Mrs. Pennington," he said gravely. "I wonder if I might have a word with you in the morning room?"

Pleasure flooded the woman's face. It was true! It was all too obviously true! She managed to control her joy long enough to say, "But of course, my lord." And with an almost regal and very self-satisfied smile to the others, she allowed herself to be led from the room.

The scrutiny of the company now turned on Priscilla. She could not bear their speculative glances. Turning to her hostess, she said, "The sun has come out, Your Grace. If you have no objection, I think I shall take my sketchbook into the garden." Sarah nodded, and Pris skittered from the room.

Before anyone could even speculate on what might have happened, Francesca and Caspar reentered the room arm in arm. They were not smiling. In fact, Caspar looked a little dazed.

Sarah was the first to speak. "Is it not incredible, Cesca?" she whispered as her friend sat beside her. "I do think Devlin has actually offered for Pris. I cannot for the life of me think why." Although privy to Francesca's own absurd matrimonial plans, the Duchess had had no idea what Devlin was up to.

"Because he wants to marry her, I would imagine," Francesca replied sullenly. "Why else does a gentleman offer for a lady?"

"I suppose," said Sarah in a doubtful voice. She gave Francesca a penetrating look, a sad look. "Well, they will most likely wish to announce it tomorrow evening if it is true. Perhaps I should have more flowers brought up."

The word "flowers" brought Caspar back to attention. "I should be very happy to go and choose some for you, Your Grace."

Sarah looked at his glum face, then at Francesca's. "Why, thank you Mr. Maltby," she said finally. "Come, I will show you what I have in mind." And she led him off.

Both Caspar Maltby and Priscilla Pennington, having bowed to their duty as they saw it, had accepted the inevitable. Caspar did not really suppose his marriage would change his life overmuch, although Lady Francesca was not quite what he had had in mind when he left home. Pris had decided that marrying Lord Devlin was at least preferable to remaining at home for the rest of her life under the domination of her Mama. At least now there would be no more harp lessons, no more ill-chosen gowns. She would have more time for her art, her only joy. She would make it fill her days.

Priscilla had a great ability, developed from necessity over a long period of time, to block all her unhappiness from her mind as soon as she picked up a sketchpad and pencils. Sketching had become her haven, and she turned to it now, setting down in perfect detail on overblown Persian rose in the hothouse. It was there that Caspar came across her as he searched out the most perfect specimens for Sarah's ballroom.

Despite their whirling heads and confused moods, they fell into easy conversation about the flowers and the drawings. It was odd that Pris never felt shy or awkward or tongue-tied with him. He complimented her again on her drawing. He made a small suggestion about some feature of the rose, which she implemented at once, to the improvement of the piece.

"Why, thank you, Mr. Maltby. I cannot think why I did not see it myself. It makes a very great difference."

"You would have seen it soon enough, I am sure. You have a remarkable eye for such work, Miss Pennington."

She flushed with pleasure. Her drawing was the one thing at which she excelled and in which she felt any confidence at all. "It gives me much joy."

Suddenly Caspar had a thought. "You know, I have for the past several years been compiling a collection of the wildflowers native to the south part of the country. I hope to publish a volume on them soon. I have long sought a competent illustrator to work on the collection with me. Do you suppose you might be interested?"

"Oh, how wonderful! I . . ." She cut herself off. How could she possibly accept such an offer, much as she would like to? She would soon be a married woman, living in . . . She realized that she did not even know where

Lord Devlin lived, where she would live. "I don't know if that would be possible," she said quietly, much of her earlier animation gone, but she did not look away from him.

What very beautiful eyes she has, thought Caspar, and he added in unwonted poetical strain: like the first, freshest cornflowers of the year. The object of his poetry caught his eyes and held them in a more compelling yet far more comfortable manner than Francesca's had ever done. He smiled at her. "I do hope you will consider it, Miss Pennington."

"Thank you, Mr. Maltby." After a moment she picked up her sketchpad to go. "Mama will be wanting me," she said. "Excuse me."

He watched her go, noticing how small and round and soft she was. Not like Francesca. Not at all like Francesca.

18

The morning of the final hunt was almost as grand an occasion as the opening meet. Once again the farmers and serving maids and anyone else who could manage it came from miles around, bundled up in the clothing that would take them into the winter. The grass glistened with the first frost of the year, little more than a light dusting of white but portending an early cold spell.

A bonfire structure some ten feet high was set upon the lawn; it would be lit after the hunters returned. A feast would be awaiting them as well. Already a large pig was slowly roasting in a pit dug beside the lawn. The scent of it perfumed the morning air.

And tonight, while the locals danced to a fiddle and flute on the lawns, the gentry would have a fancy-dress ball.

Sarah had agonized over every detail of the entertainment and had, with Francesca's helpful advice, planned a day to be long remembered, a fitting end to such a brilliant hunt.

While the hunters plied themselves with great helpings of food, then went off eagerly to join the mounted throngs, upstairs maids and valets were hard at work. Not only must fancy costumes be put into perfect order for this evening's romp, but there were trunks and valises, portmanteaux and bandboxes by the score to be packed. Tomorrow all the guests would bid their adieux and begin the long trip south.

Francesca was not eager for the journey. It would be an uncomfortable one, long and cold, with nothing but her maid and her own dark thoughts to keep her company. Or worse, Caspar would offer to accompany her south. She was loath to say her good-byes to Sarah; the next time she saw her, Sarah would be a mother. And try though she might to push the idea aside, she could not deny that she would miss Richard Devlin, miss him quite dreadfully. She would miss their little strategy meetings, their easy badinage, the promise that every moment with him seemed to hold. The next time she saw him, she would be married. So would he. To someone else.

Soon she would be traveling even farther, into Somersetshire to meet Caspar's mother. That was bound to be a tedious trip too. She could only hope she had not saddled herself with a silly nit for a mother-in-law.

Well, no need to worry about all that just yet, not when it was a glorious morning, not when there was hunting to be enjoyed. She stepped out onto the porch and breathed deeply of the frosty air.

There was more than a hint of winter about this riders hung on the air. Francesca was thankful for the morning. The steam set up by the horses, dogs, and high fur collar on her deep burgundy habit, styled à la Russe, and her warm gauntleted gloves.

She looked around for her horse and groom but could not find them in the milling throng. She did, however, spot Lord Devlin. He was leading out Arapaho, who was obviously eager for a good run. Isaac followed close behind him, with the reins of Morning-Sun-on-the-Water in his hands.

"Good morning, Devlin," she said, feeling happy to see him in spite of herself. "Who is to have the treat of riding this little beauty this morning?" She patted the palomino's golden nose and offered her a lump of sugar from her pocket.

Devlin grinned at her. "You are," he said simply. "That is, if you wish to. I took the liberty of sending Desdemona back to her stable."

"Ah, your usual high-handed self, I see," she remarked, but she could not be angry. "But I thank you for it. I have been itching to try her ever since I first set eyes on her."

The horse gave her a wet kiss, obviously begging for more sugar. Devlin laughed. "The feeling seems to be mutual. Come on, then."

He tossed her up onto the mare's back, then mounted himself, and off they rode.

The Duke of Hockleigh had not lied when he promised his guests good hunting. With but one exception, every run had been spectacular. The closing day was no exception. They flew over fields and through woods, down steep rocky ravines and heather-covered hillsides. There were more than a score of good jumps over ditches and streams, walls and hedges, and a pair of bullfinches that would have daunted any but the very best of hunters.

Francesca and Devlin were in the lead and side by side for the whole of it. The two horses moved as one; the two riders did as well. Each was able, at least for the moment, to block out the problems that had kept them awake most of the night, to block out everything but the pure joy of riding beside each other in such perfect harmony.

Priscilla, now completely in her Mama's good graces again, her own dear sweet child, had been given the entire morning at liberty, an unaccustomed luxury. She bundled up in her oldest, warmest coat, gathered up her sketchpad and pencils, and headed for the woods and its wildflowers, ferns, and mosses just waiting for her. If such freedom was to be her usual lot now, perhaps marriage would not be so bad after all.

Caspar, having done the duty for which he had come to Hockleigh—and whatever would his mother think of Lady Francesca?—allowed himself the luxury of spending his last morning collecting specimens for his botanical studies. He had been neglecting his work shamefully of late. But now that the business with Francesca was settled, he could get on with what was important in his life.

He had a thought that stopped him, frowning, in his progress toward the woods. He hoped Francesca would not expect him to go up to London for the Season. That would never do. The very best specimens would be available for collecting just at that time of the year. And his gardens would just be coming into their own. The science of botany really was something more than a hobby with Caspar. Some few might laugh at him, he knew, but he was convinced that one day he would be one of the most respected botanists and horticulturists in England. Others would study his collections and read his notes and remark his name on the roll of members of the Royal Academy of Science.

It was, of course, inevitable that Priscilla and Caspar would encounter each other in the woods, and that they would fall into discussion of their mutual interest. While Francesca and Devlin sailed over hedges and took a double oxer with ease, Caspar and Priscilla picked grasses and studied lichens and oohed and aahed over the veiny leaves crackling under their feet. Caspar could not help noticing the pretty pink tinge that the cold had brought to Priscilla's cheeks. She could not help noticing how intelligent his eyes were and how they sparkled with enthusiasm when he spied some especially fine specimen.

All four of the young people ended by being very well satisfied with their morning.

Devlin was smiling and laughing at some comment of Francesca's as they walked from the paddock area toward the house. She was beaming with the pleasure of her morning. As they rounded the corner of the house, a laugh, light and feminine and full of real pleasure, reached their ears. They looked across the lawns to see Caspar and Priscilla, in perfect and natural good humor, approaching from the woods. The sight stopped them.

"Odd," said Devlin quietly. "I've never heard her laugh before."

Francesca saw Caspar retrieve a leaf that Pris had dropped, then smile down at her. He had often smiled at Francesca, but never in quite that way. It was not a bemused lover's smile. It was a warm, open, and . . . well, very *genuine* smile.

The laughing couple espied their no-longer-laughing counterparts. All smiles faded from the scene. Priscilla, her pretty pink cheeks once more suffused with red, lowered her head and looked guilty, though she could not imagine why she should feel so.

Francesca, though she did not blush, was feeling very much the same way. "Good morning, Caspar," she said a little too heartily.

"Good morning, my dear," he answered softly. "You have enjoyed your little ride?"

She looked surprised. How could anyone describe the perfectly glorious chase they had just experienced as a "little ride"? But she only said, "Oh, yes, very much. And you? I see you have been gathering some more of your weeds. How nice." She meant no harm. She wondered why he frowned and looked down in such a proprietary way at the handful of old brown grasses and wispy things he was carrying.

"And you, Priscilla?" said Devlin. "I imagine you've been amusing yourself with your sketchpad. A pleasant diversion, I'm sure." She looked up very briefly, certain he was making fun of her. "Yes, my lord . . . uh, Devlin." She really must stop calling the man she was going to marry "my lord."

Devlin noticed that his hand was still on Francesca's elbow. He let go as though it were a hot coal. "Allow me to escort you inside, my dear," he said to Priscilla, offering her his arm. "You will like to hear about the hunt, I'm sure. It was a splendid ride, over twenty-five miles. The dogs were spot on. I was awarded the mask. . . ." He led her away, chattering madly and saying nothing that was of the least interest to her.

"Well," said Francesca, "shall we go change as well? I do hope that pig will be ready soon. I for one am hungry enough to eat the whole of it myself."

Soon the bonfire was lit; the roasted pig was carved into succulent pink slices. Hot roasted chestnuts were peeled and popped into willing mouths, and toasts to the fox were drunk with hot hearty cider. But before long it was time to retire upstairs. One did not make a proper impression at a fancy-dress ball without considerable preparation. The great house quietened while these were begun.

"Oh, George," said Sarah, seated before her mirror and putting the final touches to her hair. She was appearing at her party as Lady Hamilton to the Duke's Lord Nelson. "I simply do not know what to do!"

"There is nothing you can do, my dear," said her noble husband. "If she has decided to have him, she will have him." He laid his hands on her shoulders and smiled at her image. "It is really none of our affair."

"But of course it is our affair!" she contradicted him, spinning around to look at him more directly. Her face had a determined set to it, and her husband cringed. He could see what was coming. Sarah's conversation might be liberally sprinkled with what "George says," but in reality what George said was most often what Sarah had convinced him he should say. "They are our friends. How can we sit by and watch Devlin throw himself away on a sweet little mouse of a nobody like Priscilla Pennington? And you surely cannot expect me to allow Cesca to marry Caspar. Caspar! I mean, I know he is your cousin, darling, and a very bright fellow and all, but really! Cesca!"

"But my love—" he began.

"And *especially* when it is so clearly obvious that Cesca and Devlin belong together. I never in my life saw two people more perfectly suited."

He smiled at her vehemence. "I have," he said, and kissed her nose.

"Oh, George, do be serious," she said, but she gave him her dimply smile. "Of course I did not mean to include us."

"Cesca and Dev, eh? So that's the way the wind blows."

"No, unfortunately it does not! And it never will start blowing that way if we let them go through with this silly nonsense they have gotten themselves into." She reached up and adjusted his eyepatch. "Do you know, you look decidedly rakish in that?"

"Can't see a blasted thing," he grumbled, but smiled in spite of himself in what he was sure was a devil-may-care manner. "And how the devil am I supposed to dance with you with only one arm?"

"I am sure Lord Nelson managed it. They say he was terribly clever. So clever that I cannot imagine Nelson seeing his friends falling into such a scrape and doing nothing to pull them out again."

"Sarah . . ." he started in a worried tone. He knew her expert wheedling only too well.

"Now, darling," she cooed. "You know the doctor said I ought to be humored in my condition. There is no telling what may happen if I become too upset."

"You are a baggage!" he declared. "Just like Emma Hamilton." He kissed her again, this time not on the nose. "Very well. I'll do what I can. But I don't know what that will be."

"You must not let them announce these silly betrothals, for a start."

"I can try. They do seem determined, though."

"I know you can do anything you set your mind to,

my darling." She handed him his huge cocked hat. "Just like Lord Nelson."

An air of expectation rippled through the house. Tonight was sure to be a memorable evening. Even Francesca, despite the pall that seemed to have descended over her spirits, was not untouched by the excitement. True, her heart did not leap up at the notion of waltzing in the arms of her betrothed. But she needn't spend the entire evening with him, after all. There would be plenty of gentlemen to swirl her around the floor and make her laugh. There always were. And although she got little pleasure from picturing Caspar in the guise of Charles the Second and felt fairly certain his pulse would not quicken at sight of her, she at least had the pleasure of knowing that she was looking her best.

She had chosen to appear as Diana, the Huntress. Her height and regal bearing made the role an ideal choice. She felt, with a wry smile at her reflection in the pier glass, that a huntress was exactly what she had been of late, and not just on the field. She had taken careful aim at Mr. Maltby, and with Dev beside her to sharpen her arrows and steady her aim, the poor fellow hadn't a chance.

And now Dev had bagged his quarry as well. Priscilla Pennington would soon be Lady Devlin. Oh, yes. Between them Francesca and Devlin made an unbeatable team. And they had won.

Why, then, was the image of the Huntress, peering back from the glass, not smiling in truimph?

She willed the frown to remove itself from her face at once: She forced a bright smile to take its place. She *would* enjoy herself tonight. After all, why should she not? She had achieved a major desire. The smile glittered all over her face, missing only her eyes. She picked up the bow of the Huntress and strode from the room.

The bubbling high spirits of the costumed dancers rivaled the champagne that was flowing so copiously.

Everywhere one looked were Cavaliers and Cleopatras, Roundheads and Robin Hoods, and nearly every other character worth thinking of. And all of them smiling, laughing, flirting.

Lord Devlin, in a simple black cloak and a wide-brimmed Spanish hat, was struggling to put at ease the shy young shepherdess who was his betrothed. It had actually been Priscilla's own idea to dress as a shepherdess. The simplicity of such a costume appealed to her quiet nature, and she was pleasantly surprised when her Mama agreed to the scheme.

She should have known better than to hope. Mama's idea of a shepherdess was not Priscilla's. The poor girl now stood under the blazing chandeliers looking like something from Marie Antoinette's Petit Trianon. Layer upon layer of skirt and petticoat was beruched and beribboned and swagged up one over the other to create a little round pouf of bright color that left showing rather more foot and ankle than Priscilla could feel comfortable with.

The mouse-brown hair had grown to an immense height, was heavily dusted with powder, and supported a hugely flowered and fruited straw bonnet. And she hadn't the least idea what to do with her crook.

Had she but known it, things could have been a good deal worse. Mrs. Pennington had seriously considered asking the Duchess for the loan of a lamb for the evening. She had thought better of it only when she realized that she might well have it dumped onto *her* when Priscilla went off to dance with Lord Devlin.

"That is a most fetching bonnet, Priscilla," said Devlin in an attempt to unfreeze the girl's tongue.

"Th-thank you, my lord," came the barely audible reply.

"My lord? Come, my dear. We are betrothed, and no one will fault you for calling me by name. It is Richard, by the by."

"Y-yes . . . Richard." She could not bring herself to

look at him. She felt horribly conspicuous in this ridiculous costume. How ashamed he must be.

"I had thought perhaps, if you should care for it, we might . . ." But Priscilla was not destined to hear what they might do if she should care for it, which she was fairly certain she should not. For at that moment Diana, the Huntress, with the face of Lady Francesca Waringham, entered the room. Lord Devlin seemed to lose all power of speech.

She was lovely, perhaps the loveliest thing Devlin had ever seen. She entered the room like a queen, her golden head, wrapped into Grecian braids and knots, held high. Her gown of ivory silk fell in graceful folds, revealing as much as it concealed of her magnificent figure. He was reminded of that night in her bedchamber with the candlelight shining through her nightdress, and he smiled at the memory. A fine gold cord crossed her bosom and was tied at her waist. A small golden quiver hung from one shoulder. Thonged sandals adorned her otherwise bare feet, and she carried a small, delicately curved golden bow.

There was no need to aim her weapon. Devlin was quite sure every masculine heart in the room must be pierced by the mere sight of her.

Francesca had to be gratified by the reaction she had created. She was surrounded at once by her usual throng of admiring suitors, all of them clamoring for the right to add their names to her dance card. Even Lord Devlin, fearful that the card would be filled before he could get to her, managed as diplomatically as possible, to pry himself away from Priscilla and approach the goddess.

It seemed the only gentleman in the room who was not smiling at the lady was Mr. Maltby. Oh, there was no denying that his betrothed looked quite beautiful, Ravishing, in fact. But he could not think such a gown was *entirely* suitable for an unmarried lady. He was sure he had seen the glitter of gilt nail varnish on her toes as she entered, and the silk of her gown seemed to him to be of an unnecessarily *clinging* variety. Of course, he was most likely behind the times as far as the world of Fashion was concerned. Perhaps such dash was all the go in London. Still, he was not quite sure he could approve. Mama was likely to be just the tinest bit scandalized by his lovely Francesca. The notion made him frown.

In turning away from the brilliant sight she presented, his eye fell on Priscilla, standing in a corner while her mother lectured her and fluffed her skirt and tweaked a powdered curl into place. She submitted to her mother's ministrations with utter patience. It came from long practice, and what choice did she have, after all?

Now, here was Mr. Maltby's idea of a properly costumed young lady. No dash at all about Miss Pennington. He knew his Mama would approve. Perhaps if he asked her in just the proper way, she might be willing to speak to Francesca, give her a bit of friendly advice.

"Gentlemen, please!" fluttered Francesca, smiling a little too brightly, laughing a little too loudly. "I cannot dance with all of you at once. Yes, Graham, you may have the quadrille. I am sorry, Algy, but the *boulanger* is taken. Would you settle for a country dance? No, no, the first waltz is for—"

"The first waltz is mine," said Lord Devlin firmly, speaking out over the protests of the masculine throng. Francesca started to protest. Under the circumstances, she really ought to bestow the first waltz on Caspar. And Devlin should stand up with Priscilla. But then she caught his eye. It was as though the crowd around them disappeared, along with her free will. She felt as though she were floating, with nothing but his strong blue eyes tethering her to the ground.

"I am sorry, gentlemen," she said softly, her eyes still on his, "but his lordship is correct. The first waltz is promised to him."

The music was struck up at that very moment, and she moved so easily, so naturally, into his arms. She knew she should scold him, but she could not bring herself to do it. She didn't want to spoil this moment. Tomorrow she would be gone from here. Heaven only knew when she would see him again, or dance with him, or feel him holding her in his arms. She knew she would never again know the feeling of his lips on hers, except over and over, forever, in her memory.

He knew he should speak to her, apologize, say something. She felt so wonderful in his arms, so warm and feminine, so *right*. He felt so close to her, closer than touching. He could not bring himself to break the spell.

They danced as if they were the only people in the room, locked in a dream. It was like no other dance either of them had ever known, full of melancholy and delight.

Sarah, who had just taken the floor with her lord, watched them and smiled.

Caspar, fully expecting to do his duty and open the ball with his betrothed, was more than a bit taken aback when she waltzed off in the arms of another man. He was also strangely relieved, though he would not have been able to explain why. He turned to Priscilla. "Would you care to waltz, Miss Pennington?" he asked in his grave way.

Mrs. Pennington gave the girl no chance to answer. "Oh, sir. I am afraid Priscilla and his lordship are . . ." Devlin and Francesca waltzed by, oblivious both of Priscilla and of her mother. "Well!" the woman exclaimed.

"Thank you, Mr. Maltby," said Priscilla very quickly to cover her embarrassment and even more to keep her mother from saying anything further. "I should be pleased." She laid aside her crook and hurried away with him before she could be stopped.

To her surprise, she found herself enjoying the dance. It was a rather unique experience in her young life. Caspar found it pleasant as well. Miss Pennington was really such a very *comfortable* girl.

When the waltz finally ended, Francesca and Devlin reentered the realm of reality with something of a thud.

Before long they could expect the Duke to call for attention and make the momentous announcement of the double betrothal. They would then find themselves besieged by well-wishers. They would be required to stand hand in hand with their soon-to-be-spouses and be congratulated and accept it all with a happy smile. They neither of them felt overly happy.

They had, however, convinced themselves of the rightness of their action and they were ready to get on with it, impatient, even, to have the thing over and done with.

But the Duke seemed in no hurry to accommodate them. In answer to their queries, he found ways of putting them off. "Got to be just the right moment, y'know," he said to Devlin. "Drama. Sarah likes that." To Francesca he explained, "Make a big climax to the evening, y'see. More impact that way." As His Grace had come up with no way to avoid what he saw as inevitable, he was doing what he could to put it off as long as possible. Sarah did not want the announcement made, and there was nothing the Duke would not do for his beloved Sarah. He wasn't the brightest fellow around, he well knew, but Sarah thought he was, and he was in no hurry to abuse her of the notion. Given enough time, he might even come up with something that would do the trick.

And so the evening wore on in a swirl of color and sound and romance. Sir Algernon Pett danced again and again with his lovely wife, defying anyone to laugh at him for doing so. The Honorable Miss Lettice Hollys received and accepted an offer of marriage from the Honorable Mister Graham Symington, pending the approval of her father, which Mr. Symington intended to waste no time in obtaining. Jane Magness and Julia Dalton, seeing the hopelessness of their cause with Lord Devlin, turned their considerable charms to the other eligible gentlemen in the room, to gratifying effect.

Lord Devlin danced with Priscilla; Francesca danced

with Caspar. It was to be expected that they would. But Mr. Maltby also danced with Miss Pennington. In fact, Pris so far forgot herself as to dance with the gentleman *four times*! Her mother, assuming that Pris's future was now secured, so far relaxed her vigilance as to adjourn to the card room, where she could sit comfortably over a hand of whist and ease her feet out of their too-tight shoes under the table and give up worrying over her daughter. Soon she would have to return to the ballroom to receive congratulations on her daughter's good fortune. But until then ahhhh . . .

Thus, there was no one about to shoo Caspar off nor to insist that she refuse him. It never occurred to Caspar to stay away on his own. Dancing with Miss Pennington seemed the most natural, harmless thing in the world. Actually, it very nearly was harmless as far as the censorious eyes of the others were concerned. No one but the two most directly involved even noticed. Both partners were so nearly insignificant that they drew no attention to themselves at all except when in the company of their betrotheds.

Francesca and Devlin, both of them in a reckless humor, did not notice either.

Lady Aurelm was the first to see the snow. It was just before midnight. The Duke had been growing very nervous, still thrashing about in his underactive imagination for some means of avoiding making the announcement. His worrying was quickly drowned out by the excited exclamations of delight and dismay that issued from the crowd at sight of the fluffy snow drifting down outside the long wall of windows. The younger members of the group crowed with pleasure; the oldsters worried and muttered about the difficulty of getting themselves home.

The drifting flakes were heavy and wet, and they clung wherever they touched. In no time at all, the ground was dusted with white, a veritable fairyland to complement the enchanted ballroom within. Sarah ran lightly to the window, her husband right behind her. "Oh, George!" she sighed, "How perfect!"

"Perfect?" he asked.

"Yes, of course. For the neighborhood guests will now all be anxious to get away before the snow grows too heavy. And we cannot be expected to make an announcement of any kind while we are bidding our guests good-bye."

"By Jove, you're right!" She put her hand on his arm and beamed up at him with such force that for a moment he almost believed that he had summoned up the snowstorm just for her benefit, clever fellow that he was.

Sarah was right; the ball did begin to break up almost at once. Carriages were called for, and wraps were fetched, and extra bedrooms were made ready for those who feared they would not be able to reach their homes in safety. Sarah rushed about here and there, prettily beseeching Francesca's assistance and handling everyone and everything in a masterly fashion.

When the last guest had left and the last resident had gone upstairs to bed, all four members of the quadrille found themselves officially, or at least publicly, still *un*engaged.

19

Francesca arose early next morning with a light heart, an unusual circumstances of late. She couldn't think why she should feel so optimistic. It must be the weather. The unexpected snowstorm had lightened her spirits; winter had always been her favorite season. She hopped from her bed and went to stand at the window.

The world had lost all its color; everything as far as she could see was draped in crystalline white. Bare branches were lacy with the snow; terraces and balustrades were smothered in it. Everything looked new and fresh and pure, unmarred as yet by so much as a single footprint.

In truth, there had not been more than a pair of inches, and it was so early in the season that even that much had been something of a freak occurrence. The snow would not last long. But it was enough for Francesca. She threw open her windows and breathed in the new winter.

A sound came to her ears, a light laugh. The snowy world below her was not quite deserted. She stepped out onto the small balcony outside her window and looked off toward the source of the happy sound. A heavily bundled figure appeared around the corner of the house, followed by another. Why, it was Caspar! There was no mistaking him even under the heavy overcoat, hat, and muffler he wore. And with him was Priscilla. She was wrapped up in an old woolen redingote, a serviceable hat, and thick mittens. Her mother must be still abed, else the girl would never have been allowed to be seen thus clothed.

The young couple did not see Francesca—odd how people never seem to look up—and she watched them with interest. She had never seen Caspar so informal, so relaxed. He was even laughing. With amazement she saw him scoop up a handful of the wet snow, form it into a serviceable ball, and throw it at his companion. He was pelted in return, with rather good aim as it happened, and they both laughed.

"Shall I make a snow angel?" came Priscilla's clear happy voice.

"A what?"

"You do not know about snow angels?" she said. "Watch!" She threw herself onto her back in the snow, laughing delightedly all the while, and swished her arms back and forth. "There!" she said triumphantly. He took the hand she reached up to him and pulled her to her feet, being careful not to disturb the snow. She stepped back to show off her handiwork. "You see?" she said. "That is a snow angel."

When Caspar looked down at her with the snow clinging to her head and shoulders and her eyes shining with her high spirits, he did look rather like a man gazing at an angel, but a decidedly warm and living one.

Francesca, who was almost directly over their heads, began to feel distinctly uncomfortable. She was clearly not meant to witness what she was witnessing. But if she moved now, she would only draw attention to herself, and that would make for a very uncomfortable encounter. She remained where she was.

Caspar never did know what got into him that morning. He was acting totally unlike himself. But when he looked down at this girl, at the damp brown curls that escaped her hat, at the round cheeks pink with cold and pleasure, something he could not control made him lean over and kiss her. It was a pure, simple kiss, a sweet kiss, so much sweeter and more tender than the kiss he had given Francesca. It was a kiss filled with joy.

But then the lighthearted joy disappeared and it became a kiss filled with horror. What was he doing? He was a cad of the worst sort! He was engaged to marry another woman. What must Miss Pennington be thinking of him?

Priscilla closed her eyes and savored the kiss, the gentlest, kindest kiss she could imagine. But when she realized what she was doing, her eyes flew open in dismay. She let out a gasp; she covered her face with her hands; and she ran away, her quick steps silent on the snow.

Caspar watched her go. Francesca watched him watch her go. She heard him exclaim, "Damme!" in a totally uncharacteristic fashion, saw him shove his hands deep in the pockets of his overcoat and walk away in the opposite direction.

Alone again, Francesca shivered from the cold and let out a long sigh. But the tiniest of smiles was creeping, almost unbidden, up one corner of her mouth. And the cold did not seem able to penetrate to her insides. Her mind told her over and over how terribly upset she was by the little scene she had just witnessed. But a definite glow seemed to be warming her from somewhere deep inside, somewhere in the vicinity of her heart.

The freak snowstorm had temporarily put an end to all plans for immediate departure. Trunks and valises were reopened. Abigails and valets were sent scurrying to repress pantaloons and morning dresses so that their masters and mistresses might keep up their sartorial splendor.

The breakfast table buzzed with chatter about the weather and speculations about the state of the roads and how long the snow was likely to remain on the ground. Everyone seemed in high spirits, even Francesca, though she could not imagine why she should be.

She was anixous for a moment alone with Devlin. She really must inform him of the surprising development she had discovered that morning. But Pris was seated next to him, unsmiling and silent as the grave. And Caspar was beside Francesca, pouring out her coffee and trying unsuccessfully to smile. He conspicuously avoided looking at Priscilla. Francesca frowned. How to get off alone with Devlin? She could scarce come out and say, "Meet me in the library," in front of everyone. She must bide her time yet awhile.

The others at the table were busily making plans for their morning. Sarah suggested having runners put to one or two of the carriages for a sleigh ride. Jane Magness thought a snowman-building competition would be amusing. The enthusiasm of the company was infectious.

"I say, George," said Lord Devlin. "You must have a sled or two about the place. There's a perfect sledding hill just back of the house."

"Oh, yes!" cried Lady Aurelm, who had grown up at Hockleigh. "Remember how we used to race each other there, Georgie?" she said to her brother. "Do find the sleds. The children would love it so."

"The children?" exclaimed Devlin. "I would love it. I hereby challenge all comers to a sledding race down that hill."

"You're on!" came a chorus of voices.

The company dispersed to change into attire somewhat more suited to such hoydenish behavior and high spirits. When Francesca came down again, warmly and prettily attired in a fur-lined cherry pelisse and a shako hat edged with sable and with her hands tucked into a large sable muff, Caspar was waiting for her.

"The sleighs are waiting, my dear," he said gravely. "I was persuaded you would wish to join the outing."

"Then you were persuaded wrong, dear Caspar," she replied. "I am going sledding."

"Sledding?" he asked. It did not exactly fit his idea of an activity suitable to a young lady.

"Certainly. Who would choose to ride along in a sedate old sleigh when one can be whooshing down a hillside at great speed? I intend to beat Lord Devlin to the bottom."

"But surely, my dear . . ."

"Oh, don't be so stuffy, Caspar. You need not whoosh with me, after all. I know very well it is not in your style. Take Priscilla for a sleighride. I'm sure she would like it of all things."

As Priscilla was standing not ten feet away, and as Francesca was smiling at her encouragingly, he could not simply ignore this surprising statement. In a low voice he began, "I am sure Miss Pennington—"

"Come, Pris," said Francesca. "Would you not like to join the sleigh ride? I would count it a very great favor if you would keep Caspar company for me." She sent up a prayer of thanks that Mrs. Pennington was nowhere to be seen.

Priscilla raised her eyes to Francesca, then to Caspar, then looked down again. She dared not speak. Caspar, despite his preference for the country over town, was a well-brought-up gentleman. Good manners dictated that he invite Priscilla to accompany him. He did so. She nodded her acceptance.

"That's settled, then," said Francesca briskly, shooing them out the door. She saw them safely ensconced in the sleigh, making quite certain that they were seated side by side, then headed up the sledding hill with an easy heart.

She reached the top of the hill to find Devlin directing the disposition of sleds and the laying out of routes down the steep slope. He had donned a heavy fisherman's pullover under his coat and knotted a long knit muffler around his neck. His cheeks were glowing under their tan, and he was laughing. She thought he looked just like an eager schoolboy granted an unexpected holiday.

"Hey, Cesca! Over here!" he called "Where's Caspar? Not up for a bit of sport?"

"He's gone for a sleigh ride with some of the others." She looked at him thoughtfully. "I really must speak with you, Dev."

He looked at her and stopped smiling. "Serious?"

"Quite serious, I'm afraid."

"Well, then, it must wait. Nothing serious is allowed on a sledding hill, you know. Come on." He grabbed her hand and pulled her to a sled.

Before long she was lying on her stomach on a silly red bit of board, careening down the hillside and loving it. She screamed with delight when her sled ran into a drift and flipped her into the white powder. Devlin laughingly pulled her out and brushed her off.

They sledded for nearly two hours, the most purely joyful hours Francesca could remember spending in years. She carried Gussie's children down the hill with her several times, delighting in their delight, getting very wet and dirty along with them, and enjoying herself hugely.

As the merry group finally trudged back to the house, ravenously hungry and ready for lunch, the sleigh riders pulled up the drive. Unlike the fun on the hill, it had been a largely silent ride, at least on that side of the one sleigh carrying Caspar and Priscilla. But their eyes had been chattering madly away at each other for the whole drive, declaring all those things they would not allow their mouths to utter. The major message they both conveyed was, "God help me, I love you."

Priscilla had never expected to find love. Now that she had, she was wretched. It seemed that she was destined to go through life with nothing ever turning out right. Why must she discover Mr. Maltby only after she had been persuaded to marry someone else? More importantly, why must Mr. Maltby discover *her* just when he had offered for Lady Francesca?

When Lord Devlin had informed her of Francesca's

betrothal, she had felt little. She barely knew Mr. Maltby then, and she was too wrapped up in her own problems to give the matter much thought. That was before she realized what a warm, intelligent, thoroughly wonderful gentleman he was.

Could one really fall in love so quickly? she asked herself. Especially with a man one had met several times with no reaction whatever? Apparently one could. Apparently one did.

Caspar's thoughts were not far different from those of the girl beside him, though perhaps tinged rather more heavily with guilt. He knew very well that Priscilla was engaged to another man—the man had told him of it personally—and he knew even better that he was engaged to another woman. As a gentleman, he could never honorably cry off from his betrothal to Francesca. He wasn't certain how the entire thing had come about. It was very unlike him to act so rashly. But that was just what he had done. And now he must live with the consequences of his own folly. He must live without Miss Pennington.

Francesca, standing near the window of the dining room, where a hearty buffet luncheon had been laid on, saw Caspar tenderly lift Priscilla from the sleigh. Setting her on her feet, he allowed his hands to remain a brief moment on her waist while he gazed down at her. Then he suddenly dropped his eyes, and Priscilla hurried away into the house.

I really must speak to Dev, Francesca told herself.

A loud and lively luncheon gave them no chance for discussion. Devlin, totally unaware of the situation, was attentive to Pris, carving her thin slices of ham and chicken, bringing her wine, and making her altogether miserable.

But as the meal finally ended and each of the company began drifting off to his own early-afternoon pursuits, Francesca looked pointedly at Devlin and said with great deliberation, "I think I shall repair to the library. I've some letters to write."

He could not mistake the summons in her voice. He very shortly followed her thither. When he reached the library, she was pacing back and forth before the fire, thinking furiously. She was also smiling. He sank into a comfortable leather-covered Chesterfield chair and waited for her to speak.

"Well, Dev," she said, facing him squarely and flashing a rueful smile. "We have well and truly made a mess of things."

A bright warm autumn sun, defying the attempt of the new winter to assert itself, poured out of the sky that afternoon, working its magic on the snow and quickly clearing the roads with its warmth. Trunks were packed up again and stood ready for departures.

Lady Francesca and Lord Devlin were closeted together in the library for the better part of an hour. They were planning how best to untangle the Gordian knot they had managed to tie themselves into.

Neither of them was possessed of the smallest streak of cruelty, and despite Lady Francesca's elaborate theories on the innate selfishness of mankind, she could not think of forcing anyone to throw away his own happiness so that she might have a try at some of her own.

As soon as she explained to Devlin the scene she had observed that morning, he agreed, and not too reluctantly at that, that they must immediately put an end to their two engagements. But how best to get the thing done? Devlin could not cry off. It just was not done.

There was only one way to set about the task, and they spent some time sorting out the details.

They had no opportunity, however, to implement those plans until after dinner. It had been a meal rippling with constraint from certain sections of the table. The Duke had spent a good part of the afternoon worrying that Devlin and Caspar would insist that he make the announcements this evening. Sarah had been flailing about in her mind for some word that would convince Francesca of her folly and make her change her mind. She cast her friend a good many covert glances and wondered how she could possibly appear to be in such high spirits. She *could* not be truly happy about this whole thing.

Francesca was indeed in high spirits. In fact, she was almost giddy with relief. She and Devlin both laughed a good deal throughout the meal, both of them unsuccessfully trying to prod a smile from their fiancées. Priscilla and Caspar, however, both swallowed their meals in almost total silence.

The meal concluded, the ladies adjourned, and the gentlemen had their smoke. They did not seem inclined to dawdle over their port, and when they arose to leave the dining room, Caspar was surprised to find Lord Devlin beside him, chatting affably and steering him purposefully toward the library.

When the pair of them entered that room, Caspar was surprised, astounded even, to find his betrothed awaiting them, together with his love. It was not at all a comfortable position to find himself in. Priscilla did not look particularly at ease either.

"Sit down, Caspar," said Francesca pleasantly, taking on the role of hostess. "Have a glass of brandy." She handed it to him, and though he did not care overmuch for brandy, he took it. He even drank some of it.

"Perhaps you had best have some as well, Priscilla," said Devlin, placing a glass in her cold white hand. Her eyes were like saucers as she looked from one gentleman to the other. Was Lord Devlin able to see into her mind? she wondered. Had he somehow divined the fact that she was in love with another man? And was he now about to call poor Caspar out? She didn't think she could bear to sit here any longer. But she would have to bear it. She had to *know*.

"I'm certain you are both wondering why we have brought you here," said Devlin. "Francesca?"

She looked down at Caspar with a kind smile. "Caspar, you have been a perfect gentleman to me, honorable and kind. I have been flattered and very pleased to be betrothed to you." Well, surely one small lie was acceptable in the circumstances, she told herself. "Now, I am sure you will be pleased to know that I am bringing our engagement to an end. I am not a cruel person and have no intention of asking you to sacrifice your own happiness for me. I will not hold you when your heart has so obviously been bestowed elsewhere."

"But, Francesca, I didn't—" he began.

"Please," said Devlin. "Let us complete the whole of it." He turned to Priscilla, her eyes now even wider than ever, if that were possible. The still-evident confusion within them was now lightened by the tiniest ray of hope. "Priscilla, obviously I, as a man of honor, cannot cry off from our engagement. I have no intention of doing so. But you can, and I pray you will. I stand ready to accept your decision to end our betrothal."

The seated pair were now given a chance to speak. They did not take the opportunity, however, at least not for a rather protracted period of time. They simply did not know what to say. Caspar drank his brandy—or gulped it rather. Francesca calmly poured him another. Priscilla nearly dropped her glass but slowly and carefully set it on the table with trembling fingers before the damage could be done.

Caspar found his voice first, even though he scarcely recognized it when he did. It had become a kind of croak. "I am sorry, Lady Francesca, that you find you cannot like being affianced to me," he managed to get out.

"Stuff!" replied Francesca, smiling and airily waving a hand at his nonsense. "You know very well, Caspar, that you have been regretting your rashness practically since the moment you offered for me."

"My lady!" he protested.

She cut him off. "Just as I am certain that Priscilla has been regretting her acceptance of Lord Devlin. Now, Pris, do you not think it is time to explain to his lordship that you cannot marry him? It is hardly fair to leave the poor man dangling, you know."

It was only too clear that Priscilla truly wished to do as she was told—it was in her nature, after all—but one quite formidable obstacle stopped her. "Mama," she said softly, the tears beginning to well up in her eyes.

"Ah, yes, Mama," said Devlin. "You will leave Mama to us, if you please. I am sure that Francesca and I can deal with her between us."

"You don't know Mama."

Francesca thought she heard Devlin mutter "Thank God," which she disregarded. "I know her better than you suppose, Pris," she said. "You must not think she is unkind. She would not wish to see you unhappy."

"But she does wish to see me married," said Priscilla.

"It is only natural that she should. And so you shall be," said Francesca.

"And you might just keep in mind, my dear," added Devlin, "that a viscount outranks a mere baron."

"A viscount?" said Priscilla, puzzled.

Devlin and Francesca looked at Caspar. "A viscount," he said softly, thoughtfully. "A viscount," he repeated, louder. Suddenly his face lit up with understanding and pleasure. "By Jove! So it does! Miss Pennington, a viscount beats a mere baron all to flinders!" It was the first time in his life he was truly grateful for his impending title.

Francesca could not help smiling at his boyish enthusiasm, so blatantly absent from his offer to her. Why, the man was positively glowing!

Priscilla, as usual, was speechless. But she was smiling, a language easily understood by everyone in the room. And soon she too was glowing. With an exasperated laugh, Devlin took her hand. "Really, Pris, we must do the thing properly, you know. Now, repeat after me. I am thankful for the honor you do me, but I will not marry you, my lord."

She beamed up at him. "Oh, I am *truly* thankful, but I will not marry you, my lord."

"Well, thank God for that!" he exclaimed. Then he took the hand he still held in his, brought her to her feet, and led her to Caspar, who had also risen. Then, very much like a father—horrid image, that, but accurate—he bestowed the small white hand on Mr. Maltby, who did not seem the least bit loath to take it.

"Well, at last!" said Francesca, applauding. "I think we can leave them to get on with the business now, Dev."

As they left the room, being careful to close the door after them, they heard the first words of what would undoubtedly be a very interesting and very silly conversation.

"Miss Pennington," said Caspar. "Priscilla . . ."

"Yes, Caspar?" she replied.

As the door closed behind them, Devlin and Francesca each became suddenly and ferociously aware of the other. It was too silly after all they'd been through together, but they felt acutely uncomfortable in each other's presence just now. They didn't seem to have a word to say between them, so they said nothing.

A few eyebrows inched up a notch or two as they entered the drawing room together, most especially those of Mrs. Pennington, who sent hers flying nearly into her turban. Devlin grimaced, but Francesca gave him a little push in the woman's direction.

He bent over her hand and cleared his throat. "Might I speak to you, ma'ma, in the morning room?" he said, much as he had said once before. As he led her from the room, Francesca gave him a sympathetic look that said clearly, "Call me if you need me."

Her assistance was not required. Mrs. Pennington was

not stupid. She was quickly brought to see the advantages of having a soon-to-be viscount for a son-in-law. Truth to tell, Mr. Maltby was much more to her taste than his lordship had been. More down-to-earth, so to speak. And she did like a nice garden. And then, Somersetshire was so much prettier than Kent.

She scurried off to the library to congratulate her daughter on the perceptiveness of her choice.

It was a lucky thing that the woman proved so amenable. Had Devlin needed Francesca's help, he would have had a deal of trouble finding her. She had persuaded herself into the headache and sought the solace of her bedchamber. In truth, she could not bear the idea of finding herself alone with Dev. She knew very well he would have no trouble with the Pennington woman, but he might well seek her out after the deed was done. So, with an uncharacteristic lack of bottom, she turned tail and ran.

When Devlin returned to the drawing room, his eyes immediately sought out Francesca. Without her there, the evening soon became intolerable. He tried flirting with Jane Magness and Julia Dalton, to their surprised delight, but his heart wasn't in it. He took himself early to bed.

The great house bustled next morning; one would have thought the very foundations of the venerable old house would tremble with the activity. Though most of the snow had melted, there were still bound to be bad patches on the roads. The guests were eager to get away as early as possible and make their way as far south as they could before nightfall.

All, that is, except Francesca. And Devlin. Rose had packed the last trunk and strapped the last portmanteau preparatory to their departure, but Francesca still lingered over coffee in the breakfast room. Most of the good-byes had been completed and the guests waved off, and still she did not send for her carriage. She should go.

She told herself she would do so as soon as she had had a last private cup of coffee with Sarah.

Isaac had Lord Devlin's curricle harnessed and ready, the trunks strapped on behind, but no word came from the house to have it brought around. Devlin wandered rather aimlessly through the rooms and corridors of the house, scowling fiercely and conspicuously avoiding the breakfast room.

Sarah, absolutely delighted by the events of the preceding evening, quickly saw that there was yet more to do before things would be set completely aright. And it must be done at once. No time like the present, as the old saw went.

"You know, my love," she said to Francesca casually as she sipped at her coffee, "one of the oddest things about being with child. I seem so much more affected by the cold these days. Is it not strange?"

"I am sure it is normal, darling. You must not let it worry you. You need only put on a shawl."

"Yes, I know. But I am the silliest thing. I have left my warmest shawl in the conservatory, and it is right at the other end of the house."

"I shall get it for you, love," said Francesca, right on cue, and rose to leave the room.

"Oh, but Cesca . . ." Sarah began a feeble complaint. But not too loudly.

"I shan't be a moment," said Francesca, and off she went.

No sooner was she out the door than Sarah sprang to her feet and scurried after her. Listening a moment at the door until Francesca's footsteps had died away, she came into the hall and began peeking quickly into one room after the other. Her luck hit on only the third chamber she tried.

"Ah, Lord Devlin. Here you are," she said brightly to his scowling face. "George has been looking for you everywhere."

"Has he?"

"Yes, I believe he was last headed for the conservatory."

"The conservatory?" said Devlin, thinking it decidely odd.

"Oh, yes. Do go and find the poor dear before he covers the whole estate."

Devlin couldn't think why the Duke could be wanting him, and more especially why he would think to look for him in such an unlikely place. But he nodded his agreement and headed off after George, as he thought.

One can readily imagine the dismay/delight with which the would-be lovers found not that which they had sought in the conservatory, but each other.

"My lord," Francesca greeted him, then turned to look out the window.

"My lady," he replied, and came to stand beside her. They gazed silently out on the world. The bright sun bounced off the remaining patches of snow to bathe the room with light, almost as though it were summer. One of the windows was open—the chill air had warmed considerably—to admit a soft breeze that ruffled Francesca's hair and the muslin of her gown.

They stood there a long while, neither speaking, neither looking at the other, neither daring to. Finally he slid his eyes down to look at her, glowing there in the sunlight. God, but she was beautiful!

"Well, Cesca," he said when he felt he could trust his voice, "we have certainly made a hash of things, haven't we?"

"We certainly have. I have been feeling uncommonly stupid all morning."

"Thank God we were able to untangle the knot in time. They really are very much better suited to each other than they ever would have been to us."

"Oh, yes, certainly." They fell silent again.

Finally Devlin said, "What do we do now? Try again?"

"Oh, Lord, I don't know if I can stand to go through all that again. I am far too old for such antics, I think."

This brought about his first grin. "Yes, you are positively ancient."

She ignored the remark. "And besides, I have lost much of my confidence in my own judgment." She was genuinely upset, he could see. "Oh, Dev! The hurt we might have caused!"

He placed an arm lightly about her shoulder to comfort her. "But it is over now. And it has all turned out for the best, you know." Almost unconsciously she laid her head against the comforting solidity of his shoulder, so conveniently near. Almost unconsciously he began stroking her hair.

From a small tender embrace to a kiss of almost excruciating passion is not really such a great leap. Especially for two people so obviously meant for each other as Cesca and Dev. A small turn here, a slight movement of the arm there, and the thing is done.

Suddenly the room was filled with light and birdsong and the scent of honeysuckle. He smelled of spice; she tasted of strawberries. Five years of living fell away in a moment, and they were once more back in a gazebo in a garden on a lazy summer day.

The kiss went on and on. Francesca wondered if she would die of it. Perhaps she already had. Surely she was now in heaven. His hands moved down her arms and over her body, burning her skin through the thin muslin of her gown, then moved around her again to hold her close, so close, as though he would never let her go again. Please don't let me go, her mind shouted at him.

His brain was singing: She is here; she is mine; she will always be mine. He kissed her all the more as if he would swallow her whole.

Faintly at first, then louder, came a sound, breaking through the music of the kiss. Someone was whistling, a little off-key. It was not a hymn, not like that hapless curate so long ago, but it did jolt them back to reality. They broke apart and stared at each other.

In a moment, George Albert John, fifth Duke of

Hockleigh, appeared around the corner and whistled himself across the lawn and out of sight. They still stared at each other. Then Devlin grabbed her by the shoulders, almost painfully hard, as though to shake her. He said in a fierce hoarse voice, "You are not running away from me this time, Cesca! You're not!" He looked angry. And afraid.

But this time there was no answering fear in Francesca's eyes. They shone with a very different kind of light. She smiled, a slow happy smile of the purest joy. "No, Dev, I'm not."

He seemed not to have heard her. "You are going to stay right here, and you are going to marry me!"

"Yes, Dev, I am."

"And there will be no nonsense about being my slave or apron strings or any of that. You will be my wife, and I will be your husband, and that will be that."

"Yes, Dev, it will."

Her words finally appeared to penetrate his fevered brain. He stared at her in wonder, in awe. He clasped her to him and gave her another kiss that threatened to take the solid ground out from under the both of them. "Oh, Cesca, Cesca," he finally let loose of her long enough to say. "How have I lived these five years without you?"

"You haven't, Dev. Like me, you have merely existed. I do think it is time we got on with a bit of living now, don't you?"

"High time."

They did not hear the door click softly open. Neither did they hear Sarah's soft sigh of pleasure, nor George's low chuckle. The door clicked shut again. The two lovers were far too occupied to notice.

An hour later they were still in the conservatory, though they had managed to move to a more comfortable spot on the sofa. "When shall we leave for Kent, my love?" murmured Francesca. "When shall we go home?"

"One does not go home until after the honeymoon, sweet," he answered. "I am going to give you the most exciting, most adventurous honeymoon in the world. It is high time you had a bit of it for your own."

"I think I should like that."

"How convenient that these old ducal mansions always have their own chapels. I shall get a special license at once. You will be my wife before nightfall."

"Arranging matters in your usual high-handed way, I see."

He looked sheepish. "Sorry. I am very used to having my own way, you know."

"So am I." They smiled a gentle challenge at each other. "So. We are going on a honeymoon. I think I should like to go to Egypt."

"Egypt?"

"Yes, Egypt. I have wanted to see it ever since Napoleon rediscovered it. Now that I shall have a respectable husband in tow, I think I shall do so."

"I shall enjoy seeing you on camel. Though I must warn you the creatures are nearly as stubborn and independent as you."

"Well, if I am tossed off, I shall simply find a convenient Bedouin or some such to pick me up again."

"That you shall not, my girl! I have had quite enough of your 'convenient' gentlemen. *I* shall pick you up myself."

She dimpled prettily at him. "I think I shall like that very much. For it means you will have to stay close at hand to keep an eye on me."

"I shall stay *very* close at hand. I warn you, Cesca, you shall never be rid of me again."

"Good," she sighed.

And he proceeded to show her just how close he intended to remain.

About the Author

Megan Daniel, born and raised in Southern California, combines a background in theater and music with a passion for travel and a love of England and the English. After attending UCLA and California State University, Long Beach, where she earned a degree in theater, she lived for a time in London and elsewhere in Europe. She then settled in New York, working for six years as a theatrical costume designer for Broadway, off-Broadway, ballet, and regional theater.

Miss Daniel lives in New York with her husband, Roy Sorrels, a successful free-lance writer. Her other Regency novels—*Amelia, The Reluctant Suitor*, and *The Unlikely Rivals*—are also available in Signet editions.